BROKEN

BREAKERS HOCKEY #1

ELISE FABER

BROKEN
BY ELISE FABER

This is a work of fiction. Names, places, characters, and events are fictitious in every regard. Any similarities to actual events and persons, living or dead, are purely coincidental. Any trademarks, service marks, product names, or named features are assumed to be the property of their respective owners and are used only for reference. There is no implied endorsement if any of these terms are used. Except for review purposes, the reproduction of this book in whole or part, electronically or mechanically, constitutes a copyright violation.

CHAPTER ONE

Luc

HE WAS FORTY YEARS OLD.

He was single.

He was happy that way.

Sighing, he lifted his beer to his lips and internally shook his head at himself. He wasn't actually happy. He was miserable and lonely. Oh, and he might as well add fucking pathetic to that tally.

Because the woman he was in love with was married.

To a perfectly nice man, who loved her and cared for her and treated her like the fucking queen she was.

But that didn't help Luc or his loneliness problem.

So, he was sitting on his front porch drinking a beer, trying to forget the woman he'd fallen for two years before, only to find out she was married two weeks later. Lexi was with the legal department for the Baltimore Breakers, the NHL team he was the GM for. He'd fallen hard when witnessing her skills at contract negotiations, fallen harder when she'd proven to be whip-smart and hilarious in equal parts.

She was beautiful, smart, funny. She was everything he'd ever dreamed of.

And . . .

Then he'd met her husband while grabbing a beer with Lexi and some coworkers.

"*Luc,*" she'd said, smiling up at him, its intensity punching him right in the gut, "*this is my husband, Caleb.*"

Caleb?

What kind of name was that?

"Fucking hell," Luc muttered, taking another sip of his beer, hating the other man, and yet respecting him, because there was love between them.

Deeply rooted love that spoke of a happy relationship.

Luc hated it.

Cue lonely, pathetic asshole.

Mainly because he was a glutton for punishment, or maybe he just couldn't resist Lexi because he'd spent the last two years becoming friends with both Lexi *and* Caleb. Backyard barbeques? Yup. Holiday celebrations, exchanging birthday presents, baking flipping Christmas cookies together. Certainly. Random dinners and errands and meetups for drinks. Check, check, check.

See? He *was* a glutton for punishment.

But he'd gotten to spend time with the woman he loved, so much time, in fact, that they'd become best friends.

He was a forty-year-old man who was practically on the edge of exchanging BFF bracelets with a woman he was pathetically in love with and yet could do nothing about.

Part of him still hated Caleb, but he'd never mess with Lexi's happy. Would never be that person who fucked up a good marriage.

So he contented himself with his single status, with their friendship.

With phone calls and board game nights, text chains that ran into the thousands of messages, GIF wars and bursting out into laughter at the worst moments.

Because he and Lexi just clicked.

Because everything with her was fucking perfect.

Except . . . that she was married.

Sighing, he stood up and turned toward his front door, was just reaching for the handle when he heard the screech of tires.

Spinning, he watched the car pull to a stop, the driver's door open, and Lexi tumble out.

He was running before he realized he'd moved, reaching her in seconds.

"What's the matter?" he asked, noting the tears, the reddened eyes, the mascara blackening the skin beneath her eyes. "Lexi, are you hurt?"

She nodded, threw herself into his arms.

"Where, honey?" he asked. "Where?"

Lexi tore herself away, and the pain in her gaze shredded his insides. "It's Caleb."

CHAPTER TWO

Luc, Two Years Before

HE WAS HAVING A SHIT DAY.

The worst.

He'd fucked up and made a piss-poor decision, and now the team was going to suffer because he hadn't gotten his shit together to pick up the player they'd wanted.

There were safeguards in place, a solid plan A—*and* plans B-Z—that were supposed to prevent this. But still, he'd played his hand too early, and the three-way deal had fallen through. Which meant they were going into the trade deadline without the roster they wanted.

And he still had contract negotiations to go through.

His *fucking* favorite.

He sighed, scrubbed a hand over his face, and forced himself to take a deep breath. He was meeting with Todd, head counsel for the Baltimore Breakers. They needed to hammer out some final details for shit he didn't want to deal with, but shit that somehow fell under the umbrella of his job description.

None of which was Todd's fault.

Another sigh, another scrub of his face.

Then he pushed into the conference room.

And immediately felt as though he'd been cracked over the head with a frying pan.

She. Was. *Beautiful.*

A sleek, black suit jacket, a crisp, white shirt, tailored black trousers with a white stripe on the side. Shining brown hair, a lush, red-stained mouth, and eyes—warm, golden-brown eyes that were filled with humor when they lifted from the page in front of her—and Todd, Luc realized, obliquely, the lawyer was there, too.

"Luc!" Todd exclaimed, smiling widely, the happiest lawyer he'd ever met, and moving around the table to shake his hand. "This is Alexis," he said, pulling away and indicating the beautiful brunette. "She's finally agreed to be my associate counsel."

Alexis smiled, moved toward him, hand extended.

Sparks, the moment their fingers touched, nearly making him jerk back. But then he was frozen again because Alexis was smiling widely, those beautiful eyes open pools he was suddenly quite desperate to dive into. "I go by Lexi," she said, with a look at Todd. "Even though my boss hates it."

Todd nudged her shoulder. "Gotta give my old law school buddies a hard time."

Luc forced his fingers to open, to release her hand, moving to the table and taking a seat. "Law school buddies," he said, "why can't I wait to hear about the stories that come along with that designation?"

Todd grinned. "Probably because Lexi was way cooler than I was."

Lexi snorted. "It wasn't like that at all—"

"That somehow doesn't surprise me," he teased, smirking at Todd, and chuckling when Lexi just sighed and sat down at the table, as though she'd been through numerous iterations of this same conversation.

And maybe she had.

Because Todd didn't miss a beat.

"Lexi was popular," he stage-whispered. "I was the old man."

She squeezed his arm, rolled her eyes. "Not old," she said. "Just aged, like a fine wine."

Todd chuckled, shook his head, and Lexi's gaze drifted to Luc, her lips curved into a smile that made Luc's heart thud in his chest. "And if by popular he means, the librarians knew everything about me from my cat's name to my favorite book, to my preferred color and size of Post-It Notes then, yes," she said, her expression filled with mirth, "I was the *most* popular girl on campus."

Todd started busting up.

Luc fought a smile.

She turned to him. "You can laugh," she said. "I promise, I don't take myself too seriously."

Todd slung an arm around her shoulders, gave her a noogie. "And *that's* exactly why you'll fit perfectly in here."

"Hair!" she exclaimed, smoothing it down, and Luc couldn't hold back a chuckle, drawing her gaze. She elbowed Todd in the side. "Come on now, you're making me look bad in front of the boss."

"Technically, he's not your boss." A grin. "He's your boss's boss."

"Technically," Luc said. "Legal is a separate department from my own, though we work closely together."

Golden-brown eyes drifted to his, amusement danced in their depths . . . and then Todd gave her another noogie. Her glare whipped over to Todd. "Oh, law school buddy, you may be fifteen years older than me, but you're so dead."

Todd, to his credit, just grinned. "Pick on the senior citizen, why don't you?"

"You know me," she said with a shrug. "I'll take advantage of any loophole."

Todd said something back, some crack that Luc barely heard, probably because he was so surprised and taken by the conversation, so enamored of this bright, *alive* woman in front of him that he didn't give a shit they were eating up precious time in a meeting that couldn't be pushed back because he had several more meetings right afterward. He just wanted to sit across the table from her, to hear her joke and laugh with Todd, to watch her smile.

He wanted to be friends with her.

He wanted to *fuck* her.

He wanted—

She turned those golden eyes toward him, and some of the humor faded from her expression, though her lips were still curved. "We should get to work, huh?" she said. "Don't want to make the big boss, who's not really my boss, mad on my first day."

Luc tried to summon some joke, some light sentiment that would bring all of her amusement back.

But . . . he had meetings to get through.

He had a team to run.

He . . . didn't have time for women, even if they were gorgeous and didn't take themselves too seriously. Even if there was something about her that had his entire soul paying attention.

So he nodded and said, "We should get to work."

Then they got down to the business of contract negotiations.

CHAPTER THREE

Luc, Present Day

HE WAS GOING to commit murder.

Okay, he wasn't, though he *was* contemplating with excruciating detail all the ways he could dismember Caleb—slowly and painfully—without going to jail. Toes. He'd start with the toes. Then maybe the fingers.

Caleb's dick.

Yeah, *that* needed to be high on the list of priorities.

Because Luc now understood why part of him had always hated Lexi's husband, even after they'd spent so much time over the last few years together.

And it wasn't just that Luc was a miserable, jealous bastard.

Caleb was a dick.

Caleb had been putting *his* dick into other women.

Several other women.

So, returning to the whole concept of dismembering and murder.

Caleb had cheated on Lexi. Wonderful, smart, funny Lexi, who had a heart bigger than any person Luc had ever met and was now crying in his arms, his shirt soaked through from her tears, her fists pounding against his chest.

Broken.

He'd heard of sobs being described that way, but he'd never known it was actually true. He'd never known it would make him willing to commit murder, to do anything within his abilities—and probably a few things beyond them—just to make the sound stop, to take away her pain.

Before she'd calmed down enough to tell him what had happened—shoving away from him and pacing across his porch—he'd managed to grab her purse, close the driver's door, and lock her car.

Then when she'd crumpled, her pacing faltering as she'd fallen back into his embrace, beginning to cry, the rest of the story coming in ragged bursts, he'd swept her up against his chest and carried her inside the house to the couch. Where they still were. Where the sobs never seemed like they were going to end. Where her pain had become his, slicing through him like a thousand tiny blades.

Lexi sniffed, finally beginning to quiet, her breathing slowing.

He continued holding her, kept running his hand up and down her back.

She pushed away from him, met his gaze, her eyes swollen and red, her makeup a total mess, and she still absolutely took his breath away. Her chest rose and fell on an inhale and exhale. "Want to hear the worst of it?" Pain glimmered in her golden-brown eyes.

Fuck the toes.

He was starting with Caleb's cock.

"Tell me, honey," he said, trying to keep his tone gentle, to keep his fury buried. She'd been dealt enough bullshit without having to deal with his raging emotions.

Lex sniffed, slowly sat all the way up, shifting so her hip was pressed to his and they were sitting side by side. Her throat worked, those eyes glimmering with tears, and he slid an arm around her shoulders, tucking her against him as she said, "The worst is that Girlfriend Number Three is pregnant."

Fuck.

Fucking *hell*.

Luc knew they'd "been trying" for several months now, that Lexi had been so excited at the prospect of having a baby.

And now, the asshole was going to have one with another woman.

A tear slid down her cheek.

"Lex," he murmured, reaching for her, intending to pull her close again.

But she pushed to her feet, resumed her earlier pacing, only this time across the blue and gray area rug in his living room instead of the composite material that made up his porch. "I just don't know how I couldn't have known." She fisted her hands at her sides. "*How* couldn't I have known? Am I just that oblivious? There had to have been some signs." She spun back around. "But *what* fucking signs? I keep thinking that I'm so stupid because there had to have been something and . . . a-and—"

Luc stood, wrapped an arm around her shoulders. "Come here," he murmured, pulling her into a hug. "You're not stupid," he said into her hair. She always smelled like roses, and today was no exception. "You're far from it."

"I—" Her voice broke. "I feel like it."

"It'll get better," he murmured. "It'll take time, but it *will* get better."

She tilted her head back, her brown hair catching on his unshaved jaw. "Is this a platitude or personal experience?"

He tucked an unruly strand of hair behind her ear. "Personal experience," he said. "Which is why I can say that the only cure for this is a beer, copious amounts of pizza, and a funny movie you've seen a hundred times before."

Her lips parted, and fuck, it was so hard not to kiss her.

Usually, he didn't allow himself this close, not when she was too fucking tempting, not when she wasn't *his*.

But this right here, right *now*, would be the absolute worst moment to show his hand.

She didn't need anything else to deal with.

And his two-year, unrequited love for her was a giant *anything else.*

So, no kissing. No touching that wasn't specifically comfort related.

Which was why—although it went against every fiber of his being—he released her, stepped back, and asked, "So, will it be *Stepbrothers* or *Tommy Boy?*"

Another breath, her eyes still sad.

Then she lifted her chin, asked with a trace of her trademark lightness in her eyes, "Will there be pineapple on the pizza?"

He groaned, dropped his head back so he was staring up at the ceiling. "Why, God? Why do you do this to me?"

"Because my husband is a fucking liar and cheat," she said, her tone still watery, but at least there was a glimmer of humor in it—even if that humor was the result of torturing him, "and I've wasted seven years of my life thinking he was the best man I knew."

Thunk.

An arrow to his heart.

Luc wanted to be the best man she knew.

But . . .

Timing.

Professionally, his had usually been on point.

Personally? It had always been the absolute shit.

"Pineapple it is," he murmured, tugging on that unruly strand of hair. Turning, he snagged the remote off the table. "You pick the movie. I'll order the pizza."

Her lips curved. It wasn't her normal smile, but the pain in her gaze wasn't nearly as pronounced, so he'd take what he could. "Thank you, Luc," she said. "I don't know what I'd do without you." A little hurt seeped back into her expression, prompting him to nudge her toward the couch.

"You would be fine," he assured. "You're the most capable woman I've ever met." He snagged her blanket—yes, *hers*, since he'd bought it specifically for her after seeing her fawn over it in the store (side note: three hundred dollars for a blanket was insanity, but she loved it, so he'd had no problem making it happen)—and tucked it around her shoulders. "Movie," he prompted.

"Pizza," she countered.

He pulled out his phone, held it up as proof of his intentions.

She got busy on the remote.

And later, after she'd fallen asleep, exhaustion deepening the lines around her mouth, after he'd slipped her shoes off and lifted her in his arms again, he made the trek up to his bedroom, tucked her under the covers, and . . .

He grabbed some clothes and slept in the spare bedroom.

Even though he wanted, more than anything, to slide in beside her and take her into his arms.

CHAPTER FOUR

Lexi

SHE WOKE SLOWLY, her throat feeling like it was on fire, her eyes also burning.

For one second, she thought she'd just woken up with a cold.

Then she inhaled and smelled not the scent of Caleb, but the spice and sandalwood that was intrinsically Luc and, all at once, she remembered *everything*. Mere stinging turned into an inferno in her eyes. Her throat went tight. Her stomach twisted and knotted, nausea rising. She slipped out from beneath the covers, stood, and surveyed the room, inhaling slow and steady.

In. Out.

In. Out.

Do not *puke on the rug you helped Luc pick out.*

Focusing on the inane thought calmed her insides. She managed to not vomit on that pretty rug then slowly made her way to the bathroom. The air within was sticky, its humidity speaking to someone—to Luc—having showered recently. And just the thought of a shower created the desire to stand under the hot stream of water, feeling it pound against her skin, sluice over her body, and take with it all this agony and betrayal that was slicing at her.

She went to the tiny room on the side that housed the toilet, did her business, flushed, and came out, her heart skipping a beat when she saw Luc through the open door of the bathroom. He was wearing a pair of sweats, half naked as he moved through the bedroom, pausing for a heartbeat to tug a T-shirt over his head.

She must have made a noise, a slight movement, and he heard or caught the action out of the corner of his eye, because his gaze arrowed up, his face going soft.

"How are you doing?" he asked quietly.

"I'm okay," she lied.

Which he knew.

Because his lips pressed flat, his eyes went gentle, and she braced herself for more of the careful words, the easy tone from the night before, knowing it wouldn't take much for her to morph back into that sobbing mess who'd ruined Luc's shirt. God, she'd cried *so* much, first during the drive, having to pull over a half dozen times before reaching Luc's house, although they barely lived five miles apart. Then on his porch and his couch and in his arms and during the movie—

Seriously, who in the fuck cried during Chris Farley's fat-guy-in-a-little-coat bit?

It was physical comedy gold.

So, anyway—she took a deep breath—she was done with crying, was firmly ready to move into plotting to eradicate her soon-to-be-ex-husband from her life.

"There's a toothbrush in that top drawer you can use," Luc said, almost brusquely instead of the tender, gentle voices she'd expected, as though he'd known she was one nice sentiment away from going to pieces. But then again, he probably *did* know. He was her best friend and knew everything about her, from her obsession with pineapple on pizza to her asshole father . . . and now to her asshole of a soon-to-be ex. Two assholes, one life. Oh what a lucky girl she was.

Sighing, she met Luc's eyes, saw they were kind but devoid of pity, thank God. He nodded toward a narrow door on the far end of the bathroom. "Towels and girly shit are in there."

Her brows rose. Why would he have "girly shit?"

He wasn't seeing anyone, and in all the time of their friendship—nearly two years they'd been all but inseparable—she'd never seen him with a woman. Well, she also hadn't spent much time in his bedroom. It hadn't exactly been appropriate for her as a married woman to be chilling in a man's boudoir, even if Luc was just her friend. The extent of her experience with the space was when she'd helped him measure it for the new rug a month before.

Usually, they'd been at her place, and the times she'd come over, they'd stayed downstairs or had camped out next to the hot tub in the back yard.

So, maybe he had loads of women parading through his bedroom.

It wouldn't surprise her in the least.

After what she'd found out yesterday, every man in her circle probably had a secret life.

"My sister's," he said, moving to the cabinet. "She left it behind when she stayed last month."

Her brows relaxed.

He opened the door, took out towels—two, she noticed, because of course he'd know that she'd need one for her hair and one for her body, same as he knew that she'd prefer "girly shit" to wash up with. Caleb hadn't gotten that, not even after seven years together. But Luc . . . well, he noticed all those little details. He paid attention. He cared, and she had no clue why he was still single.

He was a good guy.

Her best friend.

And the one person in the world she hadn't even hesitated to turn to when the three women had shown up on her porch.

"I can use the guest bathroom."

A shrug. "This shower's nicer."

She bit her lip, had the sensation of his eyes going to the spot. "The rug looks good," she whispered, her gaze darting away.

"Yeah," he murmured, and she glanced up in time to see him moving across the room, hanging the towels on the top of the shower. "Mostly because I had someone who actually has a sense of style help me pick it out."

That made her smile, to relax enough to follow him over and bump her shoulder with his. "Liar," she said. "I've seen your suits."

The man had style in spades.

He cupped her cheek, green eyes sparkling. "Just a little kid playing dress-up."

Lexi snorted, her eyes dropping down and then back up. "There's nothing *little* about you."

The air around them shifted, somehow going taut and loose at the same time, and she found herself drifting closer, her body leaning against his. Embers of heat in his eyes, a tendril of desire sliding down her nape, her spine, her ass, curling in and—

She skittered back.

Luc's hand dropped to his side, fingers clenching into a fist.

"Enjoy your shower," he murmured.

And then he was gone, the door *clicking* closed behind him.

CHAPTER FIVE

Luc, Two Years Before

IT HAD TAKEN him one meeting to realize that all his talk of not needing a woman and not wanting a relationship was complete and utter bullshit.

Because . . . Lexi.

Holy shit, she was smart.

She'd figured out a solution to a clause in the contract with one of the team's vendors—a laundry service they'd decided to try out when their equipment manager had gone on maternity leave. It had turned out to be a disaster, and they wanted out, had hired extra hands to deal with the laundry on site. Tired of paying double, they'd gone to cancel the contract and had received nastygrams from the company's attorneys.

Never fail, though, Lexi had found some language in one of the clauses that could have been interpreted one of a couple of ways—"Ambiguity is usually not our friend," she'd said, pointing out the line. "But in this case, it should give us the space to push back."

She *had* pushed back.

And now, they were out from underneath the contract.

And when he'd gone to her office earlier, intending to thank her, she'd waved him off, invited him out for a celebratory beer with Todd and a few others.

Smart. Confident. Didn't take herself too seriously.

Normally, he wouldn't have accepted the offer. There were some lines that needed to be kept unsmudged, and boss or not, those within the realm of work should stay firmly in place.

Today, however, he couldn't say no.

Maybe it was her eyes. Maybe her smile. Or . . . maybe it was the invite without any pressure. The sense that he could relax in this woman's presence.

So . . . he'd said yes.

Then for the first time in a really, fucking long time, he'd actually put down work he'd been in the middle of in order to make it to the bar on time. Mark the fucking day down in history.

That just didn't happen.

But for this woman, he hadn't even thought twice of it.

He'd actually been watching the clock, counting the minutes until he could go to her.

Now, he was stepping out of his car, shoving his wallet and cell into the pockets of his slacks, and moving toward the bar. It was spring, an unseasonably warm day, and the heat had him rolling up his sleeves as he moved to the door, tugging it open.

Music filled the space, loud enough to make him squint— illogically, like turning down the radio when he was trying to find a place to parallel park downtown.

He searched the space, saw Todd first.

Then Lexi.

Thud-thud.

His heart twisted in his chest, squeezed tight then relaxed.

Todd and Lexi sat kitty-corner at the high-top table, two pitchers and a stack of glasses in front of them. The table was full except for two empty seats on either side of Lexi. She had shrugged off her jacket, slung it on the back of her chair as she laughed at something someone said.

Thud-thud.

Jealousy tore through him. He wanted to be the one to make her laugh. The one by her side. Even though he knew it was just friendship with Todd, the other man happily married, his kids grown and his first grandbaby on the way (law had been a second career for him). Even though he knew there was no reason to be envious of Todd.

Luc still was.

That deep-rooted, intense feeling had his feet sliding to a stop.

He'd had five meetings with Lexi—four with Todd at her side, only one with her alone—and every time he'd entered the conference room, each time he'd laid eyes on Lexi, Luc had felt the same focus, the same forceful draw to her.

As though every cell single-mindedly pointed in her direction, fixated on what she was saying, gleaning every bit of information he could about her.

She drank her coffee black.

She liked gummy worms.

She always wore black slacks, but she had pairs with pink, blue, and red stripes as well as the white-lined ones he'd seen that first day.

Her nail polish had changed every time he'd seen her, but the color was always topped with glitter.

And now, she was drinking a beer with Todd, seeming totally at ease.

Something else he respected. That she seemed totally comfortable with herself, regardless of the environment she was dumped in. Which, look, he understood was a generalization, considering he hadn't seen her outside of work and now this one bar, but Luc prided himself on being a good judge of character.

He wanted to get to know her better.

He wanted to ask her out on a date, regardless of the complications their work lives might bring.

He was willing to weather some pretty intense storms, considering their two-week acquaintance, considering that after his divorce, he'd vowed to never wade into a situation with complications and ties again.

Bottom line.

This woman was different.

So, all of his careful rules were going out the window.

Lexi laughed again, the noise sloshing over him like liquid sunshine.

Thud-thud.

His feet began moving again.

Yeah, maybe it made him a romantic fool, but he had absolutely no doubt that this woman would be worth burning up his rulebook.

He stepped up to the table, inhaling the sweet, floral scent of her, feeling that rightness boiling in his blood, coursing through his veins, propelling him into the chair next to her.

She smiled, and it was an arrow to his heart—but not in a painful way, in the sudden *thunk* of air freezing in his lungs, his pulse speeding. "Luc," she said. "You made it! Do you want a beer? We have . . ." She named two types, both of which he didn't process because he was watching her mouth move instead of actually hearing the words.

"The second one," he said when she paused, obviously waiting for a reply.

She nodded, poured him a glass and set it in front of him, joining back in on the conversation around them. Every other chair was now occupied, though the faces weren't familiar.

He listened, only half paying attention to the words exchanged.

Instead, he was focused on the smell of her hair, the heat he could feel coming off her body, the nude nail polish topped with pink sparkles, the half-moon of red lipstick on the top of her glass.

Luc was staring, but he couldn't find the strength to stop.

Then the conversation lulled, and she turned back to him, golden-brown eyes focusing on him.

He smiled.

She smiled back, lifting her left hand and reaching for the man next to her.

Luc felt like he'd been gut-punched as he noticed something he'd missed before. Something on that left hand—a hand, he realized now, that had always been on the opposite side of him, one he hadn't bothered to pay attention to because he'd been too focused on everything else.

Because he'd never even considered the alternative.

She laced her hand through the elbow of the man next to her, tugged him toward Luc. "Hey," she said, turning the man in Luc's direction, joy in her eyes. "Luc, this is my husband, Caleb."

Heart seizing, his gaze fixed on the sparkling diamond ring on her left finger, Luc managed to stammer out a hello.

Caleb looked at Lexi the way Luc was desperate to—with love, with adoration, with devotion—and it fueled the bright light inside Lexi, grew that sunshine within her until it seemed to fill the entire bar.

It took one conversation for Luc to see that Caleb was her perfect match.

He chimed in at the right times, complimented Lexi perfectly, refilled her glass, held her hand, gently stroked her cheek when he had to slip out for a phone call.

Love there.

Adoration between them.

But still, Luc couldn't pry himself away from Lexi. Maybe he liked self-flagellation, maybe he just couldn't move from the sunlight into the shadows. Regardless, he stayed in that chair, much longer than he'd intended, listening to her, soaking in every second of her warmth as he worked to shove down the desire, the way her body made him feel, made his cock ache. Instead, he filed away everything he learned about her, made sure he was kind and funny and friendly—*only* friendly—in return.

Even if the thought of being friends with Lexi made it feel like his heart had been torn from his chest and tossed into a blender.

But she was married.

She couldn't be his.

She was happy.

So . . . friends.

If he wanted any part of her in his life, he'd have to be content to only be friends.

CHAPTER SIX

Luc, Present Day

"Enjoy your shower?" he muttered, stalking down the hall.

Fucking, seriously?

Who said that?

Dumbasses, that was who. Dumbasses like him. The last thing he needed was to be thinking about her naked and in his bathroom, too fucking tempting, though he wouldn't lay a finger on her, not when she was broken.

Broken because of that fucking bastard, Caleb.

How had he ever thought the other man was perfect for Lexi?

Caleb had hurt her, and Luc should have recognized the fucker for what he was, should have stopped him before—

Cursing, shoving that guilt down to deal with later, he pounded down the stairs, desperate to put distance between himself and Lexi. *Fuck*. More regrets, because what the hell was he thinking? Touching her like that, drifting close, her tempting body pressed to his.

She was heartbroken.

She was hurt.

She didn't need him getting a hard-on because her breasts had accidentally brushed his chest.

Fingers grasping the curved, metal handle to the back slider, he prowled onto the deck. It was full of greenery and flowers, fucking fairy lights overhead, colorful pottery dotting the space.

Because of the woman who was probably naked in his shower upstairs.

"Fuck," he muttered, moving across the space he'd paid through the fucking nose to create because he, Caleb, and Lexi had gone to the state fair once, because as they'd wandered through the garden section, through the displays local land-scapers had put together, she'd mentioned liking it. It had been one of those scorching summer days, the humidity bearing down on him, sweat soaking through his T-shirt, dripping down his spine. Then they'd stumbled upon that shaded space, a breath of relief slipping out of him when the air had been cooler as they'd stepped through the gate.

And Lex had arrested.

Just stopped immediately in the middle of the path, people streaming around her, lips parted, eyes wide in awe.

"This is the most beautiful thing I've ever seen," she'd breathed.

Caleb had laughed, taken her arm, and drawn her forward. "Come on, crazy. You can't possibly want any more plants. The house and yard are filled with them."

And they were.

Lexi's house was an explosion of greenery and flowers, both inside and out.

But he'd seen the disappointment on her face when Caleb had laughingly led her from the displays. Just a flash of sadness, the barest blip of anything before she'd laced her arm through her husband's, her lips curving into a wide smile, her head resting on his shoulder.

Luc had been three paces behind them, alternating between wanting to tear Caleb's spine out for introducing that flash of despair onto her face, and wanting to give Lexi his credit card and turn her loose in the local garden center.

The latter of which he'd done.

Which was why he was walking across his lush deck, descending the three stairs that led to the in-ground hot tub, also surrounded by greenery and flowers and fucking twinkly lights above his head.

It was an oasis.

Built by the woman who'd had sadness on her face last night for far longer than the blip that day at the fair.

Who'd probably be wearing that despair for many more days and nights ahead.

Which was why he *kept* walking.

Past the hot tub, beyond the tiny herb garden he'd never once so much as plucked a leaf of basil from, moving farther to the small, wooden bench in the back corner of his yard, almost completely concealed by the grouping of oak trees. More twinkling lights, this time hung through the branches overhead. The bench's seat was covered with a thick, brightly-colored cushion that was a "dream"—Lexi's word—to recline on, a small round table perched next to it. On top of which currently sat a paperback of Lexi's.

She'd accidentally left it when her house had needed to be fumigated for termites and Caleb was out of town on business. She'd stayed in the guest room, had been here for seventy-two hours, had spent hours in the yard gardening and reading. Their time together had been long enough for him to build the fantasy in his mind, to dream about what it might be like if she could stay forever.

Then she'd gone home.

And he'd done what he always did when she left, when she went back to her life—he'd locked that shit up and shoved it deep down. Because it *was* a fantasy, and it would never be reality, not with her so in love with her husband.

Friends.

Best friends.

That was it.

He'd resigned himself to the fact it was all they'd ever be.

But now—his fingers ran over the spine of the paperback, traced the bright letters on the front, shoving—now maybe—

No.

She'd just found out her husband had cheated on her. *Yesterday*.

Only an asshole would prey on her now, when she was vulnerable, when she'd had her life shattered and—

Sighing, he stepped past the bench, the table, the book, and then with anger flooding through him—fury that she'd been hurt, rage at the situation, at knowing that this wouldn't change anything between them, not right then anyway—he did the only thing he could.

He stepped up between those oak trees.

And he slammed his fist against the trunk.

Over and over again.

Until the pain in his hand masked the pain in his heart.

CHAPTER SEVEN

Lexi

SHE FELT SORT OF human by the time she emerged from Luc's shower.

The steam-filled stall and "girly shit" had gone a long way toward that, but it was also the numbness that had settled inside her.

Caleb.

She just couldn't believe he'd had a whole other life outside of her.

Multiple lives.

And he was going to have a baby—or Girlfriend Three was. Brittney. A slender blond with huge boobs, a beautiful face, and who was twenty-two.

Twenty-two.

Lexi hadn't felt old, had actually felt in the prime of her life at thirty-six, but seeing the trio of women, all in their early twenties, all far more beautiful than her, and a whole wealth of insecurity had swept forward to encompass her.

For one moment, she'd hated herself, hated her body and the way she looked.

Had thought there was something clearly lacking, if Caleb had needed to seek out someone else.

But then it had hit her that he'd sought out *three* other women. Not even those young, gorgeous early-twenties beauties had been enough to satisfy him. So, it was that kernel she was holding on to as she stepped out of the shower and began the process of starting her life over.

Again.

Once after her mother had died and her dad had pushed her away.

And now, she began anew again, after spending seven years with a man who was apparently a douche canoe—actually, no. There was no apparently about it. He *was* a douche canoe.

She glanced at her clothes, not wanting to pull her dirty things back on, not wanting to be wrapped in the same fabric that had seen the shattering of her happiness.

Not wanting to wear old underwear.

Ew.

That at least, tugged her from her sad state.

It was over with Caleb. Even if Brittney hadn't been pregnant, it would still be over. And yes, Lexi thought that name with a sneer, even though it probably wasn't fair, especially when it seemed like all of the girls had just recently found out about each other and Lexi, and had actually done a decent thing by coming to tell her.

She was still sneering, still upset.

Because Brittney was going to stay with Caleb.

Stay with Lexi's husband.

"Not anymore," she whispered, staring up at herself in the mirror, wincing at the still-swollen eyes, the dark circles, the pale skin. Brittney could have him, and Lexi could even understand why the girl would stay with him. She was pregnant and twenty-two and . . . he was Caleb.

Charming, sweet, kind, so fucking good at making people feel good.

At making *women* feel good.

But also . . . if Lexi looked closer, she recognized that he'd also been good at making her feel bad.

Never outright.

Just quiet, soft, slivers of conversation, planting a seed of insecurity, twisting something she said into a fight, but then the next day acting like it had never happened, praising her to excess, showering her with kindness and compliments, until she'd forgotten all about those barbs, until he'd made her feel like the luckiest woman on the planet. So, she'd tiptoed around during those spiked times, so damned careful, and then when the switch flipped and everything was fine again, and . . . she'd convinced herself their marriage was fantastic again.

He wasn't like that all the time.

Everyone had bad days, right?

Sighing, she ran the towel over her hair, knowing she needed to remember those bad times, those kernels and the switch flipping, needed to focus in on them so she could move on.

But all the good stuff kept flashing into the forefront of her mind.

Caleb bringing back her favorite cheesecake from New York, chilled on dry ice, just because he knew she loved it.

Caleb finding her a rare book on gardening, the pages so fragile she was almost scared to turn them.

Caleb proposing to her with a tree. An actual tree in a pot because he wanted her to plant it in the house they bought, to watch it grow tall and strong over the years. That tree *was* planted in their back yard, thriving, its branches wide and thick and—

He had other women.

Inhaling, she nodded to herself in the mirror, wrapped the towel tighter around her, and bypassed her pile of dirty clothes. Later, she'd collect them.

Right in this moment, she would see about borrowing something from Luc.

She pushed out of the bathroom, just in time to catch Luc bending over the bed, straightening the covers. He glanced up when she entered the bedroom, started to turn for the door.

"Sorry," he said, his eyes deliberately away from hers, even though he'd seen her in much less clothing—toweling?—when they'd spent hours together in the hot tub. "I just thought you might want some clean clothes." He nodded toward the end of the bed, and she noticed for the first time that he'd left a stack of items there. "They're probably too big, but at least they're clean."

"Thanks," she murmured, and he was already striding to the door when she groaned.

"What?" he asked, his gaze seeming to linger on her legs for a couple of heartbeats before lifting to meet her eyes.

"I just realized that I need to find some place to live."

Luc's lips pressed flat. "You're not going to kick him out of your house?"

She probably should. But she didn't want to be surrounded by that lie, that sham of a relationship. Plus, she couldn't afford it on her own, especially if she had to buy him out.

More than that, living there again, knowing it would all be a sham.

"No," she said. It would be more than she could bear.

He didn't press her for an explanation, just nodded firmly and said, "Then you'll stay here."

Her eyes widened. Her lips parted in protest.

Luc was suddenly in her face, his body very close to hers, the spice and sandalwood of his scent surrounding her, and any words stoppered up in her throat. "You'll stay here," he said again, cupping her cheek, and she saw that his knuckles were split open and raw, and she wondered what had happened. Was about to ask when he jostled her lightly. "Lexi, honey, you're staying until you get on your feet again. Are we clear?"

She wasn't a woman who liked orders.

But this was Luc.

And it was a command that allowed her to finally take a full breath, to not feel so fucking broken.

So, she nodded and said, "I'll stay."

He smiled, and it made something in her heart unfurl.

Something that was chased by a blip of fear and prompted her to add, "Just until I get my feet under me."

Those fingers stroked gently across her cheek. Just once before his hand fell back to his side. "I have no doubt that will be very soon."

She wished she had his confidence.

CHAPTER EIGHT

Luc

IT WAS TWO DAYS LATER, and Caleb had been following Lexi around, excuses tumbling off his tongue as she gathered up the things she needed.

Luc had offered to come and do this for her, so she didn't have to see her soon-to-be ex-asshole, but she'd wanted to do it herself.

And he got that, understood she wanted some sort of closure.

But . . . fucking hell, he didn't want Lexi within a hundred yards of the bastard.

Still, Luc was waiting where she'd asked—on the porch—and listening through the open door as Caleb kept talking, the fucker continuing to follow Lexi as she strode through the ground floor, gathering up the things she would need immediately.

They'd agreed it would be best to just get the essentials, and Luc almost smiled when he watched her pick up an indoor plant—one he'd bought her and one she apparently considered to be essential—and carried it out the front door, her eyes meeting his.

He lifted his brows in question, silently asking if she was okay.

She nodded, handed him the plant. "Too delicate to be left to its own devices," she said softly.

"Want me to grab the others?" he asked.

Teeth nibbling on the corner of her mouth. "Just the ones on the table," she murmured. "The others will be fine for a bit."

He squeezed her wrist, knowing that the *bit* would be until Caleb's next business trip. They planned to move the rest of her stuff out then, and though he knew Lexi was worried about where they'd put her belongings, especially if she hadn't found an apartment to rent by then, Luc didn't give a shit. They'd get a storage unit or cram them into his place. He just wanted Lexi to have this break be as painless as possible. "Got it," he murmured, ignoring the pleading look that Caleb was tossing him, having trailed Lex into the front hall.

As though Luc would put a good word in for him.

Never. Going. To. Happen.

The man was dead to him.

But Lexi didn't need any more shit heaped onto her, and that included Luc brawling with her not-yet ex-husband. Not that it would be brawling, he knew. His fury was a deep, ice-cold sort of rage, and he had absolutely no compunction about wanting to make the other man pay. It would be a bloodbath.

Just . . . not today.

Inhaling sharply through his nose, Luc moved to his SUV, opened the tailgate, and carefully stowed the plant.

Then returned to the house and snagged the remainder of her pots from the table—along with a few others that were nearby that he could fit in the back.

Once he'd filled the trunk, he returned to the house and saw that there were a few packed totes in the hall. Most looked to be filled with makeup and hair stuff, a blow dryer, a metal tonglike thing, some brushes, and a toiletry bag, all shoved in along-side several wrapped up towels that appeared to be for her hair.

The next bag had clothes—no, *underwear*. Colorful, lacy underwear that had heat curling down his spine.

He punched it down.

Extinguished it as best he could.

Then grabbed both bags and the one with kitchen stuff, things he probably had at his place, but wasn't about to argue with her over. If Lex wanted her blender, then she'd have her blender.

Luc went onto the porch and stowed the bags in the back seat then followed the noise of Caleb's whining and excuses all the way upstairs and into their bedroom. He'd never been in this space before, but it was intrinsically Lexi. The bright floral painting on the wall over the bed, the soft purple rug, the crisp white linens, the pale gray dresser and nightstands.

Caleb was standing next to her as she emptied that dresser, shoving things into a suitcase, even as he was still pouring out bullshit, though Lexi was giving absolutely no indication that she was listening to him in the least.

The bullshit halted when Luc cleared his throat and let his fury bleed onto his face.

His hatred. His rage.

That Caleb would have the gift that was Lexi and to treat her like *this*.

Oh, Luc was very close to murder, to that aforementioned bloodbath.

But he stifled it, because when Lexi glanced up from her suitcase, he didn't miss the relief in her eyes.

Luc nodded encouragingly. "You've got this," he mouthed.

Her shoulders lifted and fell on a breath, and then she opened the final drawer, scooped out her clothes, and shoved them into her suitcase.

"Lexi," Caleb said, "please, don't do this. It's not what you think."

Luc started to move, to go to her side, but his strong, capable Lexi had it.

"Caleb," she snapped. "You are so full of shit that you don't even recognize its taste on your tongue." She zipped the suitcase closed, stood. "You cheated on me. You got another woman *pregnant*. When we were—" Her throat worked, and Lexi's eyes glimmered with tears before she sucked in a breath, straightened her shoulders. "There's never any going back from that. Not with me. We're done."

There was a finality in her words that had Caleb's shoulders slumping.

But then the bastard reached for Lexi's suitcase, whether to carry it out or hold it hostage, Luc didn't know. Instead of waiting to see which way it would go, he strode across the room, snagged the bag and positioned himself between them. "Ready?" he asked, glaring at Caleb.

Lexi nodded, headed for the door then paused, spun back to the bed and snagged her pillow.

"Now, I'm ready," she whispered. "Ready to move on with my life."

———

HE UNLOCKED THE DOOR, exhaustion heavy on his shoulders.

It had been two weeks since Lexi had found out about Caleb. They'd returned the previous Friday to clear out the rest of her stuff from the apartment.

Then he'd gone on the road with the team, finished out the last three games of the season, while she'd gone back to his house, and had hopefully made herself at home.

The Breakers hadn't made the playoffs—a pathetic undertaking—and Luc now had some tough decisions to make. The board, the coaching staff, the scouts all would have opinions about what the next season's roster should look like, but ultimately, the final choices would be down to him and what type of deals he could negotiate.

And who he had to cull.

Normally, he would have gone straight into his back yard—well, he would have stopped by the kitchen, snagged a beer, and then proceeded to the back yard to get drunk enough to clear his mind.

Today, however, his pit stop—and his pitying—was interrupted by soft humming.

He moved into the kitchen, saw Lexi swaying, her hips moving to whatever music she was listening to, her earbuds bright white against the brown wisps of her hair that had escaped her ponytail.

Something was boiling on the stove, the oven was on, and she was wearing an apron over her dress, heels on her feet.

It was his actual 1950s caveman fantasy, all born to life.

A woman in the kitchen, waiting for him.

A dress that could be lifted, heels that could be pressed into his back when she wrapped her legs around his hips as he thrust deep.

God, he was a fucking pig.

Lexi was still humming, dancing, slowly spinning in his direction.

Her eyes widened when she saw him, one hand going up to tug the earbud out. "Hey!" she said brightly, though he didn't miss the ring of red around her eyes that showed him she'd been crying.

Again.

Fuck.

"I'm sorry about the team," she murmured, her face soft. "I know the season didn't go how you wanted."

That was the understatement of the year, but Luc just smiled and said, "Shit happens."

A blip of bleak in her eyes. "Yeah, it does."

Fuck. *Again.*

Only this time because he was the one causing her pain. "Did you watch the game?"

"I—you know I'm not—" She broke off with a wince, and he just chuckled.

Because despite her job, she wasn't much of a sports fan.

He tugged the end of her ponytail. "It was better that you didn't see the slaughter."

Her brows raised. "The score didn't seem so bad."

It pleased him that she'd checked the score, more than it probably should. Especially when she didn't belong to him, when she wasn't all that into hockey. "It was bad," he said. "Trust me when I say the score cannot properly encompass the absolute horror that was my team on the ice." He shook his head. "I don't understand. We have the talent, and they were really beginning to gel at the start of the season." He sighed and turned for the fridge. "I can't pinpoint what it is that made it fall apart, and if I can't do my job"—another sigh as he yanked out a beer—"how the hell can I expect them to do theirs?"

He spun for the drawer, dug through until he held the bottle opener, but Lexi's soft voice stopped him before he could use it.

"Luc?"

He turned . . . and she walked into his arms.

Later, he would swear his heart stopped, skidded to halt when her arms wrapped tightly around him, when the scent of her filled his senses, but in that moment, all he could do was wrap himself around her in return and breathe deeply.

He wanted to hold on to her forever.

"I'm sorry things didn't work out the way you wanted," she murmured, squeezing him tight. "But you're a good GM. You'll figure out how to bring the team together."

Luc slumped, his forehead resting against hers, and she gripped him tighter.

"I see you don't believe me," she said, staring into his eyes. "But you haven't seen the way the guys look at you." Her breath puffed against his lips, soft puffs of delicately scented air. "They respect you."

He snorted, not in the mood to feel better.

She smiled, her fingers coming to his cheek. "I mean it."

"Thank you," he said, covering her hand with his. He forced a smile. "*I* mean it."

A swat to his shoulder. "Snarky bastard."

"You bring out the best in me." He didn't dare move, not when the hand that had smacked him still rested on his shoulder, when the other remained on his cheek.

Her mouth turned up.

Her fingers lightly kneaded, and their bodies drifted closer.

Her chest brushed against his, her breasts so fucking plump and lovely . . . and his cock went hard.

He tried to will it down, to ignore the lush feel of her.

He never wanted her to leave his arms.

But then she felt it, felt his cock stirring. He knew it the moment her eyes widened, her mouth parting in a tempting O that he was desperate to kiss.

Then she lurched out of his hold, face going pale.

And he was forced to make a joke. "Men," he said with a laugh that sounded strangled. "Unfortunately, even men of my advanced age never seem to grow out of our proximity issues."

Her color returned, pink flaring on her cheeks, her breathing elevating, but she searched his eyes then nodded as she turned back to the stove, stirring one of the pots.

Fuck. It seemed to be his perpetual thought around her, ever since his body had fought him on shoving down the urges, on understanding that just because Caleb was out of the picture, it didn't mean she was available.

He opened his mouth to apologize, but she beat him to speaking.

"I was hoping you might be up for a movie marathon tonight," she said lightly, and without seeing her face, he couldn't tell if it was forced or real. "I bought that special mix for the popcorn and set up the projector in the back yard."

Luc perked up. "The cinnamon sugar one?"

She glanced over her shoulder, nodded.

He fist-pumped, and she laughed, and it was genuine for sure this time. Then he froze and narrowed his eyes at her in mock suspicion. "What kind of movies for the marathon?"

The spoon hit the counter, and she drifted over again, squeezing his arm, close enough for him to smell roses in her hair, close enough that he didn't miss the caution in her expression.

When he didn't move, when her eyes flicked down, probably checking the state of his erection (now, thankfully, nonexistent . . . at least for the moment), the caution faded, as though she needed to prove to herself that she could touch him without it being weird . . . or without him pouncing on her like a horny, rabid beast.

"The only kind that matters," she said, smiling wide enough to make his heart thump. "Anything with Farley or Sandler."

He grinned. "And *that's* why you're my best friend."

Something flashed across her expression—disappointment? despair? relief?—but then it was gone, and she was shoving the beer into his hand. "Go get started without me," she ordered. "Swimsuit on. Beer down the hatch. Feet in the hot tub. I'll be out with the food in a few minutes."

He opened the beer, took a sip, but didn't leave. "What can I do to help?" he asked instead.

Her brows lifted. "You can let me take care of my best friend." The slightest emphasis on friend, and whether it was for him or her, he didn't know, didn't have time to process, anyway, because she was already nudging him toward the stairs. "Which means, following my orders."

Luc's heart thudded. "You're the best, Lex."

She smiled, but it was minus the majority of her usual playfulness, tinged instead with sadness. "I'm just thankful you see it."

As opposed to the man who hadn't.

He wanted to hug her again, but she turned her back on him once more, focused on the food on the stove, and he wanted to make her happy, to not drudge up the unhappiness all over again.

So, he took his beer and followed her orders.

CHAPTER NINE

Lexi

LUC TOOK one look at her face and pushed his way into her apartment, the paper bag of food in his hand crinkling, the door *clicking* closed behind him.

It had been a month.

She should be done with crying.

God, Caleb hadn't even reached out to her again since that day at the house when she'd grabbed anything she could think off, ending up with a random mishmash of belongings.

Winter sweaters and summer pajamas.

Heels and one half a pair of sneakers.

Thick wool hiking socks, but not her boots.

Luc had been at her side a week after that, Caleb in London for business—or perhaps to make another family—when she'd collected the rest of her things, and then had helped her make one final trip, just this morning, to oversee the movers picking up the furniture she'd brought into her marriage.

A small love seat, the kitchen table, the bed that had resided in the guest bedroom, and her plants.

Every single one of the potted plants she'd spent so long tending.

They were already looking worse for wear, though Luc had gone with her a few times to water and feed them—like pets, he'd teased. But her green pets were safe in her apartment now, and although she'd insisted he go home, that he stop worrying about her, he was here.

"You're supposed to be living your own life, Luc Masterson," she said. "Not coddling me and worrying about mine."

He tugged a strand of her hair, one that always seemed to escape her ponytail, no matter how hard she worked to contain it. "You're my best friend. It's my job to worry about you."

Then he pushed by her, strode into the kitchen, and began unpacking the bag. "Where did you put the plates?" he asked, not waiting for her to answer as he turned and began opening cupboards. "Ah." He pulled down two, started dishing up Chinese food.

She could smell the spicy tang of orange chicken, her favorite. The one that Caleb had never ordered because he couldn't stand the scent of citrus.

But then again, Caleb hadn't done anything he didn't want to, had he?

He'd just been really good at making her think she hadn't wanted to do it in the first place, that it had actually been her idea *not* to do it.

The memories made her eyes burn.

Because, dammit, she hadn't been smart enough to understand the manipulation, or worse, she hadn't been strong enough to leave because of it. And she was supposed to be both of those things, and yet with Caleb . . . she would have given him everything. Stayed forever.

And that made her—

She didn't want to think the word, because she was damned tired of feeling pathetic.

"Hey." Calloused palms cupping her cheeks. "This, Caleb,

none of it was your fault. I didn't see it either. Neither did Todd." He tilted her head up, until she was forced to meet his intense emerald eyes. "You have to stop beating yourself up," he ordered. "If he couldn't see what a fucking gem you are, then he doesn't deserve to have you in his life."

The words . . . they unlocked something inside her, something that she shouldn't be feeling, and yet a truth, perhaps, she'd always held deep inside.

Oh, why couldn't she have met Luc before Caleb?

Why couldn't she call this man *more* than a friend?

She jerked.

She'd never thought that. *Never* ever even considered it. She *couldn't* consider it, not when she was married, not if she'd wanted to keep Luc in her life. Because she wasn't a cheater, and because she'd respected her marriage, had loved Caleb with every part of her.

But . . . Caleb hadn't loved her back, hadn't respected her or their marriage, and he certainly hadn't loved her as he should have.

Another certainty? Caleb wasn't like Luc.

For a moment, she considered what it would be like to cross over to Luc, to wrap her arms around his waist, and feel his strong, hard body against hers. To taste him. Every *single* inch of him.

Desire, heady and viscous, slid down her spine, trailed down between her thighs.

She wanted that, was desperate for it.

She felt so much for him, admired him so much, held so much affection for him in her heart. He was the one person she'd let in—all in—to her heart, perhaps even more deeply than she'd let in Caleb.

He glanced up from dishing out the food and smiled.

So much warmth.

And that was the moment she realized the *perhaps* part in the letting him into her heart more deeply than anyone else was extraneous. There was no perhaps about it. He was stitched into the organ, into her soul.

And . . . he would eviscerate her if she lost him like she'd lost Caleb.

She couldn't walk into his embrace, couldn't kiss him, couldn't be anything more than his friend.

Because . . . she wouldn't be able to walk away when he left.

And if the story of her life played true, he *would* walk away.

So, she stayed where she was, shoved down that urge to be more than friends, and when it was tucked safely away, when her heart was carefully surrounded in barbed wire and reinforced with concrete, she walked over to the tiny kitchen and accepted the plate.

From her best friend.

Only her best friend.

CHAPTER TEN

Luc

HE WAS SHIT AT SKATING.

But he managed, sort of, to not make a fool of himself.

It hadn't used to be that way, not during his playing days. He'd been one of the faster players on the ice, able to dodge and weave with the best of them. But to be truly skilled at skating, two good knees were critical. Especially, for the sort of navigation that the sport of hockey required.

And Luc didn't have that any longer.

Instead, he had one good, one bad. Well, one good, one shit.

The only positive of the entire situation was that he at least still had decent hands.

Decent enough that he managed to dance around a few of the other old bastards currently on the ice before passing the puck over to his teammate and former Breaker retiree, Mico Storm, who easily slammed it home in the net. Because of that goal, his team in this charity hockey tournament had now pulled ahead in the game, and even though they were playing solely *for* the Breakers' charity—the Lil Wavemasters—Luc wouldn't be Luc if he didn't want to win the whole thing.

He was a competitive bastard, and that wouldn't ever change.

"Fucker," Frankie Bullard, another former player who was on defense for the other team, called as they all skated to the bench for a much-needed line change.

"Hey," Luc said, slashing him—somewhere between light and hard . . . okay, more *hard* than light, if he were being honest. "I used to sign your paychecks!"

"Liar," Frankie said, lips tipping up into a smirk as he batted Luc's stick away. "The finance department arranged the direct deposits."

Considering that Frankie was now in charge of that exact department, Luc supposed he would know. Not that Luc would admit such a thing, especially not when he was on the ice, surrounded by shit-talking former players and friends, all of whom—including him—were out of shape and too fucking old to be fun to watch.

But, for some reason, the stands were still full in the small practice arena they were playing in, the tickets completely sold out, and though the crowd was still cheering, it was a cheap imitation of the roar of the fans at The Crest—the home arena for the Breakers. When the team was playing well, when they were winning, Luc would swear it was the loudest rink in the league.

But it had been a while since they'd truly been winning.

Sighing, he climbed over the bench, sucked down some water, and concentrated on catching his breath.

Fuck, he was getting too old for this.

There was a tap on the glass behind him as he set down his water bottle, and he turned to see that Lexi was there, smiling. She mouthed, "Nice pass."

He shrugged.

She rolled her eyes, and he imagined her saying, more than was able to read the words on her lips, "Accept the compliment."

He nodded.

Her smile widened, and then she tilted her head in the direction of the exit, and he knew she was taking off to the library where she volunteered every Thursday.

See? Even the charity tournament's big game didn't merit a weekend game.

They were small time.

"Have fun," he mouthed.

Smiling, she mouthed back, "I will." Then with a wave, she disappeared back around the rink, heading for an exit.

Mico nudged him. "GM's got a girlfriend?"

"GM—if I'm talking in this weird pseudo-third person—has got a best friend and that's all," Luc told him.

"Damn," Mico said. "She's gorgeous." A smirk. "I didn't realize you'd lost your touch. Getting old, are you?"

Luc rolled his eyes but didn't engage.

Mico's gaze drifted across the rink to where Lexi was pushing out the rinks' double doors. "Isn't she from legal?"

"You know she is," Luc said, scooting down the bench when another line jumped on the ice. "You've had meetings with her."

"That why's she not your girlfriend? It's not like you'd be dating an underling. Legal is a completely different department from the team."

Luc tore his eyes from the game—okay, from where Lexi had disappeared—and glanced at the nosy little fucker. "She's my friend," he said simply.

Brows lifting, questions in Mico's brown eyes.

And Luc knew Mico wouldn't let it go, would just keep pestering him with questions until he spilled, so he added, "Plus, she's married."

Those brows and the knowing in his gaze went higher. "I heard she was getting divorced."

The fucker.

He *knew.*

Luc inhaled. "You're a prick."

"Damn right."

"Asshole," he muttered.

"And *that's* my wife's pet name for me," Mico quipped. "How did you know?"

Luc snorted, shook his head.

"Just saying, she's into you as much as you're into her." The whistle blew, and they stood to hop back onto the ice. "And if all that was stopping you for going after her before was her husband, that's out of the way now."

Mico was right about that. Or at least, *that* part.

Caleb was out of the picture, and Luc would hurl him back out if he attempted to return.

But even without the bastard around, time didn't magically heal hurts, and though it had been three months since her separation, the damage was still there, and more extensive than just from a divorce and a cheating husband.

Because she also had deep wounds from her father, who hadn't been much of one after her mom had died. Luc didn't know everything, but he knew enough, knew that *that* bastard had pretty much disappeared the moment her mom was in the ground, that he seemed to assuage his conscience for doing so solely with monthly phone calls.

Lexi hadn't had much of men sticking around, and certainly not enough of them doing right by her.

So, he wouldn't push, wouldn't take their relationship somewhere she didn't want.

Even if *he* wanted, so fucking much.

"You should go for it," Mico said. "Unless you want someone else"—he coughed—"*me*"—another cough—"to go for it."

"You're married," Luc muttered. "And Tiffany would slice your dick off if you *go for it.*"

"True," Mico countered. "Though, even if *I'm* out of the picture, someone else might not be."

That was Luc's most intense fear.

That he'd lose his chance with her, miss his opportunity.

Luc shot him a death glare. "You should mind your own fucking business." His death glare got even deathlier. "And tell all those other fuckers to keep their fucking hands to themselves."

Mico smirked. "Touchy."

"She's not ready."

Mico's expression evened out, understanding in his gaze.

The whistle blew before he could say anything else, and Luc blinked, lining up at the hash mark and focusing on not embarrassing himself for the final few minutes of the game.

He didn't.

They won . . . the championship *and* the bragging rights.

But when the trophy ceremony was over, and they were back in the locker room, Luc was hard-pressed to ignore the "unless you want someone else to" part of Mico's teasing.

He didn't want to share Lexi.

He didn't want to wait and watch her with someone else.

It would fucking kill him.

Except . . . what could he do? She needed time to heal, not him pressuring her for what she might not want to give, what she might not be *ready* to give for a while. Even *if* sometimes he thought that he glimpsed some heat in her eyes.

Because aside from those few and far between glimpses, she hadn't given any indication she wanted anything besides friendship.

So, he would just show her that he wasn't going anywhere, show that she could trust him.

He wouldn't push.

Not yet, anyway.

CHAPTER ELEVEN

Lexi

THE KNOCK on the door wasn't welcome.

She was having a pity party for one in her recently-acquired apartment.

Because she'd filed for divorce.

Officially.

And she shouldn't be crying, even though she'd had a moment of weakness and had actually considering calling Caleb and asking him to take her back (seriously, what the fuck, Lexi?), she'd gotten the paperwork filed, and her attorney thought everything would be finalized in three months or less.

Go her.

Single at thirty-six. *Exactly* what she'd dreamed of.

Which was why she ignored the knock and went back to her pity party for one—which consisted of a bottle of wine and eating straight out of her gallon of rocky road. Maybe she'd buy herself a pack of party hats online and keep drinking until they showed up in two days.

Then at least she could be festive.

The knock came again, and unfortunately, she knew who

was on the other side. Or at least, she assumed she did, still ignoring it while tapping away on her cell's screen.

The knock came a third time before the lock clicked open and the door pushed wide.

Luc walked inside, took one look at her face, and plunked a pizza on the counter.

"That good, huh?"

She rubbed her nose on her shoulder, oh so cute. "Go away," she snapped.

He ignored her, moving to the cabinets and pulling down two plates before dishing her up pizza—with pineapple. He set one in front of her. "Eat," he ordered, "and something besides pure sugar."

She clutched her ice cream closer. "You're not the boss of me. And anyway, wine's not pure sugar."

"Care to reconsider that statement?"

A smile. Even when she was feeling mopey and pissed off, his smile was still a beam of sunshine straight into her soul.

And *that* was the wine talking.

Because look at that, she'd almost finished the bottle.

"No," she muttered.

His eyes went to that nearly empty bottle. "Drinking your dinner?"

"Yup." A beat; her eyes narrowed on his. "Gotta problem with that?"

"Nope." He nudged the plate closer. "Though you might want some bread to soak up the booze for the morning. We're too old for hangovers."

"I can have a hangover if I want." More muttering.

This time his smile pissed her off.

That was also the wine talking.

"I'm staying drunk until my party hats come in two days. 'Cause I'm supposed to be celebrating instead of feeling like shit." She held up the phone, gestured at the screen. "See? They're pretty with sparkles and everything. But they're not coming for two days." Her cell dropped onto the counter with a clatter. "So, I'm staying drunk until they come, and that's that."

"That doesn't sound like a good plan."

"I don't care," she muttered, scooping up a giant bite of ice cream. "Drunk until party hats."

"Lex—"

She dug back into the carton, glaring at him. "I think I already told you to go away."

There was that grin again, so fucking bright and lovely and—

"I hate your smile," she grumbled, stuffing the spoon into her mouth.

He laughed, grin widening. "Well, I love yours."

She sniffed, put down her spoon, and began glugging wine. Was she feeling tipsy? Damn right, she was. Did she give a fuck right at this moment that she'd probably have that hangover Luc was talking about? Nope.

"Nope," she repeated with a *pop* on the p.

"Nope, what?"

"Nothing," she slurred and then since the bottle was swimming in her vision and she didn't trust herself to reach for it, she held up her glass and added, "Since you're not leaving, at least give me a refill."

"Nope." It was his turn to *pop* on the P . . . right as he snagged the bottle and moved it out of arm's reach. She could see that much, even if everything else was still floating and drifting like a buoy on the waves. "Not until you eat something that's more filling than ice cream and wine," he said, pushing the plate a little closer. "See? It's even got pineapple on it. Your favorite."

She shoved the plate back, staggered up to her feet, the wine glass in her hand. "Stop it."

He brought it close again. "No," he said, his eyes flashing. "You need to take care of yourself."

"I *am* taking care of myself." And so what if her words were slurred. She was a grown woman who could live her own life as she wanted, and if that involved two days of drunkenness and party hats and red wine and rocky road ice cream, then that was just perfectly fine.

She nodded, agreeing with her inner monologue.

"The fuck you are," Luc said, snagging her arm *and* the glass.

The latter he set on the counter, the former he held as he picked up the plate and shoved it in her face. "Eat. The. Fucking. Pizza," he ground out.

"Fuck you," she said through gritted teeth.

His brows rose, and he rocked back slightly on his heels, but he didn't let her go. "That's fine," he said after a moment. "You can be pissed at me, at your situation, at the world if you want." His eyes came to hers, something hard and molten in those emerald depths. "But you're still eating the goddamned pizza."

Something inside her snapped.

Maybe it was the slice of pizza an inch from her nose. Maybe it was the divorce filing. Maybe it was her father and Caleb and every other man who'd tried to ingratiate himself into her life.

Who the fuck knew?

What she *did* know?

That she wasn't eating the fucking pizza. She didn't give a shit that it smelled delicious or that it was her favorite or that Luc had been kind enough to bring it to her.

No one had any right to tell her how to live her life.

"I'm not."

"You are."

She smacked the plate out of his hand.

She must have surprised him. Hell, she'd surprised herself. She'd never done anything like that before. Never *ever*. But it was done, and she could only watch as the ceramic disc flew down onto the tile . . . and shattered.

The pizza went one way, the plate's remnants scattered in a hundred different directions.

Some of the haze of alcohol faded, and shame poured in.

"That was a supremely stupid thing to do," Luc growled, his eyes going to her bare feet, the glass shards all around. She'd never seen such a furious expression on his face. Not *ever*.

Tears welled in her eyes, but she didn't apologize. *Couldn't* apologize.

Instead, she just lifted her chin.

And . . . waited for him to leave.

"Fuck," he hissed, scooping her up. His shoes crunched on the glass as he carried her over the debris of the plate and pizza, moving to the couch and plunking her on it.

"Luc," she whispered when he turned away, knowing this would be the moment when all of those fears came true, the moment he decided she was too much trouble.

And he would go.

And she would be alone. Again.

His eyes, blazing emeralds, came to hers, but he didn't say anything.

Instead, he moved back to the kitchen and picked up the shards of ceramic, the ruined slice of pizza, tossed them all in the trash. He retrieved the dustpan she kept beneath the sink, swept the space, and when she started to get up to help, he glared at her, snapped, "Stay."

She sank back down onto the couch.

Watched in silence as he grabbed the vacuum from the hall closet and ran it over the floor.

Back and forth no less than ten times.

Then he calmly grabbed another plate, filled it with pizza, put the ice cream in the freezer, and topped off her glass.

"Eat," he ordered again, bringing the wine and pizza over to the coffee table.

She hesitated, and he crossed his arms, fury dancing in his eyes.

Lexi picked up the pizza, took a bite.

Only after she'd chewed and swallowed did he bring his

plate over and settle down next to her. Without a word, he turned on the TV, pulled up the reality show she'd been bingeing of late, and they sat in silence as they ate and watched.

As he refilled her glass.

Over and over again, until she shook her head in silent refusal.

Then they sat in that continued silence as he pulled the ice cream back out and got her a fresh spoon.

And stayed quiet . . . when the tears came.

When he wrapped his arms tightly around her as she ruined another one of his shirts.

The silence was only broken when he carried her to bed, brushed a kiss to her forehead, and ordered—more orders—softly, "Sleep."

Luckily, it was an order she didn't mind heeding.

She let her eyes close as the blankets were tucked around her, sleep rising up to drag her under.

And in the morning when she woke up, definitely hungover, though not nearly as bad she would have been if Luc hadn't demanded she eat, she hobbled her way into the kitchen and smelled the coffee he'd made. A greasy breakfast sandwich that she knew instantly would be the best hangover cure ever sat next to the still steaming pot. Sighing in relief, she poured herself a cup, took a sip as she turned, saw the blanket folded neatly on the end of the couch, the pillow next to it.

And next to that . . .

She blinked, crossed over to the coffee table and frowned at the purple hat, almost identical to the ones she ordered last night.

It was propped up next to a bottle of ibuprofen, a note on the wood next to it.

So you can stop drinking.
-L
P.S. You can push me away, but I'm not going anywhere.

She ran her finger over the glittering hat, tiny purple sparkles gathering on the tip. It was just a gift, a silly, what should be meaningless but was instead a ridiculously important gift—because it showed *again* that he paid attention, that he listened and gave a shit what she said.

Because she was finally getting that it was a gift . . . from the one man in her life who'd proven he would stay.

CHAPTER TWELVE

Luc

IT WAS SEPTEMBER, time for a new season.

Fresh beginnings and a chance to start over.

Luc had high hopes for the team. They'd picked up some good players, their rookies were looking good at training camp, and their experienced guys were solid.

"What do you think?" he asked Oliver, when the captain skated up to him, leaning back against the boards as the young guys played on.

Most would spend the majority of their time in the minors.

A few would find permanent positions with the team.

Marcel Aubert was one of them. A talented forward, he would make a good addition to the offense, and while their defense was mostly untried, they had a couple of older players that Luc would be relying on to bring stability.

Oliver nodded. "I've got a good feeling about this season. May take us some time to find our groove, but most of the guys are genuinely motivated."

The *most* in that sentence was concerning, but when he

glanced at Oliver, the other man shook his head. "Just some personality clashes, I think."

"You let me know if it becomes too much to handle."

Oliver opened his mouth as though to say something, but then Tommy, the team's head coach, blew the whistle to gather up the rookies. Oliver straightened, readying himself to skate over and join them.

"You know you don't have to be here for every practice, right?"

Only a few of the full-time roster guys were here, mostly those recovering from injuries who needed the extra ice time.

Oliver met Luc's eyes. "Leaders lead by example."

Then he skated over and joined the players huddled around the red line, taking a knee and giving his full focus to Tommy.

Luc smiled, approval sliding through him.

Yeah, he had a good feeling about this season, too.

———

SHE WAS TENTATIVE TONIGHT.

Probably because he hadn't been alone with her since that night at her apartment, when she'd tried to push him away.

They'd both been busy with work since then, trying to get everything settled for the new season, and though he'd stopped by her office and they'd eaten lunch together with conference calls rolling in the background on speakerphone, they hadn't spent time like this in nearly a week.

This meaning at one of their places.

This currently meaning his back yard, their feet in the hot tub, and beers in their hands. Along with soft pretzels dunked in the cheese dip he'd picked up on the way home from one of their favorite restaurants.

"Did you . . ?"

He glanced up from where he'd been studying the bubbles

in the heated water, and met her gaze, lifted a brow when she hesitated. "Did I what?"

She gestured at the pretzel that remained. "Did you want the last one?"

Since they'd stopped being that polite around each other, stopped the dithering do-you-*no*-do-you civility a long time ago and just ate what they wanted, Luc waited.

Teeth nibbling into a lush bottom lip. "I mean, if you're still hungry, then you can—"

"I saved it for you." He shifted, nudging the plate closer. "I always save it for you."

Because the woman had a hollow leg and could eat him under the table.

Because he would never deny her anything.

Because she loved these fucking pretzels.

Because he loved her.

"Why?" she whispered.

And he couldn't tell her that.

Not yet. But . . . they were getting close to that time, to when he would push, when he would make it clear just what he wanted. That gave him the strength to just smile and say, "Because you have a fucking hollow leg and can eat me under the table?"

She nibbled at her bottom lip.

"What?" he asked, smoothing back a strand of her hair.

She didn't back away, just shook her head and reached for the pretzel.

"I'm not mad," he said softly. "I wasn't mad then, and I'm certainly not mad now."

"You were definitely mad."

"I was . . . frustrated that you weren't taking care of yourself," he told her. "That was all." He nudged her shoulder as she took a bite. "You were pretty spicy yourself, if you remember."

"I was a total asshole," she murmured, dropping the pretzel, shame washing over her face. "You've been so nice and under-standing and amazing, and I treated you like—"

"No," he said, stopping with a hand on her wrist.

"*Yes*," she countered.

"*No*," he said again. "You lost your cool. You've had the shit piled on you, and you lost it *one* time. I'm not a baby. My feelings aren't hurt. I promise."

"But it wasn't right, and I hurt your feelings . . ."

"No." He cupped her cheek. "You didn't. I'm sure there will be a time I freak out, that I lose my cool." He sure as hell hoped not, but shit happened, and he wasn't dumb enough to think he was completely immune to it. "You just return the favor when I do, and we'll be good, okay?"

Her eyes studied his for a long moment.

Then she nodded, released a shaking breath. "Okay."

"Good," he grumbled. "Now, eat the fucking pretzel. We need to catch up on our couples."

For the dumbass reality show she'd hooked him on.

She took a bite of the pretzel, smiled up at him with such warmth in her eyes, such affection, so much that he nearly felt blinded, as though he'd looked into the sun, and he knew he couldn't tell her he loved her. Not quite yet.

But soon.

Soon, he'd find the perfect time.

CHAPTER THIRTEEN

Lexi

SHE STARED at Luc's back, sweat seeping through his T-shirt, causing it to stick to all those yummy muscles there.

Yummy?

No.

She wasn't supposed to be thinking anything about Luc was yummy.

He was her friend. That was it.

Even if he *was* yummy.

He glanced over his shoulder, lifted a brow. "Coming?" he asked.

Yes, she totally could be *coming* with him, if only she made the first move. Her gaze dipped down to the firm globes of his ass, outlined to a delicious degree in his workout shorts.

Lex froze, forced her gaze back up, shoved the heat away.

Because *one*, nose wrinkle. When had she gotten into childish innuendos? (Side note: probably right around the time she'd stopped having regular sex). And two, her decision to keep Luc firmly in the realm of friendship meant that she shouldn't be thinking about yummy muscles and delicious curves and definitely shouldn't be thinking about anything remotely related to *coming*.

"Lex," he said again, his tone teasing, his eyes still on hers. "Did I break you on this paltry hike?"

She scowled, wiped a hand across her forehead, and started walking again. "You know only insane people hike in the middle of summer. This humidity is my seventh circle of hell."

"It's technically almost fall," he pointed out with a sly grin.

"Tell that to the weather," she grumbled, moving to catch up with him. "I'm sweating like a pig."

He smiled, and just like always, her heart blipped. "Worried about your hair?" he teased.

No. *That* worry had worn off about five minutes into the first hike she'd taken with Luc, nearly two and a half years before. Now, she didn't bother with makeup or anything other than a hat and ponytail.

"Worried about *yours?*" she countered. "I think you have a gallon of product in it." She sniffed and moved alongside him. "It's probably melting all down your spine."

He tilted his head back and laughed, loud and true, and the sound of it slid right into her soul.

God, he was such a nice guy.

He'd seen her at her worst. Multiple times.

And yet, he'd stayed.

Even when she'd done her level best to push him away.

That was something she had been thinking about lately. More than she probably should be, considering that she was clinging desperately to the whole friendship thing.

Because the fact still remained. She was terrified of what might happen if she lost him.

Was afraid that it would shatter something inside her.

Yes, she was fully aware that made her a coward.

No, she wasn't ready to stop ostriching any time soon.

Inhaling deeply, she tugged down her hat and kept hiking. They were almost to the top of the hill, and she'd already spotted the place where she'd rest her weary feet. A large boulder that overlooked the forest, green for the foreseeable future.

"Come on, slowpoke," she said, prodding him in the side. "I want my PB&J."

He laughed. "Who says I packed them?"

She tossed her head, smiled at him. "Because I packed the gummy worms, and if you don't have my sammy, then I'm not sharing."

"Meanie," he said, then stuck out his tongue.

"You're the—"

She stumbled on a tree root, catching herself in the next instant, but Luc's hands were already there, wrapped around her waist, ready to steady her, even though she didn't need it.

Normally, he released her almost immediately.

This time, he lingered, sweat and male filling her nose. His skin gleamed golden in the sunlight. His breathing was slightly elevated from the climb.

But then again, so was hers.

And she was starting to question whether it was truly the climb, or if it was just this man.

Despite the brightness, his pupils were huge, his emerald irises darkened to almost black, making his eyes look other-worldly.

His thumbs moved just slightly, and she shivered, body drifting forward.

"You're beautiful," she murmured, stroking her fingers over his jaw.

He blinked, lips parting, hands tightening, but didn't say anything, didn't back away.

"That's really not fair, you know, right?" she murmured as she ran her fingertips through the bristles on his cheeks, loving the sensation on her skin. "You shouldn't be so pretty."

His hand covered hers, pressed her palm flat. "You realize

that you're the pretty one, right?" His breath puffed on her lips. "*My* nose is a wreck, and I'm covered in scars."

She shouldn't be this close. Shouldn't be in his arms, touching him.

But a wildness had overtaken her, and she couldn't move, could only drift closer, could only continue to touch him.

"The scars make you look rugged."

One side of his mouth curved up, highlighting the thin white line at its corner. A line she was tempted to kiss.

A tiny scar she'd actually risen up on tiptoe *to* kiss when a noise had her jumping out of his arms.

A family came around the corner, two young boys skipping down the trail, their parents following them, holding hands as they descended. Maybe it was seeing the parents with their fingers interlaced, or perhaps it was the kids, reminding her of what she didn't have. Either way, the sharp slice of pain that slid through her had her keeping her distance from Luc as they continued their hike.

Friends, she reminded herself.

Only friends.

Even if she was starting to realize that she wanted so much more.

CHAPTER FOURTEEN

Luc

DESPITE ALL THE promise on their roster, the team wasn't off to the greatest start.

They'd lost their home opener on a few bad bounces, and it looked like they were going to lose this matchup, too.

"Damn," he muttered, knowing the fans wanted a win at home.

It always meant something more when they were in The Crest.

The timer counted down, the buzzer sounding on the three-one loss, and Luc pushed out of his seat, leaving the team box and heading to his office, hopeful that the team would sort out their failures.

It was a new system for most of the team. It would take time to sort out the mistakes and hiccups.

At least their goaltending was solid.

Martin Robinson was the only reason the score hadn't been seven to one.

Sighing, he headed to his office, cleared out his inbox while watching the guys and Tommy be interviewed by the media, their pressing questions annoying and presumptive.

"Will this be the year the Breakers make their comeback?"

"Do you honestly think the team will have a chance at the playoffs after the way last season went?"

"What could have improved tonight, and will those changes have an impact on the remainder of the season?"

No one knew the future.

The only thing they could do was put their best foot forward and hope things would come together. The pieces were already in place, and now they had to see how they played out.

Oh sure, they could make shifts as the season went on, but they would all be reactive to circumstances (in response to matchups, injuries, trades, chasing points as they headed into the post-season) rather than proactive (locking in the strongest roster possible before the year began).

None of the changes from here on out would give them the same strategic effect.

He sighed, rubbed his forehead, and knew it was time for him to get the hell out of the office. To go home. Overthinking this for the hundredth time wouldn't make the least bit of difference.

Sleep then refocus in the morning.

He picked up his suit jacket, moved to the door, and was just about to leave when there was a knock on the metal panel. Frowning, wondering who would be trying to see him at this late hour, his usual quiet, uninterrupted time as the arena cleared out, he opened it slowly.

Lexi was leaning against the doorjamb, looking sexy as hell in tight jeans and a royal blue Breakers jersey, a blue ribbon tied around the end of her braid.

"Hey," he said, surprised.

"Were you leaving?" she asked.

He nodded, and she stepped back, letting him flick off the

lights and shut the door behind him. "What were you doing here?"

"I figured I'd better check out this whole hockey thing," she said lightly.

His brows pulled down. "You watched the game?"

"From the nosebleeds," she said with a nod. "Still don't understand most of the rules, but it was fun to be with the fans. Quite an atmosphere." A smile. "Though they got a little rowdy toward the end."

"A multitude of *'you sucks'* being shared around?"

That smile widened. "A chorus of them, all in perfect harmony from the littlest chitlin to the oldest, grayest man."

Luc snorted. "They must have really loved how the team played."

"There might have been a few *'you sucks'* about our boys." She winced when she saw his expression. "But only a few."

"We'll rebound," he said. "It'll come together."

"I know."

"I could have gotten you tickets, you know." Could have had her in the box next to him, an idea, he had to admit that he liked far too much.

"I know," she said again. "But I had it."

He brushed his knuckles down her cheek when she paused, glanced up at him. "I know you do."

"Luc?" Her hand rested on his shoulder.

"Yeah?"

"I—"

A door slammed in the distance, and whatever she'd wanted to say disappeared as she turned forward and continued walking. They were quiet as they turned the corner that would lead them to the exit, but just before they made it there, she snagged his hand. "Wait."

He stopped, frowned. "Everything okay?"

"Of course." She tugged him toward a stairwell. "There's just something I wanted to show you. Is that okay?"

Luc nodded, letting her tow him along, lead him up several flights of stairs. His knee ached with the exertion, not happy at the pressure it put on the joint to ascend them all, but he didn't say a word, even when she drew him through a hall and then beyond another door, the cool air of the arena surrounding him . . . and the narrow metal staircase.

"Come on," she murmured, when he paused at the base of them, releasing his wrist to grip the handles as she climbed, not stopping until they were on the metal gangway, high over the ice below.

She sank down in the middle of the platform, and he mirrored her, though with a bit more discomfort.

"Your knee," she murmured. "Shoot, I'm sorry." She rested her hand there, rubbed the joint.

"It's okay," he said, even though he liked her touching him, enjoyed the little bit of fussing. "Have you come up here a lot?"

A nod. "Well, not *a lot*, but a handful of times. I find that sometimes it's the only quiet place to be found here."

Luc snorted. "That's for damned sure."

She shifted a little closer, her gaze on the arena, her fingers still working on his leg, and his cock was becoming a problem. Not that he'd ask her to stop. He'd just have to do some strategic shifting so she didn't spot the tent in his slacks.

"I like to look around and see how big this is, even when my job, my part of it all, seems so small." Her free hand swept toward the rafters.

Luc glanced at the banners, at the flags that showed the retired numbers, at the others that showed their accolades— some of the hangings emblazoned with "Division Champions," a few with "Conference Champions," and one with "Stanley Cup Champions."

The team's accomplishments, displayed there for the world to see.

"You did that," she whispered. "You were *part* of that."

"You were, too," he said.

"A small part." She smiled. "You, good sir, are a large part."

And a large part of the losses since, he thought, stifling a sigh.

Her shoulder bumped his. "Don't do that."

"Do what?"

"I didn't bring you here for a pity party." A sly look in his direction. "The hats are still are at my apartment waiting for that true celebration."

He chuckled.

"I brought you here so you could see," she murmured. "See that you're having an impact and bringing some joy to those who love the game, making it a good place for the guys to play." She yawned, and he almost coaxed her back down those stairs, bundled her into his car because she was tired and needed a good night's sleep. But then she melted slightly, resting her head on his arm, and he couldn't move, not when she was like this. "Sorry," she said. "What I'm trying to tell you is to not take responsibility for every part of this. The team is a unit that has to be working together in order to be truly effective."

He opened his mouth.

She pinched his arm. "And don't say that it has to be led by someone effective to *be* effective." She sat up, cupped his jaw with one soft palm. "You *are* effective. You're one of the smartest people I know, *and* you live for this team."

"Are you trying to stroke my ego?"

Not a good choice of words, especially when her other hand rested just above his knee.

"That depends."

He stared at her, brows raised.

"Is it working?"

Luc chuckled. God, he loved this woman. "Yes," he said. "Thank you." Then he turned his head, found himself kissing her palm.

Lexi inhaled sharply, the air between them tightening, desire its bowstring pulled taut.

She leaned in.

He leaned in . . . and this was the moment. This was when he would finally taste her, high above the world, her scent surrounding them.

It was perfect.

Her tongue darted out, moistening her bottom lip, her breath smelled sweet, as though she'd drunk one of The Crest's famous root beer floats. Her fingers tightened, drawing him even closer . . .

A trace of uncertainty crossed her gaze.

Fuck.

Fuck.

He pulled back.

She released a breath, and whether it was in relief or disappointment, he didn't know.

And that was precisely why he hadn't kissed her.

"Luc," she whispered.

He stared deeply into her eyes, trying to discern one over the other, whether it was disappointment or relief. "Yeah?"

"I—" She paused, didn't look away from him for what felt like an eternity, the golden-brown depths flickering with emotions he couldn't read. Then her gaze flitted away, and she murmured, "I'm tired."

Not tonight.

Not yet.

He stood, angled his hips away so she didn't see his cock pressing against his slacks, then extended a hand and helped her up. "So, let's get you to bed."

The flicker of heat in her eyes didn't help his tent situation, eroded his decision to pull back, made him curse his word choice.

But he didn't want any hesitation on her part when they took that final step.

So . . . patience.

Soon, he would have her for the rest of his life.

CHAPTER FIFTEEN

Lexi

SHE WASN'T GOING to cry.

She'd done enough of that.

More than enough of that. God, it felt like she'd done nothing but cry for the first month after she'd found out about Caleb, until she'd seriously begun to wonder if she'd filled the ocean with her tears, singlehandedly contributing to the sea levels rising.

But then, thankfully, eventually, the tears had halted.

And she'd trucked right down the six stages of grief.

Denial. Oh, God, she'd had fun with denial, thinking that she could just ignore the affairs, the baby mama, and just continue on being married to Caleb because they'd had good times, and they'd been together seven years, and it would be, it could be *them* again.

Thank fuck that phase had lasted less than an hour.

Until she'd seen the sonogram picture on Instagram, Caleb happily holding it up, the young (*young!*) redhead he'd knocked up beaming widely.

Yup. That snap had propelled her right out of denial.

And firmly into panic.

What the fuck was she going to do with her life? Were they going to have to sell the house? Oh God, not her house, not the one that had the back yard she'd planted with love and care. Not the space she'd spent hours digging out copious amounts of rose bushes, their roots going so fucking deep.

Plants aside, back yard aside, and twinkly lights she'd hung and rehung and rehung again until they were draped just perfectly, when Lexi realized she'd been more worried about losing her plants and lights, she'd snapped out of the panic.

She wouldn't be able to live in that place and not see Caleb's betrayal.

Then it was onto bargaining.

Maybe she could convince Caleb to stay married, just for a little longer, to give her enough time to figure out a way to keep that yard she'd poured her blood, sweat, and tears into. She could tear out the plants, transplant the trees.

Their tree.

Thankfully, that stage had also been short. Mostly because their tree was a lie.

But probably also helped by Luc reminding her that selling the house and buying a new place meant she would have another yard to redo, one she was able to design all on her own.

No Caleb having an opinion about a stunning water feature, just because he didn't think it was worth two hundred dollars. No Caleb making fun of a gorgeous flower, just because it happened to resemble a vagina. No Caleb grumbling about helping her haul bags of soil into the back yard.

So now, six months after her life had been reduced to shambles, Lexi had moved on to anger.

Because . . . Caleb was now a father.

A. *Father*.

To a healthy baby boy with bright red hair and Caleb's hazel eyes and . . .

She was alone. In an apartment. With a balcony full of potted plants but no back yard.

No twinkly lights.

So yeah, anger was here to stay. Rage had supplanted any bargaining and panic and denial.

Hopefully, considering she'd spent the first month filling the Atlantic with her tears, she'd leapfrog right over the fifth stage of depression and land in acceptance.

Because, *God*, she thought, looking at the envelope on her desk, the stack of papers she'd just pulled from inside. Divorce papers. She was getting ready to sign her divorce papers. Everything would be final the moment she scrawled her signature on the line on the bottom, just beneath Caleb's name.

He'd already signed.

So . . . this was it.

Seven years of her life wasted. Seven and a *half* years, if she were being exact.

And now what?

She was thirty-six. Single. Childless. Which, look, was fine. If someone didn't want to have kids, then good on them. But she'd always dreamed of being a mom, of having a partner who loved her, who went to school plays and sat for yearly portraits. After meeting Caleb, after falling for him and marrying the fucker, she'd thought that future was within grasp. She hadn't ever imagined having to start over.

What was she going to do? Start dating again? Get on Tinder and start swiping?

God, just the thought of having to meet men on an app or needing to make small talk in a bar or coffee shop or the grocery store . . . hell.

That seemed like *hell*.

But an even deeper circle of hell?

Remaining married to the asshole who'd cheated on her with three—at least, because there was always a distinct possibility that there more—women.

That wasn't even an option.

So . . . she picked up a pen and scrawled her name on the line.

Then paused, the tip of the ballpoint hovering a couple of millimeters off the paper, and waited.

For what, she didn't quite understand.

It seemed so anticlimactic. Streamers should burst forth from the ceiling, fireworks should explode over the harbor in the distance. A band should blare to life playing a jaunty tune to signify this huge moment.

But nothing happened, even as she waited a little longer. The only noise was her breathing, the *click* of the pen as she placed it on the desk, the soft rumble of voices in the hall. Perhaps she'd expected for depression to swell up and swallow her whole, to drag her into a whole new swell of emotions.

Instead, she just felt . . . resigned.

It was over.

Sighing, she tucked the papers back into the envelope and swiveled toward the window, staring out at the surrounding buildings, the blue sky with puffs of cotton-like clouds.

No fireworks.

Just another phase of life down.

One tick through a box she'd never wanted.

Divorcee.

She stood, reached for her purse. It was early, but suddenly she needed to get out of here, away from the steel and glass, away from the papers. Away . . . from everything.

After she strode to the door, her fingers were on the knob when it turned in her hand.

It pushed in toward her, making her skitter back a step.

Luc's head popped in.

Her heart squeezed when he took one look at her face and came fully in, closed the distance between them, and wrapped her in his arms.

He'd hugged her countless times over these last six months.

She'd sobbed against his strong chest, soaked more than a handful of his T-shirts, slept in his bedroom while he'd—against her arguments—taken the guest space.

They'd spent a lot of time together, her and her best friend.

So it was no surprise he was here.

No surprise that he'd known in an instant what was up.

And that strong, broad chest was her strength, those solid arms her support. Only today she didn't cry, didn't melt into him, didn't dissolve. Today felt like she could maybe stand on her own feet. She thought that . . . maybe she would be okay.

She stepped back, and his green eyes came to hers.

Assessing.

Then approval drifted across his face. "You signed."

She nodded toward the desk, toward the envelope she hadn't been able to stomach taking with her just moments before. Now, with Luc here, with the pride on his face, she found that she wanted that envelope gone, wanted the papers out of her sight.

She wanted to be done.

So fucking done.

Four more steps brought her back to her desk, one reach had her fingers grasping the envelope and then rotating to face Luc again.

He stood patiently by the door. So damned patiently. She'd never seen him lose his cool, not at work, not at home. He was always even and cool. He was always kind, understanding, even when she'd been so wrapped up in grief and hurt that she'd treated him abhorrently. Not a pushover, not in the least, but considerate and empathetic.

"Come on," he said when she neared the door again.

"Where?" she asked.

His mouth curved. "To celebrate."

"With party hats?"

He chuckled. "I do have the rest of the set. Want to match?"

He pretended to zhoosh his hair. "I think pink sparkles in particular will bring out the green of my eyes."

Lexi found herself laughing, even as she shook her head. "I think the gold one would serve you better."

"Done," he said, tilting his head. "Let's go."

She trailed him down the hallway where the law offices were located in the Breakers' facility. They had a small legal staff for the team, just one other associate counsel, a couple of interns, and a clerk, but she hoped to be promoted to head counsel in the next few seasons. Her boss, Todd, had certainly been grooming her for the position. For the moment, though, she was happy with her role as associate counsel. Sports law was interesting and intricate, and it kept her on her toes.

Pairing that with some pro bono work for a local charity that offered free legal advice out of the local library, and her professional life was full.

She waited until the coast was clear before asking, "Celebrate where?"

"I have some plans," he said lightly.

Her brows lifted.

"I've been considering this for a while."

"Oh?"

He bumped her shoulder. "Yes, *oh*."

She grinned. "You're too good to me."

"I'd do anything for my best friend," he said, and, no, that wasn't a blip of disappointment sliding through her. That was . . . *happiness*. Right, happiness that this man cared for her, that he'd been the greatest freaking best friend in the world.

Friend.

Friend.

She was really starting to hate that fucking word.

But . . . to use her least favorite cliché in all the world, it was what it was, and she was lucky enough to have him in her life.

"No," he said when they'd reached the parking lot and she turned in the direction of her sedan, "leave your car here. I'll drive you back in the morning." His smile was full of mischief. "You won't be in any shape to get behind the wheel," he said when she lifted her brows in question.

"Why?" she asked. "Because we're getting drunk?"

He tapped her on the nose. "Because *you're* getting drunk. I'm having three beers, max."

"Spoilsport," she teased.

"Someone's got to drive my drunk BFF home."

Her mouth curled up at the corners. There was something that was ridiculously funny about hearing big, burly Luc say *BFF.* "It's Tuesday," she said. "I'm not getting drunk on a Tuesday."

Now it was his turn to lift his brows.

But he didn't comment, just snagged the envelope from her fingers, opened the door with a flourish, and said, "We're dropping this off on the way."

She could kiss the man.

She couldn't, of course.

But maybe . . . kinda sorta . . . in a totally inappropriate way, she . . . really wanted to.

She sat down in his car.

The door closed.

At exactly the same time, the steel-plated one in the back of her mind, from which that dangerous thought in her brain had emerged, slammed closed.

And not a second too soon.

CHAPTER SIXTEEN

Luc

SHE WAS BEAUTIFUL.

Too fucking beautiful for the men who were staring at her as they walked down the sidewalk, her heels clacking on the cobblestones as they strode through one of her favorite parts of the city.

Fell's Point was all bright buildings and ancient streets, restaurants and bars and shops. If they moved beyond the cafés, past the temptation of the yummy smells in the air and made it down to the waterfront, they could take a water taxi, cuddle together in the cool evening air, and watch the bright lights drift by.

But that was something to do on a date.

Not something that best friends did.

So instead, he just stayed close as she perused the menus out front of each restaurant, bending at the waist and lifting the hem of her dress to levels that had his cock twitching. If she remained true to course, she'd read every single menu on the block before deciding on a place.

Which was fine with him, since he got to enjoy the view.

Pervert? Probably.

Inadvisable? Also, probably.

But though he tried to not stare, he found his gaze drifting back to her ass, over and over again. It was a dangerous game he was playing, but he couldn't stop himself.

Soon. Soon, he kept promising himself.

But sooner or later his control was going to snap, and he could only hope that Lexi was ready for it.

After they'd dropped the papers off at her attorney's office, Lexi had insisted on going back to her place to change, and he'd waited in her tiny living room, the space crammed with every potted plant that had been in her old house. They were doing as well in her apartment as they'd done in her previous home, filling the room with lush greenery and brightly colored flowers.

None of which had held a candle to her when she'd appeared out of her bedroom, her shining brown hair cascading down around her shoulders, her curvy body encased in a sinful black dress. Breasts and hips, legs and ass. He'd been absolutely starstruck, his cock hard in an instant, the urge to grab her, to pick her up and haul her back into the bedroom intense and almost overwhelming.

She'd worn a pair of strappy heels he'd never seen before, thin bands of leather crisscrossing up her calves, stopping just below her knees. He'd wanted to trace the lines, to allow his fingers to disappear under the short hem that danced around the middle of her thighs. Creamy skin, legs he'd been desperate to get in between from the moment he'd first seen them, and her breasts. Fuck, they were on display and calling for his mouth . . .

He'd turned away, focused on a plant with bright purple flowers.

Thank God she'd gone into the hall, gathering a shawl-sweater thing, covering up enough of her cleavage that the haze of his desire cleared, and he'd been able to shove the urge away, to grab her purse from the coffee table and bring it over to her.

Now they were here standing on the sidewalk, the cool drift of the evening breeze lifting the ends of her brown hair, blowing it forward and around her face, even as she wrestled it back, straightening from the menu placard she was reading, giving a small shake of her head, and then moving to the next restaurant and the next.

So much bending, so much skirt lifting, so much of his gaze heavy on her body, fueling his desire until it was a fiery thing, no matter how hard he tried to extinguish it.

Then they'd reached the end of the street, and she was straightening from the final menu, a chagrined expression on her face.

"The first one, is it?" he asked, need tempered by amusement.

She wrinkled her nose. "Is that okay?"

As if he'd ever deny this woman anything, least of all a meal in a restaurant of her choosing. Which was why he took her hand and led her down the cobblestones back to that first restaurant, the one he'd known from looking over her shoulder at the menu that she would choose.

Because . . . chocolate cake.

Because . . . champagne.

Because aside from her love of plants, those two things were her kryptonite.

Paired with homemade pasta and Cesar salads, and he'd known they would end up at this Italian restaurant.

Her heels *clacked* on the sidewalk as they meandered back, her shoulder brushing his, her soft, floral scent drifting up to his nose. People moved all around them, weaving and talking, their conversations loud and filled with laughter, but he didn't give them more than a sliver of his attention, because it was all about Lexi.

He held the door for her as they made their way inside, forced himself to tear his gaze from her face, her body when they were seated. Ordered some pasta dish and salad he didn't give two shits about.

They were here.

She was smiling.

"Oh," he said as the waiter started to turn away. "Can you bring a bottle of champagne? And our desserts first?"

Lexi's brows rose.

He shrugged. "We're celebrating."

Her smile grew, his heart pulsed, and yeah, he knew that he'd do absolutely anything for her. "Yeah," she murmured. "Yeah, we are."

———

MAYBE STARTING with champagne hadn't been the best idea.

Because one bottle had turned into two, and by the time Lexi had devoured her pasta, her color had been high, her eyes slightly glazed, and she'd been well on the opposite end of tipsy.

But she was happy.

So fucking happy and talkative, her plans for the house she was going to buy once her old one sold rolling off her tongue, plant names interspersing with paint colors and furniture styles.

"And then," she said, her fork waving through the air, "I'm going to go lingerie shopping, because I burned every piece of underwear I bought for that fucker, and now I'm stuck with boring cotton panties, and no man is going to want to fuck me in gross, granny panties."

"Any man who's worth his weight doesn't give a shit about the underwear on his woman."

Her lips turned up. "As long as it's clean?"

Laughter bubbled in his chest. "Clean would be preferred."

Preferred, but not required. Not with this woman. Which probably made him sound fucking gross, but whatever. He was already in love with Lexi, so he wasn't going to pretend.

At least in his head.

In the real world, after she'd had her heart shattered, he had definitely been pretending. To be the best friend and nothing more, until she wasn't so vulnerable.

That time was coming soon. They inched closer to it every day, every moment, until he could almost taste it on the air.

And then he'd strike.

Like a fucking cobra.

More laughter, this time escaping because of his own idiotic thoughts, but luckily it blended in with Lexi's, with her amusement over the underwear conversation.

Then he was paying, despite her argument to the contrary, and then standing up, leaving the restaurant. She took his hand, guiding him a block over toward the noise and music he could hear spilling out on the sidewalk. A bouncer stood by the door, but he took one look at Lexi and immediately let them in, and given the huge smile, the complete and utter joy that was emanating from her, Luc didn't blame the other man's gaze for lingering, not one bit.

He still wanted to punch the fucker for looking at her body, though.

"I need a drink!" Lexi said, lacing her fingers with his and towing him to the bar.

"You sure?" he asked.

Her eyes met his, a tendril of sad in her golden-brown eyes. "I want to get drunk," she declared. "Really, *really* drunk." She squeezed his hand. "So drunk that I don't remember. So drunk that this night wipes away all of the nights before. And then I want to dance until they kick us out, until the moon is high, and tomorrow becomes the first day of the rest of my life, and it's going to be fucking great!"

Heart thudding, he slid to a stop, his insides in a blender, shredded by her hurt, and yet somehow whole because she was so fucking strong.

Because despite everything, she had hope and wanted to move forward.

Fuck, he loved her.

Fuck, he loved her enough to be here, to give her the strength and support to grasp on to that hope, to ensure that this light inside her, the one that had finally reappeared after six long months, never went out. He'd be her kindling and her flame. He'd been her shield from the rest of the world, hands cupped around the tiny sparks just beginning to burn again.

"What are you drinking?" he asked, starting to walk again.

More light, more bright, more *life* bubbling up through her and filling the space around them.

"Vodka cran," she said.

"You mean a Cosmo?" he teased.

"Nah." A squeeze of his fingers. "That's too fancy. I just want a lot of vodka with a dash of cranberry."

His mouth turned up. "Done."

He made a mental note to call Todd before the night was up, telling him she'd be taking the next day off. Then he slid an arm around her waist, hauled her close, and set about turning tipsy into drunk.

CHAPTER SEVENTEEN

Lexi

SHE WAS FLOATING.

Or maybe less floating and more slicing through the sky, a turkey vulture riding the heat of the morning air, circling higher and higher until she reached the top and sailed down.

Then again, circling once more, the heat under her wings lifting her higher.

Until she was soaring, the music pulsing around her, filling her up.

Warm arms surrounded her, a spicy male scent her body identified as safe, as wonderful, as *Luc* creating the perfect little bubble around them as they danced and danced.

Her feet were well beyond aching in her heels. The alcohol had blunted the initial discomfort, and now she'd danced them into numbness.

It was glorious.

So fucking glorious.

She felt alive again, the bass thrumming through her veins, sweat sheening her body. Luc had her shawl and her purse tucked under his arm, and it should have looked ridiculous, the big burly man holding her glittery bag, but it was . . . right.

Everything was right when she was with Luc.

The music slowed, and she found her body drifting closer to Luc's. He was so much taller than her, having several inches on her, even though she was wearing her tallest heels. Strong and warm and smelling so damned good.

"Should we get another drink?" he asked, smoothing her hair back from her face.

"No." She wound her arms around his waist, rested her head against his chest. "I want to keep dancing." Her hips jutted forward, pressing their bodies together as they slowly circled.

He inhaled sharply, a sound she couldn't hear over the music, but one she felt against her chest.

But that wasn't all she felt.

Because he was . . . hard.

Now, it was her turn to inhale sharply, a bolt of desire arrowing through her insides. His cock was granite and thrusting against her stomach, and God, it had been so long since she'd had an orgasm.

More than six months.

More than six long months without a cock inside her, and if she were being truthful, if the alcohol buzzing around her brain was revealing the reality she hadn't wanted to admit before things had ended—that sex between her and Caleb hadn't exactly been soul-shattering.

She'd loved her husband.

Loved him desperately until he'd broken her trust, broken her heart.

But her marriage hadn't been all she'd hoped it could be.

That was the understatement of the year.

She snorted and nuzzled close to Luc, to the man who wouldn't break her, to the man who'd always kept her safe, who'd been her friend and sounding board and support system when the rug had been pulled out from beneath her feet.

Their hips brushed again, and she stiffened at the feel of that erection against her.

Not in fear or disgust, as he probably suspected, given how quickly he angled their hips away from one another. But because . . . she *wanted* him.

He bent, spoke directly into her ear, the heated words making her shiver and press closer. "I'm a man," he said, his husky chuckle skating down her spine. "It comes with the territory when a beautiful woman is dancing so close."

He'd said something similar once before, and it hadn't sat well with her then, just as it didn't sit well with her now.

She didn't want it to come with the territory.

She wanted it to come . . . for her. To come *in* her. To—

His mouth was still at her ear. "We should go get another drink."

"In a minute," she said, turning her head to speak into his ear, breath catching when the movement brought their lips past one another, so close to that intimate line they had never crossed.

Heart pounding, mind spinning, she let her head fall to his chest, enjoying the feel of him against her, of that warmth and strength . . . of his—her hips tilted toward his—cock, hard and jutting against her abdomen. God, he was so sexy and wonderful and—her arms tightened around him.

"Lex—" he began, his breath warm against her hair.

"Just a little longer," she said above the din, her head tilting back, her eyes meeting his.

The pulsing lights flickered across the green of his irises, reminding her of a Christmas tree, of the joy of winter, the first snow of the year, floating down and coating her skin, her hair.

His lips parted, his head dipped, and then his mouth was at her ear again. "Okay, honey."

Relief coursing through her, mingling with desire, with the

booze, with . . . Luc, and this night, this celebration. With forget-
ting everything that came before and focusing on what
could be.

What she wanted.

It finally crystalized in her mind.

What. She. Wanted.

Holy *shit*.

Whom she wanted.

She jerked in Luc's hold, gaze lifting and returning to his,
searching the green depths for some sign that his erection was
about *her* and not just that it was the result of some intimate
dancing and male biology. But . . . there wasn't much there that
she could discern, not with the dimness of the dance floor, the
flashing lights.

And if it was just biology? What then?

Did it matter?

Would it ruin things?

She knew that Luc wouldn't change, wouldn't despise her,
no matter what they did together. Still, she knew to the depths
of her Cosmo-addled brain—no, to her vodka-cran-addled
brain—but the point was that even the alcoholic buzz in her
mind understood the risk was too great to risk imploding her
friendship.

This attraction was vodka related.

This attraction was six-months-pent-up related.

This attraction meant that she needed *more* alcohol, and she
needed to find someone else to fuck.

Because it wouldn't be Luc—even if he wanted her back,
even if her attraction *wasn't* the result of alcohol, and his hard
cock the result of dancing close. Even if she were willing to risk
her friendship.

The slow song ended, shifting into something more fast-
paced, the thrumming music vibrating through her, making her
need and want and—

"More drinks," she said, forcing herself out of his arms, turning for the bar.

Luc didn't argue, just sheltered her with his body as they moved through the gyrating bodies, as they moved over to the steel and granite counter, behind which the mirrored wall held shelf after shelf of alcohol.

The bartender knew them by now, smiling as she set a glass down in front of her, as Luc pulled out some money to tip her, even though he didn't get a drink for himself, even though he'd long since stopped drinking. Even though she'd long ago stopped arguing with him over buying her drinks.

She picked it up, handling it in the careful way she moved when she was drunk. Easy, slow movements, pretending that she was far less tipsy than she let on.

Through pure dint, she managed to raise it to her mouth, to take a long, heady sip without spilling it over her dress. And fuck, it was glorious and tart, with just enough booze that she could taste the bitter bite of vodka.

Warmth slid through her, loosened her limbs, softened the draw to the man behind her.

It allowed her to look around, to focus on the other men.

To study them, to hope and pray for some sort of pull, some semblance of attraction.

No one compared. Nothing burned inside her.

Not like Luc.

Well, she'd just ignore that, would just find someone close enough who maybe didn't make her burn, but who could at least spark something, could pull off the Band-Aid of sleeping with someone who wasn't Caleb.

She set the empty glass on the bar top, straightened, and eyed the closest man.

Attractive, nice smile, a confident gaze that met hers then drifted down. Tendrils of desire slid through her. She could do this. It would be fine, and—

An arm slid around her waist, tugged her back against a firm chest. "No," Luc said. "You're not here for this."

"I need a cock," she moaned, hips tilting back, her ass finding *his* cock. Wishing that things could be different, that maybe they were more than friends. "It's been so fucking long, Luc. I need—"

"Drunk tonight," he said, hissing when her ass thrust back. "Fucking another."

"But—"

"*No*, Lexi." He dragged her back to the dance floor, far away from the man with the nice smile, the one who might have tempted her to do something she might later regret. Her body was flush to his, his cock was still hard, and she had enough alcohol in her system, was enamored enough with his body against hers that she didn't give a fuck about the man by the bar any longer.

Not when she had Luc.

"Baby," she whispered.

There was no way that he could have heard her, not over the noise bumping out of the speakers. But either he had super-human hearing or he just sensed that she'd spoken, because he kept one arm around her, used his other hand to cup her cheek.

"Dance, Lex," he said, and she read his lips more than she heard the slight rasp of his voice. "Just dance."

Green eyes.

Happy memories.

Luc.

Luc.

She moved closer, and . . . she danced.

CHAPTER EIGHTEEN

Luc

TORTURE.

Absolute torture to have her curvy, soft body pressed to his. No. Writhing against him, driving him mad, fueling his desire until it burned through his veins. He'd given up on trying to tamp down his cock, knowing he'd have to be gay or made of stone in order to not be affected by Lexi.

God, she looked so happy plastered against him.

Her eyes closed, head thrown back as she moved to the music, her hair a silken sheet over the arm he had clamped around her waist.

She was beautiful and free . . . and *his*.

He knew he'd do anything to make her his.

So it was torture to have her against him, especially after her gaze had been on the other man at the bar, when she'd said she needed a cock.

Fuck.

Had he ever heard anything so sexy?

No.

And he'd wanted to give her his. So fucking bad.

But she was drunk.

So he'd contented himself with dancing, with holding her, with—the man from the bar moved too close—that being within thirty feet of them—and Luc pulled Lexi closer, glaring over her head at the motherfucker, making it clear what would happen if he moved another inch forward. The other man paled, stepped back, and disappeared into the crowd.

Lexi just wrapped her arms around his waist, rested her head on his chest, and kept dancing.

Torture. Absolute torture.

Yet, he knew that he wouldn't stop dancing. Wouldn't stop holding her.

Until she was done.

Because it was also the best fucking night of his life.

———

OKAY, so he'd had to revise his earlier statement.

Because Lexi wasn't anywhere near being done.

But she was *done*.

She was riding that line between drunk and sloppy, and even though she'd hauled him over to the bar for another drink, he'd shaken his head at the bartender, who'd nodded her understanding and had made Lex her vodka cran with just cran. Lexi was too far gone to notice, which was why he closed their tab and tipped generously before getting hauled back onto the dance floor, intending to make her request of staying here until they were kicked out a reality.

But it was her stumble that did it.

She caught the edge of her heel, her ankle started to go over.

He shifted, dragged her against him, steadying her even as he turned for the exit and began bustling her toward it.

"Where are we going?" she asked, a slight slur in her question.

"Home," he said.

"But—"

"*Home,*" he snapped, causing her eyes to fly up to his.

"But," she began again.

He gripped her chin, kept her gaze on his. "Home, sweetheart," he said. "End of discussion."

Her lips moved, forming the words "End of discussion." Sparks of fury in her golden-brown eyes, turning them molten, and he knew her well enough to understand that her temper was one second away from rupture.

Which was why he found himself bending close, his fingers weaving into her hair, his mouth finding her ear. "End," he breathed. "Of. Discussion."

Her breath shuddered on his neck, her hands gripped his shoulders.

He nipped her earlobe, and she moaned, loud or near enough that he heard it over the music and turned his head, instinctively seeking out the sound, wanting to hear it again, wanting to make her moan again. Temptation lingered in the flush of her cheeks, in the plumpness of her lips, in the dilation of her pupils. And God, her mouth was right there. So close and alluring and . . . smelling of alcohol.

Of all those vodka crans.

Luc straightened, banded his arm around her waist again, and led her to the exit.

Thankfully, his car wasn't far, and he poured her into it with the warning, "You have to puke, you let me know. I'll pull over."

Maybe he was an asshole, but he didn't want to clean up vomit from his car.

"Lex?" he pressed when she just closed her eyes and rested her head back against the seat.

"No puking on the leather," she murmured, quieter now that they'd left the bar. "I got it."

He stroked a finger down her cheek. "I'll get you home."

And he did. He rounded the car, got into the driver's seat, and started up the engine. Then he drove her home.

Drove her to *his* home.

It only took twenty minutes, the traffic at this time of night virtually nonexistent, and pretty soon he was pulling into the garage, shutting it behind him.

Lex hadn't made a peep from the moment he'd closed her door, and he'd thought she was asleep, but when he'd parked and opened her side of the car, her eyelids slid smoothly back.

"I didn't puke," she proclaimed proudly.

He snorted, helped her from the car, guiding her up the two stairs that led into the kitchen and then up to the second story, up to where she always stayed when she was here.

His room.

He set her on the edge of the bed, kneeling in front of her to untie the leather laces crisscrossing up her legs so he could take off her heels. His fingers felt too big and clumsy as he fought with the knot, as he slowly unwound them from around her calves. Her skin was like silk, and his cock was even harder than it had been in the bar—desire a constant thrum against his insides as he knelt between her thighs, his hands on her body. Pushing it aside, knowing he couldn't do anything about it, not right then, he slid her heels off her feet, lining them up carefully next to the nightstand.

Her toes curled, pointing and flexing, and he found his hands on her again, found himself massaging the soles of her feet, knowing they must ache after the night in those stilettos.

She moaned, her thighs drifting apart, giving him a glimpse of bare skin, of black lace that clung to—

Fuck.

Releasing her, heart pounding, he stood, tugged back the covers. "Here," he murmured, lifting the blanket, indicating that she should crawl beneath them. "Get in," he said when she didn't immediately move.

"Uh-uh," she said, head flapping as she shook it.

"Lexi," he warned.

She reached for him. "Come here."

"You need to sleep, honey."

Her arms came around his waist, her mouth too close to his dick for the well-being of his self-control. "I want you," she murmured, nuzzling at his stomach.

He deserved a fucking gold medal.

"Lexi," he said again, grabbing at her wrists, starting to undo them from around him. She relaxed, arms falling away, and he let his guard down, thinking that she had released him because she was going to get under the covers.

Instead, she moved extremely fast for a drunk woman, reaching for the button of his jeans, flicking it open, and getting both hands down his pants.

He groaned, hips jerking when her cool, soft hands gripped his cock.

It felt . . . well, it felt like *everything*.

Which was why he deserved another gold medal, or whatever was better than a gold medal. Another Cup, he supposed, his name etched in giant letters on the side, much bigger than it had been engraved when the Breakers had won it six years before. Either way, he somehow managed to summon his self-control, the strength to tug her hands off him, to step back and nudge her onto the mattress, to tug up the covers, to cover the temptation of her body.

Her bottom lip slid out into a pout.

"Sleep," he ordered, buttoning his jeans.

"I can't sleep in my dress," she said, throwing the covers back and reaching for a zipper hidden under her arm, tugging it down, and before he could summon a protest, slipping her arm free, spreading the fabric wide.

Black lace.

Creamy skin.

Breasts and the gentle curve of her stomach and—

He spun away, stalked through the bathroom to his closet,

and fucking hell, why had the hockey gods decided to torture him? He snagged a T-shirt from his drawer, moved back into the bedroom, ignoring the pulsing desire, ignoring his cock telling him to get into bed, to help her get naked, to kiss every inch—

The curse burst out of him, the shirt in his hand dropped silently to the carpet because . . .

Breasts.

Breasts that would overflow his hands, rosy nipples that were hardened in the cool air of the room, tight, little furls that begged for his mouth. Her bra was clenched in her hand, her head on his pillow, shining hair spread out behind her like a fucking siren calling him to her, desperate to throw himself on the rocks if only he'd get one chance to prostrate himself at her feet.

The black lace of her underwear barely covered her pussy, and her thighs were spread wide enough to give him a glimpse of glistening pink folds.

Sweet fucking Christ.

Slamming his eyes closed, he crouched, blindly feeling for the cotton, shoring himself for the sight of the woman on his bed.

When he'd summoned the slightest bit of his control, he opened his eyes, grasped the shirt and stood, crossing over to her, tugging the material over her head. She stirred, bleary gaze meeting his as he threaded her arms through.

"Luc," she murmured.

"Hush, baby."

It was an almost painful thing to cover her body and also a relief, pulling the material over her curves before tucking the blankets over her.

"Luc," she said again, burrowing into the comforter, her eyes closed.

"What?" he asked softly, smoothing back her hair.

A yawn that stretched her lush lips wide. "Why do you always have me sleep in your bed?"

His hand faltered before he continued his stroking, continued the gentle, soothing touches, soothing her into oblivion. He continued touching her, studying Lexi's face as her lips parted, her breathing slow and steady, and he didn't answer until he thought that she was fully asleep. "Because I like you there."

Her eyes slitted open, telling him he hadn't waited long enough, that she was awake, at least slightly.

"I like it here, too," she murmured.

And then her eyes slid closed again, sleep taking her fully under.

Luc stood and went to sleep in the guest room.

For the record, he hated it *there*.

CHAPTER NINETEEN

Lexi

HER HEAD POUNDED.

Her throat felt like the Sahara.

Those were the only two sensations she could summon when she managed to yank her eyelids open.

She instantly knew that she was in Luc's bed, his spicy smell surrounding her like a yummy, masculine cloud. The blankets were tucked up and around her, safe and secure and cozy.

Always in his bed.

Never with him.

So strange, and yet, so typical. He was a gentleman, a nice guy, someone who cared enough about his friends to want to ensure their comfort.

At least, that was what she'd always figured, and he'd told her that his shower was nicer. Maybe it was as simple as that.

A thread of a conversation trickled through her brain. Had they'd talked about it the night before, about why she always ended up here while he took the guest room, even though she'd protested frequently? She rubbed her forehead, thinking maybe they had, that maybe he'd said . . . then sighed, frowning when it flitted away, the memory of coming to Luc's house disappearing into a fog of flickering lights, vodka crans, music pulsing, and a hard body against her spine.

Of Luc.

She smiled, despite the pounding in her head, the desert in her throat. They'd had a good time, she thought. She couldn't remember much of the conversation, much of anything after dinner, aside from feeling safe in his arms, her feet going numb as they'd danced, and . . . not puking in his car on the way home.

Thank God for small miracles.

And seriously, he was such a good friend to put up with her drunk ass, to take her to her favorite place and to dance and eat and drink, to celebrate one chapter ending and the next beginning without once making her feel ridiculous or like a burden. It was sad how until Caleb had done what he'd done, she'd never considered how her relationship with him hadn't made her feel the same.

There'd always been a hint of impatience, of testiness, of wanting her to make the decision *he* wanted her to make.

Not in an obvious way.

It was always a small redirection, a sigh, a joke that was maybe a bit too sharp, and she'd never realized it.

How had she never recognized the manipulation?

Well, then again, she hadn't known he'd had three other women in his life, one of them who was pregnant, had she?

And *this* was way too heavy of a conversation for the morning, as she was trying to summon her hungover ass out of bed.

She was going to focus on positive things, not on the fact that she was single and without prospects, save a best friend who was kind and probably saw her as a pity case who was needy and didn't have her own life anymore and—

"Enough," she murmured.

Luc was the one person in her life who'd become indispensable, who she trusted not to leave, and she wasn't going to do anything to fuck it up. Not by being a miserable pity partier—with or without party hats—nor by dwelling on the past. She'd used up a lot of their relationship energy the past six months, and now was the time to put that energy back in, to be as good of a friend to him as he'd been to her.

End of story.

Rolling to her side, she hesitated, waiting until her head steadied, until her blurry vision cleared, and what she saw on the nightstand made her heart squeeze tight. Ibuprofen and a glass of water.

"Why in the hell is the man single?" she murmured, reaching for the bottle, downing three pills, and draining the glass.

She moved gingerly into the bathroom, saw the towels he'd laid out for her, the hair products, and "girly shit" (*her* brand of "girly shit," since the man paid attention and had bought stuff to match what she used during the weeks she'd stayed here after Caleb had revealed himself to be a complete and utter douche canoe), and knew that her quiet question from the bedroom was doubly true.

She needed to find him a woman who appreciated him.

Selfishly, she didn't want to give up her friend, and she knew that anyone he dated probably wouldn't be thrilled to have her and her single baggage tag along. But now, she knew that she had to let that self-centeredness go. He deserved better, and they wouldn't ever be more than friends—not that she wanted anything more than friendship. For one, she'd just spent seven years in a relationship where she hadn't even understood she'd been gaslit, manipulated. For another, and the most pertinent piece of information to her inner monologue, Luc wasn't interested in her that way.

She couldn't deny she was attracted to him.

Tall and broad-shouldered, along with great hair—dark locks that seemed to sweep in a perfect arc across his forehead with just the barest gray at his temples. Big hands, powerful thighs, an ass that filled out the slacks he wore regularly to the office.

In a word, gorgeous.

But never once—even despite those two erections—had he made a move.

Maybe before, she wouldn't have expected it, not with her being married and him being honorable. Of course, she was honorable, too. She hadn't even once looked at him like that during her marriage. She hadn't been single, so while she could appreciate his body for the fine specimen it was, he wasn't ever on her radar as something sexual.

Her friend. That was it.

But even after Caleb, nothing had changed. On his part, that was.

There was yearning in her, an underlying attraction that called to her, that pushed her to make the first move.

Except, she was a coward.

And not once during the last six months had he ever given her any indication that he wanted more than friendship. Not once had she ever thought that he might want her in that way.

Was she sure about that? Because sometimes she thought—

"Enough," she whispered. *Sure* or not, this was the way it had to be.

But what if it didn't *have* to be?

Another memory flickered on the heels of that thought.

Flashing lights, strong arms, her ass brushing against his cock, him saying—

Gone.

Too much vodka.

It should be a crime against humanity to make such a statement, but clearly, she had lost her college resistance to alcohol because it had been ages since she'd drank so much that she'd blacked out, that she couldn't remember.

Pathetic.

Certainly.

But, despite her throat and head and her teeth feeling like they'd grown fur, Lexi also felt better than she had in a long time.

As though she'd excised some demon from her brain.

As though the boulder weighing down her shoulders was gone.

As though she could finally move forward with her life.

She crossed the bathroom, turned on the shower, and got on with her day. With her life.

————

SHE WAS GOING cross-eyed staring at the contract in front of her.

It was Friday, three days after her drunken escapades. Three days since she'd found out that Luc had reached out to Todd for her, had called in sick for her before he'd gone to bed.

But, despite the late night they'd had, he'd thought of her. And okay, maybe she *did* have some of her college-aged self still left in her, because she'd woken up at one-forty-five on Wednesday afternoon, the house empty, Luc long gone to work, and seriously, she couldn't remember the last time she'd slept past eight.

Usually, Lexi was an early riser.

But vodka crans and letting go of a man who'd hurt her, who'd dragged her down into six months of despair, apparently had a girl feeling as light as a feather.

Still, they'd received an offer on the house today.

She and her ex-husband (God, it felt weird saying that) had received an all-cash offer on their house for a little above asking. As is. No inspection. No contingencies. A fifteen-day closing and . . . there was no reason not to accept it.

Except . . . it was *her* house, with her garden.

And, if she were being truthful, with her final tie to the past seven years.

Her baby. Her yard and her flowers and the grass she'd spent years reseeding until it was plush and lovely and green.

Sighing, she set the contract on her coffee table and rubbed her eyes, knowing there was nothing wrong with it, knowing that because she'd already read through it, and knowing that she was only resisting signing because it was the final link with her past.

All those painful memories gone, huh?

Purged by vodka, right?

Ha.

She was delusional. She was fucked up and—

"No," she hissed. "God, seriously, Lexi? This again?"

A wave of annoyance welled up inside her, had her reaching for her cell, hitting a contact she would soon be able to permanently delete from her phone, waiting until Caleb picked up the call.

He did. On the first ring.

Probably because he'd been pushing her to make a decision since the contract had come in the day before.

She spoke before he could, raising her voice so it was over the sound of the baby crying in the background and it was strange, but that noise settled in her heart, had her free hand unclenching, the grip on her past and regrets loosening. Perhaps, she thought, finally for the last time, a puff of air dispersing dandelion stalks.

"Let's accept the offer."

Relief in his voice, the fussing baby quieting in the background. "Thank—"

"I'll call the realtor, get a signing date as quickly as possible."

"Lex—"

She was done. So done.

Finally, done.

The last strand between them pulled tight, strumming with tension, and then in stinging, painful relief, snapping free.

"Bye, Caleb."

She hung up.

Yeah, okay. Maybe, just maybe she wasn't the worst kind of coward, after all.

Maybe, she could find the strength to be brave.

Maybe she could find the strength to go for what she wanted deep down.

CHAPTER TWENTY

Luc

HIS LUNGS WERE BURNING; sweat was dripping down his spine.

Feet pounding on the sidewalk, reverberating up his legs, making his right knee ache, the old injury from his playing days reminding him of why his career was over, of how he'd obliterated the joint to the point of not ever being able to play again.

Young and promising, to broken and washed up. Alone. Abandoned.

Then slowly putting one foot in front of the other, getting an opportunity with the Breakers, and working his way up from scout to assistant coach to assistant GM and finally to GM.

Until he'd spent more years in the front office than he'd spent playing in the league.

And he'd seen one of his goals realized, albeit in a completely different form than he'd imagined—his team had won the Cup.

Twice under his watch.

So, broken had brought him full circle. By being shattered, he'd become whole again.

The pain in his knee had become a blessing.

It reminded him of how far he'd come.

Of everything he'd lost and everything he'd avoided.

Until golden-brown eyes flickered through his mind, reminding him of everything that was *important*.

He had the professional success.

But he hadn't had a serious relationship since he was twenty-three.

Not since—

The horn blared just as he was about to step off the curb, and he skittered back, that old injury flaring as the car swerved around the corner, nearly clipping him.

His knee gave way, his other leg collapsing under the sudden weight, his patella hitting the concrete lip hard. "Fuck," he hissed, leaning forward, shifting his weight and putting his hands down so he was more stable before he got his feet back underneath him. Now both knees hurt like hell.

And his palms were scraped.

Awesome.

He glared at the car that was tearing away from him, speeding down the residential street, and used that fury at the driver's lack of safety to fuel his ascent to his feet.

From big hits to fighting a curb.

How far the hockey player had fallen.

At least, he didn't need to worry about getting back on the ice tonight. He could sit in his office, in the team's box, and pop ibuprofen like it was candy.

But fucking hell, his palms stung.

Ridiculous.

Sighing, he rolled his shoulders, shook out his stinging hands, and took that step off the curb—double-checking for careening cars this time. First, he just walked, but then he slowly started jogging, even though it hurt like hell. He was three miles from his house, walking wouldn't be any less painful, and if he did, it would take fucking forever to get home . . . and to get to that ibuprofen.

So, as soon as he could manage, he began to jog and then he made himself start to run.

Thump. Thump. Thump. Thump.

Feet pounding. Pain pulsing.

But nothing came from being weak, from just giving in and shutting down, from quitting halfway through the battle. He was a man who saw things through to the end, even if the path was long and slow and brutal. So, he made himself push on, to finish his loop, although it meant adding another mile before taking the turn that would lead him back to his place.

The pain had dulled to a thrumming beat in the back of his brain by the time he'd landed back in his front yard, and he thought he was good.

Or *would* be good after a couple pain killers.

But he must have underestimated how bad he looked because the moment he walked in the front door and Lexi saw him, she freaked the fuck out.

He was smiling, because he'd seen her car in the driveway, and it was a really fucking nice surprise to have her in his kitchen. Because any time with Lexi was a good time. Not to mention the smell of whatever she was making on the stove had his stomach rumbling.

"Hey," he called.

"Hey," she called back, slowly turning toward him. "I hope you don't mind, but I thought—" Her expression was bright, cheerful, but the moment she laid eyes on him, that happiness faded, the spatula she was holding dropping to the tile. "Oh, my God." She rushed toward him, hands flapping up and down his body but not touching him anywhere. "You're bleeding!"

"I'm fine," he said. "I just took a spill—"

"You're"—she knelt in front of him, lifting the hem of one leg of his shorts—"*knee!*"

He glanced down, realized it was bleeding more than he'd thought. "It looks worse than—"

"Don't tell me it looks worse than it is!" she exploded,

tugging him toward the kitchen table and shoving him into one of the chairs. "Sit down," she ordered, moving to the sink and wetting a paper towel. Then she knelt in front of him, wiping the blood away with a gentle touch, clearing away the dirt and debris until the wound was revealed.

"See?" he said, nodding toward the cut. "It's nothing."

Her eyes shot to his, and there was such fury in the golden-brown depths that he immediately clamped his mouth shut and stifled any further words. He'd been married once, long ago, but he'd learned enough during those few years to understand when a woman gave him a look like that, the only smart recourse was to shut up.

So, he shut up and let her fuss over the tiny scratch, told her where the antibiotic ointment and the bandages were. Then continued letting her fuss over his other knee with the even tinier scratch, and his palms that were hardly abraded.

Okay, truthfully, his knee hurt like hell, along with his palms, and he knew he'd limped-run the last mile, had made it home solely because he hadn't had any other choice. And, yeah, he was pretending that he didn't like Lexi fussing over him, but he wasn't going to lie, having her hands on him, having her worried and caring about him, felt nice. Lex was generous and sweet, but she'd been so . . . reduced since that twat-waffle, Caleb, had broken her heart. Seeing her filled with fire, snapping at him and ordering him around, made something burn within him.

Because she was almost back to herself.

And that made him want her even more.

Seemingly impossible, but thus was the power of Lexi.

"There," she murmured, smoothing another Band-Aid on— the third, for those who were counting, and he certainly was. "You're going to have a bruise."

He shrugged. "I'll live."

She sat back on her heels, started to pick up the dirty paper towels, the wrappers from the bandages, the bottle of Neosporin. Luc stood, tugged her to her feet. "I've got it."

"But—"

"Baby," he said, tugging her flush against him.

He didn't know why he did that. Why the simple hug had turned into a full-body press. Why he'd held her close like she was a lover instead of a friend. Maybe it was the club. Perhaps, the dancing. Maybe it was that she was different today, something in her eyes calling to something deep inside his heart, some hope he'd been pushing down for so long.

Or maybe it was just that he'd reached his limit, and his control had finally snapped and—

Luc smoothed his hand up and down her back. "I said, I've *got* it, sweetheart."

Her breasts were against his chest.

His cock was hard.

Her smell, sweet and floral, roses with a dash of soil, was the most intoxicating perfume. He bent his head and inhaled deeply, wanting to singe the scent onto his lungs, to permanently bind it to his cells.

Lexi shuddered, her weight resting heavier against him, her head tipping back.

And . . .

Something else snapped.

His head lowered, the moment seeming to stretch, to last an eternity as he waited for insecurity to creep across her face. But it didn't, even though he kept expecting it to. Then . . . their lips touched, just the barest brush of their mouths, and for a moment . . . nothing. Absolute stillness. She was frozen in his arms, her lips against his, their mouths closed, his mind spinning, curses beginning to fly through it, excuses on their heels.

Until she moaned, the sound vibrating through her to him.

And melted against him.

Her lips parted. Her tongue darted out to trace the seam of his mouth. He opened in turn, tasted her, hands coming up to cup her cheeks, to angle her head and to kiss her with every bit of pent-up need he'd been harboring.

She was with him, her hands sliding up his chest, clenching his shoulders, drawing him near, her tongue meeting his, stroke for stroke.

It was just starting, and it was already the best kiss of his life.

No hesitation after that first moment, just desire and sensation and the realization that this was the most *right* thing he'd ever experienced.

He pulled her closer, threaded his hand into her hair, kissing her deeper, with more passion, with more *hunger* than he'd ever experienced. He was in the desert, dying and dehydrated, and Lexi was his salvation, his oasis, his pool of water far in the distance—so fucking far that he'd had to walk for miles over a scorching dune before he'd stumbled upon it, jumped into that icy pond. She was the cool kiss of the moisture on his skin, the perfect balm after years out in that roasting wasteland.

Then . . . still.

She went still again. Frozen like a statue, stiff where she'd once been warm and pliable in his arms.

She tore her mouth away, pushed at his chest.

"Luc, I—"

He dropped his arms, scuttled back. "I'm sorry," he said. "I shouldn't—" Something terrible flashed in her eyes. Something that eviscerated him, that had him shutting the fuck up before he finished saying, "I shouldn't have done that."

Lexi spun away from him, picked up her purse from the island. "I need to go," she whispered.

He reached for her.

But she'd already turned away, hurried to the front door. What right did he have to chase after her? After everything she'd been through, how could he do anything but let her run away?

Still, he found himself taking a step after her. Another.

She spun back. "Don't," she said, pointing a finger at him. "Don't do this."

His stomach seized. His heart turned into an icy bolder, sinking heavy and deep. But more than anything, the only thing he could think was, "*Fuck that.*" He wasn't going to let her run away. Not after everything they'd been through. Maybe she didn't want him. Maybe the other night had truly just been the result of too much alcohol and a dry spell. But even if she didn't want him, Lexi was still his best friend. And he wasn't giving her up.

He moved forward, closing the distance between them, taking her in his arms, as he'd done so many times before, as a friend, as a man who hated when a woman he cared about was hurting, as a man who longed to hold and touch a woman he loved, in any way.

"No," he said.

Just no. Just those two letters. Just the one word.

No.

And she shuddered, stilled, didn't fight his embrace, melted against his chest.

"Luc," she whispered.

His arms tightened.

This was right. So *fucking* right. Luc and Lexi. Her and him.

"We shouldn't," she murmured.

"We need to," he murmured back. "This. You and me. It's good. It could be really fucking good. It—"

A trembling breath. Her arms tentatively coming around him, and she rested her ear against his chest, probably able to hear his heart thundering within. Everything inside him was perched on a precipice, ready and waiting, anxious, terrified to hear what she would say next.

Then she squeezed him, bringing them closer. "We'd be perfect," she whispered.

Triumph ringing through him, church bells on a summer

day, the sound resonating through the air, filling his lungs with vibrating joy.

Joy that was squashed in the next instant.

"But Luc," she said, "we *shouldn't.*"

Breaking into pieces, the shards scattering this way and that. He'd miscalculated. He'd thought she'd responded to him, thought her not struggling, not holding back meant that she wanted him, too. He'd thought . . . too many fucking things apparently. If she didn't want him, it would kill him, but he'd shove the attraction down, he'd box it back up, because there was only one unacceptable thing.

Not having Lexi in his life.

"Do you not . . ." He paused, arms loosening, starting to step back. "That way? With me? Is it not . . . You don't want—"

She swallowed hard, deliberately not looking at him.

Fuck. *Fuck.* He froze, dropped his arms.

"Luc."

He turned away, sucked in a breath that felt like razor wire, released it slowly, even though that somehow felt even worse. "I get it." Forced the next words out. "No hard feelings. It's . . . I'm"—he forced his tone to go light, teasing, even though he despised it—"just still hopped up on adrenaline from nearly getting mowed down by a car. Ignore me." He moved into the kitchen, away from her, even though every cell in his body was telling him to turn back, to kiss her again, to kiss her until she recognized their potential, until she kissed him in return.

Until she loved him as much as he loved her.

"You're limping," she said, her voice quiet.

"I'm fine," he said, knowing he was anything but.

"It was a car?" she asked, the question barely reaching his ears.

"Yeah."

For one moment, he wished she'd just stop talking, would leave, would give him the space to wallow and be miserable.

But only for a second.

Because although it felt like she was carving his insides out with a spoon, he couldn't ignore her, didn't want her to go.

He wanted *her*.

However much of her she would give him.

As pathetic of a sop as that made him.

"Luc?"

He turned back.

"Are you really okay?"

"Never been better," he said, taking a step toward the fridge. "Did you want to eat?"

"I . . ."

He knew what her answer was going to be, even before her words crossed the gulf between them.

"Should go."

"Okay," he said, going to the table, picking up the trash and supplies that had never made it to the garbage can, back into the first aid kit. "I'll see you—"

The front door opened and closed.

He carefully put the antibiotic ointment away, threw the trash into the pail, but when his gaze made it to the beginnings of pancake batter Lexi had been putting together, he couldn't stomach finishing it . . . or throwing it away.

In fact, he couldn't stand being in this kitchen, in this house.

His stomach churned, his lungs felt tight, every muscle in his body locked down. He pounded toward the back door, took one look at the porch, at Lexi's plants, her twinkling lights, smelled the sweet floral scent, and he kept moving. Past the hot tub, into that cluster of oak trees, to the bench, fingers drifting along the paperback.

And then like that evening six months ago, he took out his rage and disappointment on the poor, abused oak trees.

CHAPTER TWENTY-ONE

Lexi

HER LIPS TINGLED. Her heart pounded.

Her legs were so shaky that she barely made it down the porch steps, barely made it to her car.

Fingers fumbling, she tugged open the door, sat in the driver's seat, but she couldn't close it, just kept her ass plunked on the leather, her feet hanging out the frame, her body twisted to rest her forehead on the steering wheel.

Sweat dripped down her nape, soaked into her shift, the band of her bra, dripped between her breasts.

That kiss . . .

Holy fucking smokes, the man kissed like a tempest, thrashing her against the rocks, weighty, crushing waves crashing over her, only to have his arms draw tighter, his feet to brace heavy against the ocean floor, to hold her steady against the ravaging current.

And that whole time, memories had crept back in.

His front against her spine in the club. Him making eye contact with the bartender, and suddenly her drinks didn't have alcohol in them. His arm steadying her as she stumbled in her heels. His gentle hands removing her heels.

His bed.

His smile.

His touch.

His . . .

Suddenly, she straightened, pushed from the car and closed the door behind her, moving up the driveway and inside, finding the kitchen empty, the rest of the house silent. There was a force propelling her as she searched his bedroom, his bathroom, the study. She even checked the guest room.

But Luc wasn't inside.

So then, her feet carried her into the back yard.

No sign of him in the lush greenery, nor in the open space to the side of the hot tub. She almost turned back, to go inside again, but then she heard it—

A quiet *thunk-thunk*, *thunk-thunk* coming from the way back.

There was a sickening feeling in her stomach, twisting and clawing its way through her insides as she listened to that constant thumping, the impacts echoing through the yard.

She hurried back, not certain of what she would find and yet also somehow, some part of her was aware of exactly what Luc was doing.

And there he was, his fists bloody as he punched the tree, his hair hanging all in his face, sweat sheening over his arms, his throat from his exertions, combining with that from the run earlier. It was raw and animalistic, almost sexy in an alpha male sort of way. Probably, she should be equal parts pissed off that he was hurting himself and grossed out, by the blood, by the sweat.

But instead, she just had a pang in her chest, sympathy for him weighing her shoulders down.

He'd given her that sign, taken that first step. And she'd—

Her eyes slid closed, opened slowly. The terror that had gripped her in the middle of that kiss was gone.

Just. Gone.

Because . . . Luc.

He'd kissed her. He'd said he wanted her—or *had* he? He'd said they would be good together, and she'd agreed.

That was the truth.

But how could they possibly be together?

Luc was . . . well, quite simply, the best man she knew. And how could she bring her broken, dumped, cheated on ass into his life? It would be cruel and unusual punishment for her to do that. She wasn't . . .

A splinter of frustration, of *fury* shot through her.

Not at the man who hadn't yet noticed her, who was wailing on the tree trunk, whose knuckles were split, but at herself.

Caleb had fucked around on her.

She'd spent the last six months being broken and hurt and . . . just wasn't that long enough? Couldn't she just let it go now? Couldn't she just do her best to create something with this lovely, wonderful man who nearly singed her eyebrows off with his kiss? Didn't she have enough courage to push through the fear of getting hurt again, especially when it was with someone like Luc?

She used to be the type of woman who courage and confidence in spades.

She used to be the type of woman to leap.

She used . . .

"Haven't you already bled enough for one day?"

The words came from behind some inner well inside her, some deep reserve of bravery she hadn't even known still existed. But to her astonishment, it *was* there, and that force propelled her into action, allowed the words to come, allowed her to lean against the trunk of the adjacent tree, to cross her arms and wait, affecting casualness.

Even though her heart still pounded, her throat was tight, and she would be lying if she said there wasn't a small piece of her that was absolutely terrified to do this, that she would *ruin* this.

But, despite that fear, she held on to that glimmer of herself.

And Lexi found courage.

Luc had stopped from the moment she began speaking. Going absolutely frozen, his chest heaving, his gaze fixed on the tree in front of him. But there wasn't any more punching, so at least there was that.

Then his head swiveled, green eyes coming to hers, slowly, oh so slowly, as though he hadn't trusted his ears, as though she were an apparition and wouldn't actually be standing there. As though . . . he never in a million freaking years actually expected her to be standing a few feet away from him.

"You're still here," he whispered hoarsely.

Intensity rippled through the air, scorching waves bursting forth from his stare, his body, his . . . heart. Wrapping her in warmth, although he wasn't actually touching her.

And that bolstered her courage, gave her the strength to lift her chin and say, "I'm not going anywhere."

Something amazing happened to his face—softening and hardening at once, determination and gentleness weaving through his expression and his eyes. God, his eyes were beautiful. Molten, the green irises glittering like the most beautiful pair of emeralds she'd ever been given the opportunity to view. She'd never seen eyes like that, never witnessed that depth of emotion in someone else's gaze.

It made her feel . . . so *much*. So much more than she'd realized.

Even as she was reeling from the impact of that realization, that flurry of emotions, he moved, closing the space between them, one hand reaching for her then stopping a few inches away, his eyes going to his knuckles. He winced, started to draw back.

Now she moved, grabbing his wrist and keeping him in

place, drawing him nearer, until that slightly roughened palm met her cheek.

"I'm here," she said, turning her head so she could kiss the inside of his wrist.

His lips parted. "Lexi."

"I'm scared," she admitted. "Scared to get hurt or to disappoint you. Scared to lose you as my friend."

His expression clouded.

"But," she said. "I'm also so fucking pissed."

Brows drawing together, he opened his mouth.

She spoke first. "I'm pissed that I didn't see Caleb for what he was. I'm pissed that I've wasted six more months on him when I should have been moving on with my life. And I'm pissed that I've spent these last six months thinking you weren't interested in me."

His fingers flexed on her cheek. "I couldn't be interested in you, Lex."

Maybe once that would have hurt, but today she knew what he meant. Because neither of them were cheaters. Because she'd been happy in her relationship and not in the right mental headspace to even consider him as anything more than her best friend.

But . . . Luc was right in what he said before.

They'd be good together.

She felt it in her bones, her heart, in the flutters invoked from his touch, the butterflies from her stomach, the joy when he was near.

They'd be *perfect*.

"I know," she said, kissing his wrist again, grabbing onto her courage again, holding it tight, using it to feed her strength, her words. "But . . . we could be something now. We could go on a date"—God, that sounded stupid after they'd spent so much time together—"or just . . . I don't know, see what it's like to be more than friends." Her teeth found her lip, bit down on the corner of it, struggling to put her thoughts into words.

Why did this feel so fucking stupid?

Things with Luc had never been awkward. Not ever and now, with one kiss, one conversation, she was spiraling. Maybe she was wrong. Maybe . . .

"Lex," he began, his tone infinitely gentle, a note of careful in his voice.

Her stomach clenched, tying itself into knots that were worse than those she'd made as an eight-year-old learning how to do up her shoelaces.

Because maybe even with that chance of perfect on the horizon, they shouldn't do this.

Except, maybe that was the fear talking.

And *maybe* she needed to continue womaning up, so she would stop being the sniveling coward she'd been the last six months.

No maybes.

All certainties.

It was enough.

Lifting her arms, she wrapped them around his shoulders and drifted closer. "Did you know that I realized a long time ago I was wrong about Caleb?" His brows drew down. "Because he wasn't the best man I knew." She slid one hand down, rested it on his chest, just above his heart. "You are." A beat. "And you've proven it to me every day from the moment I met you."

He inhaled sharply, let the breath shudder out. "*Lex.*"

She pulled on that well of courage, tugging up strands, wrapping them tightly around each other. "Do you want to date me?" she asked baldly.

The sound he made was garbled, a groan, a sound of disbelief, a noise of surprise. "Yes, baby," he said, voice hoarse. "It's all I've dreamed about since the moment I first heard you laugh. I've wanted you for years, and it feels like a fantasy for us to even be having this conversation, for you to ask that question."

Her lips parted, and her breath trembled as it left her mouth.

"So," she whispered, cloaking herself in more bravery. Just a little more. It was heady and intoxicating, making her feel like her old self again. Her chin lifted. Her shoulders straightened. "Kiss me."

A long, still moment.

The thread between them pulling taut once again.

And then his mouth was on hers.

CHAPTER TWENTY-TWO

Luc

THIS WAS A DREAM. A wonderful, unbelievable dream.

Then, in a movement that should have been choreographed in some shitty, romantic movie, he bent and she jumped, and suddenly she was in his arms, her thighs around his waist, her lips never leaving his.

Music should be blaring around them, flowers springing to life, bluebirds fluttering through the sky.

Or doves.

"Yeah," he mumbled. Definitely doves. He dragged his lips over her throat when she pulled her mouth from his, sucking in great gasps of air. His own lungs burned, but he'd rather suffer from asphyxiation than stop tasting her.

"Yeah, what?" she asked, panting.

He blinked, half-crazed from the taste of her. "Huh?"

"You said, yeah," she said, her breaths rapid puffs that glazed his skin. "What'd you mean?"

Lexi was wrapped around him, her pussy hot and slightly damp against his stomach, even through the layers between them. Her breasts pressed firmly against his chest, her mouth was close, her skin was nirvana. All of which meant he was having a hell of a time concentrating on anything that was conservation and not just pure sensation.

"Luc?" she asked, fingers sliding into his hair, her hips undulating. "What did you mean?"

He finally managed to piece together two thoughts. "Doves," he blurted.

She froze, jerked back, and nearly toppled from his arms. "What?"

This woman was going to be the death of him. He shook his head, cleared enough of the desire so he could cup her cheek and explain. "When I kiss you, I feel like we should be in a movie. Music should blare to life, doves should be circling overhead, woodland fucking creatures should tie you up in ribbons."

"Music playing?"

He nodded.

Her lips twitched. "Tying me up?"

"I meant tie ribbons in your hair." He tracked the amusement in her eyes, her expression, and knew his explanation hadn't helped his cause. He groaned, let his head fall back. "I'm never going to live this down, am I?"

"No," she said with a laugh, her hands gripping his jaw, tilting his head up again. "Though, for the record, I definitely don't mind a little kink."

His brows rose. His cock somehow got harder. "What kind of kink?"

A husky laugh. "Well, I guess you'll just have to date me and find out."

"Oh?" he asked archly.

"Yeah. *Oh.*" She lowered her head, inhaled deeply. "You smell so good," she moaned, nipping at his jaw. "I want to taste you all over."

A fire was burning inside him, *had* been burning in him for what felt like an eternity. And her words, the way she clung to him, her thighs around his hips, had him at risk of losing control. Especially after the emotions of the last half hour, the fact that she'd come back and said she wanted to date him, that she seemed to like kissing him as much as he enjoyed kissing her.

He wanted to lasso the moon for her, to capture the stars in a mason jar, to—

Her hand came to his cheek, stroked gently. "So fierce," she murmured, brushing her thumb over his lips.

"Only for you," he said, capturing that palm and pressing a kiss to the center of it before he continued his explorations, dancing his hand up her side, trailing his lips over her collarbone, using his nose to nudge the neckline of her shirt to the side.

"Mmm," she moaned when he shifted his focus, arrowed in on a sensitive spot just behind her right ear.

And he knew he was two seconds from taking her to that bench and fucking her into oblivion. His hands shook, his cock throbbed, his spine was a rigid piece of steel, his muscles taut and primed, ready to be called into action for just that noble cause.

But . . . too soon.

They hadn't even gone on a first date yet.

Lexi deserved a first date, deserved romance and care.

But . . . just one more.

He slanted his mouth across hers, tasted her, knowing he would never get enough of this woman. And then he slowly set her away from him. Gently took her hand and led her into the house.

"Breakfast," he murmured when she glanced up at him in question.

So many inquiries in those eyes, but surprising him, she didn't put a voice to them. Instead, she just weaved their fingers together and squeezed.

Then they went in and made pancakes.

Pancakes.

With syrup and butter and sticky fingers and shining lips and laughter and teasing and shoulders and hands and bodies brushing against one another.

Friendship. *More.*

As though nothing had changed . . . and yet, everything had.

———

THE TEAM WAS PLAYING like absolute horseshit.

Fumbled passes, two fucking empty nets missed—two!—and a bunch of flat feet on the ice.

It was times like this that it killed him to not be on the ice.

Especially with that morning's events roiling under his skin, making him feel alive, making him burn with the need to claim, to plunder. Yeah, he felt like a fucking Viking, ready to scorch the earth just to bring a smile to his woman's face.

So, he would give a lot to be down there, to feel the cool air on his sweat-covered skin, to take any hits thrown his way, the burning in his lungs, his legs.

To fly again.

But he'd had lots of practice with ignoring that urge.

With ignoring *many* of his urges—to play again, to claim Lexi for his own, to have something that resembled a family again.

The only bit of grace was that Lexi had given him a shot.

And he wasn't going to blow it.

His forward got picked at the blue line, and the other team's player went streaking down the ice toward the Breakers' end alone, and fuck, but Luc wished again that he'd managed to pick up Dominic Bullard at the trade deadline two seasons ago.

Two years before, when the scouting reports had come in, the kid had just been coming into his legs but hadn't burst through the rest of the pack yet, hadn't turned into the type of player that was currently down on the ice, making mincemeat of Luc's defense. Luc's best chance to get him on the roster had been before the potential he'd seen in the young player had erupted to the forefront and every other team had wanted him.

Case in point, Dominic skating through the Breaker's defense and making them look like pylons.

Tiny, little, ineffective cones.

But Luc hadn't been able to get the deal down.

Dominic hadn't come to the Breakers, and now every damn coach and scout and GM in the league could see that Dominic was going to be fucking great. *Really* great.

Another reason it also would have been nice to acquire Dominic's talent?

Because the Breakers were rebuilding.

Still. Six years after they'd won their second Cup.

It was taking too fucking long for his competitive nature, though if he were being truthful, the rebuilding technically hadn't begun in earnest until three years before. They'd made the playoffs every year, gone pretty far down the track to those sixteen wins it would take to win another Cup in the three previous years.

But not all the way.

And then three years ago, contracts had begun to expire, trades were made—some for different players, some for future draft picks or prospects. The salary cap was considered and planned for, scouts did their job, coaches adjusted lineups, and even with all that work, this year was still off to the worst start in Breakers history.

Two wins.

Two.

Out of fourteen games.

That was right. They were two and twelve.

So, circling back to pathetic . . . and the game.

Dominic streaked in toward Martin Robinson, their goalie, and Luc could see, even from way up in the nosebleeds, that a goal was imminent. A deke to the left, one slow drag of the puck, and . . . in the net.

The Breakers down two points with thirty seconds left in the game.

Not an impossible lead to overcome.

But not one his team had the will to close. Not that night.

Sighing, he wanted to get up, to go back to his office and start looking at stats and players their scouts were tracking, reviewing the millions of details that went into his job, but the team was still on the ice, still playing. So, he did what he'd promised himself he would do when he'd taken a position in the front office—he stayed.

And watched as the Breakers went two and thirteen.

"Fuck," he muttered, already hating the post-game interview that was coming his way. The questions about the direction of the team, questions the fans and investors and players all deserved answers to.

The responsibility for the team began and ended with him.

But on nights like this, after runs of games like this, that accountability fucking sucked.

Sighing, he pushed through the door, headed down the hall, and popped into his office, waiting for the players to do their interviews as he caught up on emails and requests. Then it was his turn to go in front of the cameras and take his well-earned blows from the media.

Two and thirteen.

Two and thirteen.

Fuck, *two* and thirteen.

CHAPTER TWENTY-THREE

Lexi

SHE WATCHED LUC ON TV, so calm and poised during his turn at the press conference. The post-game reporting only stayed on him for two questions before cutting away to the remainder of the coverage, but his answers were crisp, taking responsibility for the team, though he was far from the only person in the organization.

It was funny, but she hardly ever watched the team play.

She wasn't much of a sports fan, preferring to binge documentaries on Netflix and Hulu, and if there wasn't anything new, then to re-watch her favorite couples on *90-Day Fiancé*.

Tonight, after this morning, after they'd eaten pancakes and then had spent a couple of hours on Luc's back porch, talking about the offer on her house and how accepting it had made her feel, about the team and his work, and . . . about nothing, blathering away as they watched the birds flit through the garden, until he'd had to go to work and she'd needed to get to the realtor's office to sign the contract. He'd walked her to her car, had kissed her like she mattered.

And with promise.

So much promise.

Now, she was in her apartment. In her pj's and tucked snuggly under the covers, the intention to not move, to slip off into sleep had weaved lazily through her body.

They had plans for the morning, to go on a hike and then gorge themselves at their favorite brunch place. Tom's had homemade lemon ricotta pancakes and they were only one step shy of an orgasm.

Sometimes she actually dreamed about the lemon curd drizzled on top.

Tart and sweet, making her taste buds zing with awareness.

Kind of like Luc's kisses, she thought with a smile.

The hike had been his choice and based on past experiences with his "easy" hikes, frankly he was in better shape than her. *Much* better shape. Usually his choice meant her pain, so Lex had crawled into bed early, intending to soak up all the sleep she could manage. But some force had propelled her to turn on the TV, to watch the game, her heart pounding when the camera cut to Luc up in the team box, his face placid, composed.

But frustrated.

She could see the dissatisfaction even through the screen, though she highly doubted anyone else could see it. They didn't know him like she did, couldn't deduce the emotions behind the mask—

And maybe she shouldn't be tooting her own horn.

Fuck, she hadn't even known the man had any feelings for her that weren't platonic.

Wrinkling her nose, knowing that wasn't entirely true, understanding now that she hadn't had the mental headspace to even begin to consider something more than friendship for a long, long time—even if her soul had always seemed to . . . settle in his presence.

Yeah. Settle.

Not in a bad way. Not as though she were accepting something mediocre. But rather as though every cell in her body was paying attention, coming to prickling, absolute awareness, and yet also calming, relaxing.

No stress. No angst.

Just Luc and her.

So, she'd slipped into bed, intending to rest up before whatever ass-kicking trek he'd take her on and she was very much looking forward to the next day.

But those two questions the media had asked him and his responses, the slight note of misery in his eyes, had her tossing the covers back, shoving some clothes and toiletries into a duffle, her feet into her cozy boots, her hiking boots in one hand, her purse over one shoulder.

And then she was driving to Luc's house, parking at the curb so as not to block the driveway, using the key he'd given her to go inside, to turn off the alarm.

Soft footsteps took her upstairs and into his bedroom, where she tucked her bag into the bathroom.

Mischief had her shucking her pj's, sliding naked beneath the sheets.

She had no clue what time Luc would make it home, how long it would take him that night to get his post-game necessities done. But she was here, waiting, and there wasn't any doubt in her mind that he would think it was a good surprise.

Funny, that.

Wonderful, that.

Smiling, she turned off the lights, turned on the TV, cueing up a documentary she'd been in the middle of before she'd watched the Breakers lose, and then she waited.

CHAPTER TWENTY-FOUR

Luc

FATIGUE PULLED at the edges of his mind as he pulled into the driveway.

He'd finished what he'd needed to at the arena, but then he'd needed to pick up a few things for tomorrow. For his "hike" with Lexi.

He grinned, the first time since that disaster of a game, thinking about the expression on her face when she'd told him to pick what they did on their first date tomorrow. Not happy. But also not going to let him win by saying that.

He might have worried about starting off on the wrong foot, with her not being able to tell him when she was unhappy.

If they didn't have a long history of torturing each other.

Him with hikes. Her with her documentaries and copious amounts of M&Ms.

Maybe he should worry about that, too. Their affinity for torture. And probably he would, if he didn't know that she secretly enjoyed the hikes, even if she moaned about her legs for the next few days. Because there was a quiet moment whenever they made it to the top of a peak, or when they spotted a particularly beautiful bit of scenery where she went still, where joy bloomed on her face, where . . . she would grab his hand and just hold it tight as they surveyed what was in front of them.

It was why he'd paid for the pro version of the hiking app, just so he could find more trails.

She enjoyed the hikes, despite the complaining.

Same as he groused about the documentaries, though she seemed to find fascinating and bizarre films that he never would consider watching on his own, but with Lexi, they made for the perfect night in.

Paired with loads of M&Ms and plenty of wine.

Smiling, he rounded to the trunk of his car, pulled out the bags, and hauled them all into the kitchen, spending a few moments to get everything sorted for the next day's "hike."

Then he sighed, rolled his shoulders, and climbed the stairs.

His mind was focused on that date, on all the things he needed to prep in the morning, so perhaps that was why he'd missed the car at his curb, the blue light of the TV coming from his bedroom, the bag in his bathroom.

But it wouldn't be until later that he realized he'd missed those signs.

At that moment, he stumbled into his closet to strip off his suit, went to the sink to brush his teeth, and then blearily crossed the carpeting to slide into bed.

And nearly jumped out of his skin when he encountered a body beside him.

A naked body.

A naked, *female* body.

He blinked, his eyes adjusting to the dim light after the bright of the bathroom, the blue illumination from the sleep screen of the TV drifting up and over the covers, clinging to the curves of Lexi, fast asleep beneath the covers.

Naked and asleep and next to him.

A surge of greedy, predatory need coursed through him, his fingers curving into fists, his heart pounding. She was here. In his bed. But . . . sleeping. Her lips parted slightly, curled on her side, both hands tucked up under the pillow. He ran a light finger down her spine, watched as she shifted slightly, burrowing deeper into the covers, the pillow. Still asleep. Out soundly.

That was okay.

Sliding closer, he slipped one arm beneath her, brought his body close to her spine, his other arm tucked tightly around her middle. In his embrace, completely wrapped up in him.

He wouldn't wake her, and yet, it was still the best surprise ever to find this woman naked and in his bed.

She shifted again, moving closer, his name a whisper on the air, and Luc knew he couldn't have released her, not even if the world were ending, not even if a portal were opening up beneath their feet and threatening to suck them both down into oblivion, not even if a meteor were barreling toward them.

So, no, he wouldn't wake her.

Because even asleep, Lexi in his arms was still the best surprise of his life.

CHAPTER TWENTY-FIVE

Lexi

FIRE.

She was burning up with it.

Sweat pooling between her breasts, her skin threatening to scorch, to turn to ash. And more heat drifting up to her nose, spice instead of temperature, and that pulled her out of sleep, dragged her into reality.

The TV was still on, its blue light casting the room with an almost otherworldly glow.

But even as that was processing, she became aware of what was behind her.

Who was behind her.

A warm, calloused palm resting between her breasts, the heavy weight of his arm draped over her hip, his chest, the sparse hairs tickling her back, making her shiver and shift closer to—

Sweet mother of God.

Where had he been hiding *that?*

She'd seen the man in swim trunks, in gray sweats (because seriously, hello gray sweats and all the gloriousness they lovingly cupped and showed off), and never once had she caught a glimpse of the monster currently hard and pressing between the cheeks of her ass.

Instantly, her hips canted back, rubbing against it, heat now pooling between her thighs.

She wanted to roll over, to touch him, to trail her fingers south and wrap them around his cock. But her hands were trapped beneath her, his body almost pinning hers to the mattress. Not a bad place to be, all things considered; it was just that she wanted to trace every inch of him with her tongue.

Except, pinned.

The hard man on top of her. The blankets on top of them both, adding to that sweltering environment, a humid jungle beneath the covers, a fucking jungle cat behind her.

Lexi stifled a giggle.

Because jungle cat? Really?

She bit her lip. But it was just . . . he felt all big and possessive and yummy behind her, although there was nothing particularly funny about his giant cock.

More giggles. Though this time, one escaped.

She turned her head toward the pillow, stifling the sound, even as his hand dragged down her abdomen, drawing her ass even closer. "Is there a reason you're laughing at me?"

Lexi stilled, tried to roll him back so she could see his face.

He didn't let her, fingers clamping onto her hip, holding her steady, as he slowly pumped against her cheeks.

The giggles were gone. The need to stifle them dissipating, mainly because there were moans bubbling up in her throat. That hand slid up her side, making her shiver, a groan tumbling from her lips. His fingers danced, just on the outside of her breast. Her nipples beaded into tight aching buds, practically begging for his mouth. "Well?" he asked, a slow *tap-tap-tap* of those digits just inches from where she wanted him.

"What?" she breathed, hard-pressed to think of anything

besides that need raging through her. His thumb grazed her nipple, and she moaned again, ass thrusting back against him.

His groan rolled over her like hot water, his cock twitching against her cheeks. "Why were you laughing, baby?"

"I don't remember."

And she didn't.

Because the only thoughts in her brain were, *"Get that cock inside me," and "Now,"* and then, *"Please, God, now."*

His chuckle was on her skin, damp heat that echoed what was between her thighs. He leaned a little heavier against her.

She moaned and shifted, sweltering beneath him, the blankets, her desire swarming over her.

"What's the matter?"

"Hot," she breathed.

"Yes, you are." She felt his smile on her skin before he pulled the covers back, the cool air gliding over her in blissful relief. She wasn't the least bit cold, not with him against her. "Better?"

She nodded.

"Good," he murmured, brushing her nipple with his thumb again, making her jerk. "So, you want to tell me what you're doing in my bed, Lexi, baby?" His hand moved again, sliding over her breasts, down her stomach, trapping his fingers beneath her hips.

A heartbeat later and with a slight flicker of movement, he'd found her clit.

She gasped, moisture pooling. If she'd been wearing panties, they would be soaked, but because she was naked, she felt that wetness on her thighs, her labia swollen, her pussy empty and aching.

Slow circles around her clit, sparks of need and desire alighting through her. His other hand curled around her front, rolling her nipple between thumb and forefinger.

"Lexi?" he asked.

She was on fire, and her rapid breathing was the only response she could summon.

His mouth came to her ear, nibbling lightly at her earlobe. "Why are you in my bed?"

Superhuman strength.

Somehow, she found it, even despite loving the way he was touching her, fucking entranced by the weight of his hard, sexy body pinning her to the bed, she bucked up and rolled, pushing him to his back and climbing on top of him.

"I wanted to surprise you," she murmured, settling her naked pussy over the hard thrust of his cock.

He was naked, too.

And it was fucking glorious.

She teased the head of him, rolling her hips, drawing the hard length of his cock through her wetness, loving the feel of him so close and yet not *in*.

"Fuck," Luc groaned, and he was so fucking beautiful, his head thrown back on the pillows, the tendons on his neck standing out in sharp relief. He gripped her hips on a groan, and the next moment she was on her back, him huge and hard and poised over her.

Lungs seizing, her breaths in short gasps, her heart pounding, she spread her thighs.

And had the pleasure of watching his expression grow even more intense.

She hooked her leg around his hip, undulated against him.

A warm, rough hand on her waist, pinning her to the mattress. "Teasing?" he asked, the question barely more than a growl.

"Teasing is sometimes the best part," she countered, ratcheting up to slant her mouth against him. "Teasing can make every sensation stronger, every touch feel better, every orgasm more intense."

"*Every* orgasm?" His brow lifted. "As in plural?"

Considering she was ready to combust, and he was barely touching her— "Yes," she said. "As in plural." Her brows waggled. "Think you can handle that, Big Shot?"

A wicked smile, his head dropping, his nose pressing to her throat as he inhaled deeply. "I *like* you, Lexi Hallbright."

She shivered. "Well, *I* like you, Luc Masterson."

He pushed off her and stood next to the side of the bed.

"What are you doing?" she asked, frowning, suddenly feeling cold without her warm male blanket and maybe a little vulnerable with him looming over her.

"Plural," he said, as though that were an explanation, his hands coming to her thighs. She gasped when he yanked her to the edge of the mattress. "You said plural." He dropped to his knees. "So, I need to get working on all that—"

"Don't say plural again—"

He pressed his mouth to her.

"Oh, fuck," she moaned, the bristles on his jaw, the hot dart of his tongue, the softness of his lips, the sharp bite of his teeth.

It was . . . perfect and amazing and—

"Oh fuck," she moaned again.

"So *that's* the spot," he murmured, barely lifting his mouth, the words a whole new type of heated caress, one that fueled her need, one that had more curses tumbling from her lips, tangling with his name, with pleas to do it again. And when he did it again, to not stop. *Ever.*

Lucky for her, he *didn't* stop.

He continued stroking that spot with complete and total focus, winding her tighter, desire ramping higher and higher until . . . she exploded, wave after wave of pleasure flowing through her. Her nerves went taut and then relaxed millimeter by millimeter as her orgasm slowly waned. Eventually, she emerged from the fog of bliss, feeling his hands on her thighs, his mouth moving gently, his tongue oh so gentle.

Then he was shifting her back onto the bed.

Okay, less shifting and more tossing.

She bounced. He cursed.

"Fuck," he rasped. "You have the sexiest fucking tits I've ever seen."

Laughter bubbled in her throat . . . at least, until he pulled a condom out of the nightstand and set it on the bed next to her. At least, until he didn't make any move to tear it open or roll it on. Instead, he settled over her, heavy body on top of hers, trapping her against the mattress in the best possible way.

Then he put his gorgeous fucking mouth to good use, all over again.

And plural became a prayer. A benediction.

Plural became the best fucking night of her life.

CHAPTER TWENTY-SIX

Luc

SHE TASTED sweet with a hint of salt and mint. Toothpaste and woman. Flowers and Lexi.

The woman he loved.

The woman he was on fire for.

She was amazing.

Everywhere he touched her, she seemed to fall to pieces, trembling and moaning, her hips jerking, her limbs wrapping tight around him. He kissed her luscious mouth, tasting her until she broke away for air, but he was possessed, he didn't need oxygen in his bloodstream. He could inhale Lexi, survive on her alone, as he dragged his mouth across her jaw, down her throat, along her collarbones.

And then finally onto her breasts.

Tasting the silken skin of those plush globes, trailing his lips toward the tight furls of her nipples. A flick of his tongue had her groaning, clawing at his back, and she was so damned sensitive that he knew he had to move carefully, move slow and steady and *easy*. Exactly as he'd done when he'd been between her thighs.

His rewards were her moans, her nails digging into his skin, her hips bucking against him.

A hand down her side, slipping in between her thighs, finding that spot again and exploiting it until her breathing hitched in the back of her throat, until her lips were plump and red, until her fingers were tight in his hair, until she made that soft little noise that he recognized as her being close to the edge.

Then . . . redoubling his efforts.

Not stopping. Not ever.

Not a chance in fucking hell.

She went stiff, her hands gripped tighter, her moans rolled over him like the waves on a shoreline, over and over and over again until . . .

Tsunami.

"Luc," she gasped. Her head thrashed on the pillow, her mouth was wide, his name tumbling off her tongue repeatedly.

Until she finally went still, her chest heaving. "Plural," she gasped, pressing her hand to her chest. "Holy fucking shit."

He was grinning.

Like a cocky fucking bastard.

But he didn't give a shit if it *was* arrogant. Making this woman come had just become his new favorite pastime, especially when she dropped a limp hand to the side, fingers fumbling for the condom he'd placed there.

She slapped it against his chest. "Put this on and get inside me," she snapped, though her eyes were twinkling.

His fingers were still between her thighs, and he fluttered them gently. "I still need to prove I can do *plural*."

She jumped, another moan in the air. "You've proved it—"

"Hmm," he nuzzled her throat. "I'm not so sure about that."

Laughter and irritation when he lifted his gaze to meet hers, and he knew what she was going to do, even before she moved. Because he knew this woman, because he maybe knew her better than she knew herself. So, when she put her hands against his chest and pushed, he wrapped an arm around her waist and rolled with her.

She frowned. "You let me do that."

A shrug. "So?" He brought his hands to her hips, brought her flush against him. "Maybe I like the view." Then dragged his palms up, cupping her breasts. Fuck, this angle was incredible, the pouty, glorious way they hung. Heavy and round, the hardened tips so fucking tempting.

Her lips parted, a breath shuddering out. "I like the way you look at me."

He dragged his thumb over one nipple then the other with a featherlight touch that she liked. "Are we doing more teasing?" he asked, repeating the motion. "Or are we moving to the *getting inside* part?"

More shaky exhales. More moisture pooling on top of his naked cock.

More desire in her golden-brown eyes.

"Oh yeah," she murmured and tore open the condom with her teeth. "I want to do *that*."

Then she was rolling the latex down his cock, her fingers bringing it down at what seemed like a snail's pace, even though the movements were deft without fumbling.

He wanted to flip her over, to thrust into her.

But . . . patience.

He'd had two and a half years to dream about this day.

She'd had—

She pushed up, began to lower herself onto him.

Now, he was the one to say, "Oh fuck!"

She was hot and tight, a fucking vise clamping down on him, her breath hissing out, her eyes heavy-lidded and scorching on his as she slowly bottomed out.

"Too fucking big," she whispered.

"Words a man dreams to hear," he said, somehow finding some strength to joke, even when he was in real danger of exploding without even one thrust.

She leaned forward, rested her hands on his chest, slowly raising and lowering her hips, sliding up and down his length, and he'd been right about the danger of coming. He was close, *too* fucking close, especially when he'd wanted to feel her orgasm around him, her pussy clenching on his cock.

Reaching between them, he flicked his fingers over her clit, used the other to cup her breast, to tease her nipple, drew her close to taste her.

She tightened around him, broke away to moan, her breath hitching.

Thank fuck for that breath and that hitching.

Because she was close, and he wouldn't have to hold out for much longer. He thrust up, going deeper, probably too deep, but she didn't stop moving against him, bearing down, grinding against him.

"Luc," she whispered, her eyes sliding closed as she moved faster.

He kept his fingers moving, his hips pistoning up. "Come for me, baby," he murmured. "Come on my cock."

Please, God, come. Before he lost it.

"I—" She faltered, jerking against him, starting to lose her rhythm, and she groaned, her eyes flying open, her teeth biting into her lower lip.

Not waiting for her to lose her tempo completely, he flipped them, started stroking in deep and fast and hard. Because he couldn't move any differently. Because any semblance of his control had snapped. Because . . . he'd lost it, and her pussy was his fucking salvation and—

She went stiff, a moan filling the air, and then, thank God, thank *fuck*, she was coming, all that tight, wet heat convulsing around his cock, the pulsing of her orgasm catapulting him over the edge.

He came and came, unable to see straight, unable to stop moving.

Just thrusting until he could hardly feel anything, until his balls were empty, his body felt like an empty husk.

He collapsed on her, his arms shaking from the effort not to crush her.

His lungs burned, sweat sheened his body, and he somehow found the strength to roll them to their sides, tugging her against his chest, and just breathing in her scent.

She yawned, snuggled closer. "That was . . ." Her words trailed off, another yawn taking the place of any adjective she might have summoned.

"Incredible," he finished, holding on to her for one more moment before he slipped out of her embrace and went to the bathroom to clean up.

Then he slid under the covers, her naked body not a surprise this time.

And it was still the best fucking thing ever, having Lexi there in his bed.

In his arms.

The *fucking* best.

CHAPTER TWENTY-SEVEN

Lexi

SHE WAS BEING ROMANCED.

She shouldn't have been surprised.

Probably, she'd nuked all of his careful plans by slipping into his bed the night before. Totally worth it—their middle of the night shenanigans before passing out for a couple of hours —even if Luc had still woken her at the crack of dawn, pressing a kiss to her lips . . . then tugging the blankets off her, leaving her naked and chilled as he'd walked across the bedroom.

Equally as naked.

But not chilled, apparently, based on the erection he was sporting.

Still, when she'd pushed out of bed and trailed him into the bathroom, intending to jump his bones, she found a candle lit, the shower on, soft music playing from the speakers.

And a sexy man hanging towels over the glass of the shower.

Her brows rose then her lips curved into a smile.

He turned to face her, eyes warm. "Hey, love," he murmured. "How are you?"

"Chilled," she mock grumbled, flattening her smile as he prowled toward her, making her pulse leap, her lips part, pleasure and joy flutter through her like the breeze ruffling the leaves on a tree.

A stirring, gentle but with the possibility of so much more.

The backs of his knuckles slid over her cheek, down her throat, between her breasts. "Are you okay?" he whispered, and the real concern in his eyes had her dropping her faux disapproval and stepping into his arms.

"I'm perfect," she murmured, squeezing him tight.

"Promise?"

A nod.

"*Lex*," he warned, his breath in her hair, and she knew he wanted the word, knew there was power in words.

"I promise, I'll tell you if I'm *not* perfect, okay?" She leaned back, stared into his forest green eyes. "So long as you'll do the same for me."

He nodded.

"*Luc*," she warned this time.

A grin. "I promise." He hefted her up, made her squeak, her hands flying up to grasp his shoulders, her legs wrapping around his hips. He carried her into the shower, tucked her under the stream of water, the warm liquid sloshing over her shoulders, down her body, forming little hot pools between them. "Since we're going to be late for our hike"—he groaned good-naturedly—"we should make sure to conserve water."

"Is that what this is?"

She hadn't missed the condom on the built-in shelf, nor did she miss the way he tilted the showerhead toward the tile, warming it before he pressed her back to it, his hard cock between them.

He ignored her question, nuzzling her throat, nipping just behind her ear. The spot was beyond sensitive and made her shiver, even in the warmth of the shower.

Then his lips found hers, one hand slipped between them to

tease all the spots he'd discovered just hours before, displacing any thought of answers or water conservation or hiking, wrapping them into proverbial concrete and dropping them offshore. She watched them sink down, *down* into the dark depths.

But not sad or scary. Just buried by the weight of the moment, by this man who made her feel so much.

Who made her feel right.

She embraced the deep, the dark . . . because this man had led her out of it.

Her hair was wet and dripping down her shoulders, the shower's water streamed between them. His hands were gentle, considering their exploits earlier, but not any less skilled as they swept her into a whirlwind of need, of shaking, all-consuming *need*.

But never taking her over the edge.

Right up to the precipice, but never over.

Frustration and demand had her clipping out his name, arching against him. He smiled at her, a wolfish grin on his face.

She was torn between wanting to be relieved and wanting to throttle him. But he saved himself from the latter when he finally reached for the condom, somehow rolled it on without dropping her. The man had magical superhero abilities or . . . maybe just skills. Either way, the condom was on, his cock was pressing against her folds and then pushing inside.

Her lips parted on a groan, her tender insides spasming in pleasure-pain, and then he was in deep, his hips flush to hers, pinning her to the tile, one hand cupping her ass, his other propped on the wall by her head.

He moved, thrusting hard and fast, sending her up that mountain, propelling her over the other side much more rapidly than she'd anticipated.

She couldn't catch her breath, couldn't do anything but hold on to his shoulders and brace herself for the ride he was giving her, embrace the burning in her lungs when wave after wave of pleasure rolled through her. He thrust several more times, sending aftershocks of ecstasy through her before he groaned her name, pressed deep, and stilled against her, his forehead on her collarbone, breaths coming in rapid succession.

"Fuck," she whispered after several long moments. "How the hell am I supposed to hike after *that?*"

He froze.

Then his shoulders started shaking.

His laughter echoed off the tile, and it filled her, filled her with happiness, with . . . hope for the future.

————

HER LEGS WERE TREMBLING, long unused muscles protesting the physical activity after she and Luc had used up so much energy.

But though she groused and groaned, she really enjoyed being outside.

There was something about feeling the wind on her face, and whether it was that she was starting to get into better shape because of all the hikes they'd taken of late or because he'd taken pity on her and picked an easy path, she didn't know.

And didn't care, she supposed.

So long as she was with her best friend, her boyfriend, her . . . *lover?* God, that sounded weird, just as it was strange to have the label, the tone of that friendship shift into something different, something *more.*

Probably not quite as much as it should.

They'd been moving toward this, probably from the moment they'd first met, so while the names, trying to quantify what they'd become sounded odd to her brain, being with him, sleeping in his arms, having his body against hers, his mouth on hers, his cock inside her, all felt . . . weirdly enough, *normal.*

Even though they'd leaped from friends to—*yes*—lovers.

Their feet crunched quietly on the trail, the dirt and rocks shifting beneath the soles of their shoes. The trees had closed in around them, making the air cold and damp, almost clinging to her skin. She'd brought hiking clothes—leggings and a T-shirt, along with her ridiculously expensive boots and socks (both of which she'd invested in after their first hike had left her with blisters and aching feet for days), and a hoodie.

But she'd pilfered Luc's oversized sweatshirt not long after they'd begun, the chill seeping into her and the exertion of this trail not strenuous enough to have her peeling off layers like normal.

Now she was safely ensconced in warm, male-scented cotton, its arms rolled up several times at the cuffs, and even then, they still fell past her fingertips, its hem teased her legs at mid-thigh. Luc had snagged her water bottle, storing it in the pocket of his backpack before they'd even left the parking lot, and aside from one stop to drink and rest, they'd been walking for what had to be close to an hour.

"Was this a loop?" she asked, glancing over her shoulder at him, catching him staring at where the hem of his sweatshirt was brushing. "Or an out-and-back?"

"Loop," he said, his gaze slowly tracing up her body, no embarrassment for being caught staring in his eyes that matched the deep green of the trees surrounding them.

Speaking of which— "Are we going to see anything besides trees?" she asked, another look back.

Half of his mouth tipped up, flashing her a dimple. "Yup."

"You going to tell me?"

"Nope." The *p* sounding like a balloon popping.

She waited for more of an explanation.

Then wondered why she bothered. Luc wasn't the type of man to be pushed into anything, and certainly not an explanation. When he wouldn't budge, he wouldn't budge. Luckily, that wasn't too often, or she might want to throttle him.

Okay, fine, when he pulled his whole gorgeous, dimpled, half-smile bullshit, keeping mum on all the revealing thoughts and secrets in his mind, she *did* want to throttle him.

But she had other tools in her repertoire to draw from.

Plus, he was quite tall.

It would be really hard to reach that high up to get her hands around his neck.

Slowing, she spun to face him, letting her eyes show exactly what other paraphernalia she had in her toolbox. His body came flush to hers, her palm resting on his chest. "Luc," she murmured.

He merely tapped her on the nose. "Behave," he said, eyes dancing as he snagged her hand from where it rested above his heart, weaved their fingers together, and drew her forward again while she sputtered over the indignity of being tapped on the nose and told to behave.

On. The. Nose. And. Behave.

Like.

Seriously?

What the fuck was that?

She opened her mouth to ask him precisely that, but no sooner had that question reached the tip of her tongue and his lips were on hers, his tongue was sliding home, trailing along hers as he kissed her into a pile of mush of damp earth like that which lined the edges of the trail.

He broke away, leaving her chest heaving, the fingers of one hand having slipped beneath the hem of her sweatshirt to cup her ass. "Behave," he said again.

Then they were moving forward, her head spinning, her legs like jelly.

"Remind me to never give you my sweatshirt again," he said, right about the time her breathing had approached normal.

Lexi frowned.

His free hand dipped back underneath the sweatshirt. "Covers up the sweetest ass I've ever had the privilege to see."

"And touch, apparently," she said with far more dry humor

than she felt, considering the light caress was enough to nearly send her combusting all over again.

Another glimpse of that dimple.

Then his hand was out from beneath the sweatshirt, and he was tugging her forward again, up and over a small hill, and—

Her breath caught.

Not from his kiss or his body or the attraction, but from what she saw ahead of them.

Luc let her stand there in a stupor, eyeing the most beautiful clearing she'd ever seen—almost perfectly round, wildflowers having sprung up around the circumference, springy green grass in the middle, a creek babbling just beyond the trees on the far side.

"Come on," he said, after a few minutes, her eyes taking in every detail.

He brought her toward the clearing, guided her over the wildflowers so they didn't trample them, then he tugged her into the center, pausing and pulling a blanket out of the backpack. A flick of his wrist had it spread on the grass; another had a thermos pulled from his bag.

"Sit," he ordered.

She sat, and he plunked down next to her, the smell of coffee reaching her nose when he unscrewed the lid and poured her a cup.

Then he pulled a container of chocolate-covered strawberries from the backpack.

Romanced.

Holy hell, was she being romanced.

And she'd be lying if she said it wasn't the best feeling ever.

CHAPTER TWENTY-EIGHT

Luc

SHE WAVED GOODBYE, driving her little car down the street, and he wanted to chase after her, to demand that she stay at his place forever.

But . . . they'd skipped quite a few steps already.

And he'd had all day with her.

And she'd come to him the night before.

God, he'd never expected her to come to him. After two and a half fucking years of shoving everything down, after being absolutely terrified that she would run screaming for the hills when he'd first made a move, still waiting for some other shoe to drop—her realizing that it wasn't him she wanted or that they were better as friends or that she just wasn't interested in dating anyone right then.

All would be valid reasons to not take this step.

But she'd shown up anyway.

And . . . it was the same as it always was between them, and different. Completely, utterly different . . . and better.

So much better than he'd ever dreamed.

Perfect.

The woman was perfect.

Okay, so he knew that was the hormones talking, knew that she, of course, *wasn't* perfect, just like he was far from flawless. But she was perfect for him. So fucking funny and tough and smart and generous. He knew the person she was inside, knew that she had a light burning inside her. One that had guttered and nearly gone out because of that fucker, Caleb. And one that now burned bright again.

Because of *her*. Not him.

Because she was so fucking strong.

And he admired her so freaking much.

Even if she *was* leaving him.

Frowning, he turned back for the house, knowing that she probably needed the space, especially after their crazy jump into intimacy, but he'd wanted to have her stay. Which was completely a new phenomenon for him.

After his divorce, he'd done the whole different bed every night thing—at least once his knee had recovered enough to do said bed-hopping. But he hadn't done relationships, didn't think he'd been cut out for them, even when he'd gotten tired of variety and stuck with one woman for longer than a night. *Then* his dealings with women had become two people searching for mutual satisfaction with neither party interested in a relationship.

He hadn't wanted to be vulnerable.

Yet, with Lexi, he'd never been able to keep his distance.

He'd been so desperate for any connection with her that he'd opened himself wide. Pathetic, probably, especially after he'd discovered she was married. Luc certainly wasn't the romantic type—or hadn't been, anyway—but if she'd been available, it would have been love at first sight.

It was for him, he supposed.

For Lexi . . . well, she'd certainly never given him any indication of being open to anything aside from friendship. He'd need to ask her one of these days.

Making a mental note of that, he went into the house, locked up, and pulled out his computer, intending to get ready for the week. As always, there were dozens of emails, those that had piled up since he'd been ignoring his cell all day.

Ignoring, except for the pictures he'd snapped of Lexi, and then the ones she'd snapped of him and her together.

Selfies.

He was taking selfies, and he was happy about it.

But was it a selfie if it included another person in it? Or was it a doubly? An us-y? He dragged a hand over his face, knowing he was too fucking old to deduce the mysteries of young person lingo.

Forty.

Fucking *forty.* Almost forty-one.

God, when he'd been twenty, forty had seemed so old, but today, he felt like he'd just begun living.

"Romantic sap," he muttered, deliberately thinking not about his love life and instead focusing on his emails, clearing the decks, making a few phone calls when an email response wouldn't fly. About an hour later, he rolled his shoulders and neck, closing the browser and mentally shifting gears as he opened a password-secured spreadsheet.

Things My Love Loves.

The password was Lexi's birthday. January 4th. Zero-one-zero-four.

Such. A. Sap.

But he didn't give a fuck, not as he made a couple of notes, new things he'd discovered today—she wanted a candle that smelled like Christmas, she loved apple cider but hated eggnog (the latter of which he couldn't believe he hadn't known, considering they'd spent last Christmas together)—and then took a few minutes to study his list, wondering what he should do next.

They didn't have an official plan for another date, but she'd said she would see him the next day.

Should he be planning something fancy and romantic? A nice dinner? A date that didn't involve her hiking up a mountain? It was strange to feel caught flat-footed, usually he was so comfortable knowing everything about Lexi, his instincts and the fact that he paid attention driving him in their interactions.

But . . . everything had changed for the better.

And he was half-terrified he was going to fuck it up.

Which was why, even though the sun was setting and he had a full day of work the next day, he continued studying that list, continued planning his next step. He harnessed that fear of ruining things between them and focused on the fact that he knew her, that they were good together.

He'd given his players this same advice a dozen times.

Don't overthink it. Just keep your head down and continue moving forward.

It wasn't a magic pill. It didn't completely alleviate the dread in his heart, the urge to dig his claws in and hold tight for fear of losing her.

But it settled him enough so he could close the document, could head up to a bed that still smelled like Lexi.

And yeah, maybe he held tight to the pillow that smelled like her as he fell asleep.

———

MORE RUNNING.

This time without a side of nearly getting run over.

Which was why he noticed the car at the curb this time, the smell of bacon wafting into the front yard as he jogged up the walk and unlocked the door.

He strode straight into the kitchen and smiled.

Lexi was wearing a frilly apron, her hips moving to music he couldn't hear, courtesy of the headphones she had stuck in her ears.

Bacon and eggs, cheese and green onions.

As he leaned on the wall that marked the entrance to the kitchen, he watched her dump the eggs into the pan, add big handfuls of cheese and bacon and onions, then deftly flipping the mixture and letting it cook before sliding it onto the plate.

She turned, met his eyes as though she'd known he'd been there the whole time, just watching, and lifted an eyebrow. "You going to keep standing there?" she asked. "Or are you going to eat?"

"I was enjoying the view," he said, pushing off the wall and moving toward her.

"We need to go dancing again," she murmured, pushing the plate into his hands. "I promise to not drink so much, so I can actually remember all of it."

Chuckling, he wrapped his arms around her, spinning her so her back was against his chest. "It was a lot of me doing this."

She inhaled sharply, and he set the plate on the counter, before bringing his hand to her stomach and drawing her closer. "I think I like it when you hold me like this," she murmured, hips arching back.

"It was a love-hate for me." He bent to kiss her jaw.

"Why?" she asked, tilted her head to the side, giving him more access.

"Because I loved having you close, and I hated having the rest of those fuckers in the bar looking at you."

She spun in his arms, brows raised, putting a few inches between them. "Possessive much?"

A few inches too many.

He clamped a hand on her hip, drew her to him, eliminating that space she'd created. "I spent two and a half years dreaming about a woman who belonged to someone else." He crouched a little, so his gaze met hers. "Yeah, I'm feeling a lot possessive."

Her lips parted, and he couldn't resist tasting her.

Until she planted her hands on his chest and pushed him back a step.

"Eat," she ordered when he reached for her again, stepping back and grabbing the plate, handing it to him a second time.

He might have ignored her order, if not for the fact that she'd already turned away, beginning to prep her own breakfast, and he didn't want to delay her eating any further. Plus, the omelet smelled incredible, and his stomach was already growling. So, he sat down at the table, although he should have probably gone upstairs and showered instead of grinding all up against her like a sweaty asshole.

God knew what he smelled like.

"I like you sweaty," she murmured, tossing a glance at him, adding at what was probably a surprised expression on his face —it was like she'd cherry-picked that thought straight out of his mind, "I know you, too, Luc."

A grin had him pushing out of his seat, crossing to her and looping his arms around her waist. Lexi didn't retreat from his smelly ass. Instead, she drifted closer, rubbed her nose against the column of his throat.

"And I like the way you smell after you exercise." One hand cupped the side of his neck, drew him down for a short, blazing kiss, then she turned her head, running her mouth along his jaw, inhaling deeply.

When she rotated back to the stove, he moved to open the utensil drawer . . . then froze when she cleared her throat.

His eyes went to hers, and he grinned when she extended a fork wrapped in a napkin, and he took it back to the table, knowing that if she kept feeding him breakfast, he was going to have to add some extra miles to his running routine. Hell, her saying she liked him sweaty had him willing to run his whole circuit again, just so she'd come close again and press her nose to his throat again.

Both scenarios were totally worth it—the extra running *and* the sniffing.

Dork, he thought.

Biting back a laugh, he dug into his omelet.

Then nearly moaned.

The cheese was hot and melty, the bacon crispy, the green onions a nice bite to contrast with everything else. He'd pounded half of it before he made himself come up for air, and he saw that she was putting her own omelet on her plate.

A few moments later, she was next to him.

And they were eating breakfast together.

Something they'd done a hundred times before, and yet something that was completely different from a week before.

Lexi rested her palm on his thigh, smiled up at him.

Different because they were dating.

His mouth curved, pleasure in every cell.

Yeah, he could definitely get used to this.

CHAPTER TWENTY-NINE

Lexi

SHE BLINKED her bleary eyes and logged off her computer, intending to walk down to Luc's office to see if he wanted to do lunch.

Before she so much as pushed out of her chair, her cell rang.

She glanced at the screen, saw it was her dad, and then immediately remembered what date it was. These calls were like clockwork, once a month, from wherever he was.

Lexi swiped to answer the call

"Dad," she said. "How are you?"

The connection was bad, as it always was. Since her mom had passed nearly eight years before, her dad hadn't been around much. Her mom had barely been in the ground before he'd sold her childhood home in Connecticut, bought an RV, and then spent most of his time floating around different states in the continental U.S.

She'd been an adult, but it had taken time for her to come to terms with that second loss, well, the third, she supposed—if she counted the house where so many of her happy memories had been grounded—and she certainly did.

Three blows.

Her mom.

Her dad.

Her childhood.

Maybe that was why she'd grasped so tight to Caleb when he'd first strolled into her life. She'd been adrift and mourning, and he'd been so fun and alive, a total force of nature. So big that she'd been able to cling onto his wake, and some of his life had bled into her, making her feel more like herself again.

Hmm.

Things to ponder in the dark of night.

For the moment, she needed all of her concentration to focus on the conversation, on the half-broken words that were coming through the line.

"I'm good . . . in the mid . . . of Wyoming . . ."

"Yellowstone?" she asked, throat suddenly tight.

"Next up," he said, and the static cleared enough that she heard the bit of sad wind its way into his tone, the same sad that was winding its way through her.

"Fun," she said, interjecting happiness into her words. Probably sounded fake as hell, considering the memories slamming through her like a battering ram. "You going to go to Old Faithful?"

A pause, more road noise in the background. "First stop."

She sucked in a breath, whispered, though he probably wouldn't hear her, "I'm glad. She'd want you to go there."

But the road gods had obliged, apparently, because she heard him inhale sharply.

"I'm sorry," she said quickly, not wanting to cause an eruption, not when every mention of her mother previously had caused him to lash out.

She braced herself, but the eruption didn't come.

Instead, silence greeted her.

Then a long, shaking breath.

"I've been a bastard since she's been gone, haven't I?"

Another inhale, one that burned her lungs. Or maybe that was her eyes. "This probably isn't a conversation we should have while you're driving that behemoth," she said, deliberately keeping her tone neutral.

Silence.

Long and not punctuated with anything aside from the sound of the road.

And, God, how many conversations had been like this? Stilted and filled with uncomfortable quiet, her eyes drifting around whatever space she was in, hoping that she'd find a way to escape, to shove the call plumb full of pleasantries, even if it was all just pretend.

But today, she couldn't find the words to cram into that emptiness.

She just didn't have the energy to pretend anymore.

Too much of that. She'd done far too much of that.

"I should concentrate on the road," he said, and there was a note of something in his voice that she couldn't deduce. Especially, when he went quiet again, when he didn't say anything else.

"Goodbye, Dad," she said. "Drive safe."

They hung up, and she sucked in a breath, not having the mental headspace to deal with all the emotions the call had churned up. She just wanted to focus on work. She didn't even want to eat now, or to see Luc. Not when he would understand what the call did to her.

"Dammit," she whispered, trying to stuff down all of the feelings that had been drudged up.

She wanted to have something happy.

Was that too much to ask?

Turning to the window, seeing the roads and cars in the distance, she sighed and knew it wasn't too much, knew that she deserved that happy.

But usually, what she deserved didn't matter.

————

LUNCH CAME AND WENT, but she didn't go see Luc.

In fact, she found she wasn't hungry, the conversation with her dad stifling the pangs in her stomach long after they'd hung up and well into the afternoon.

She finished her work around two then began working on a couple of the projects that were approaching deadline, Todd having passed them onto her as his retirement loomed. But by the time the end of the workday came around, she still wasn't hungry, though at least she felt like most of that rawness had been buried deep again, shoved down beneath the walls she'd erected in the wake of that triple loss.

Sighing, she rolled her shoulders, shifted to her personal email, and waded her way through that.

This evening was her turn at the library to offer pro bono help. She'd be there from six to eight, and by the look of the schedule the charity had just sent her, she was completely booked.

That was perfect.

More work to keep shoving down, to continue to mortar and brick over the past. First, with her parents. Then . . . with Caleb.

Because the next email down was from the realtor.

Everything had been funded and signed. The house was gone. The yards she'd worked on were gone. The marriage was gone.

The fantasy gone.

Maybe she should be sadder about that.

Maybe she should be wailing again, instead of just reading that email with a creeping sort of numbness.

The knock on her office door, the head that poked through had that numbness cascading away. Luc studied her for a moment then moved inside and closed the wooden panel behind him, leaning back against it. "Your dad called."

Her fingers spasmed on the keyboard.

How did this man know every single thing about her?

She forced a smile, her tone light and filled with false joy. "I'm going to grab a quick bite before I go to the library. Want to join me?"

He was in front of her in the next instant, his hands on her cheeks. "Don't," he said. "Don't do that."

Lexi swallowed, her eyes drifting up and over his shoulder. "Do what?"

"You don't need to pretend with me," he said. "Not today. Not ever."

Her lips parted, a shaking exhale escaping. "Luc."

He tugged her against his chest, wrapped those warm, strong arms around her, holding her tight for a long moment. Then when she relaxed into his hold, he released her, said softly, "Let's go get something to eat."

———

HE FOLLOWED her to the little hole-in-the-wall restaurant, cramming their cars into the tiny parking lot behind the space.

Luckily, it was early, so it wasn't too tight of a squeeze.

Luc took her hand, drew her around to the front of the shop, and inside. The smell of noodles and sauce made her stomach rumble.

Thank God for udon.

The warm broth, the chewy pork belly, the soft noodles, the crunch of the vegetables.

Lexi was a pasta girl, through and through, whether it was with creamy or tomato sauce or in a briny, delicious broth like at this café. They—she and Luc and Caleb—had come here often enough that the hostess/waitress knew their orders and had put it in before they even sat down.

Their legs tangled beneath the scarred top as the hostess

brought glasses of water to the small table for two. "The third one?" she asked. "He's not coming anymore?"

Lexi's teeth clinked together, and she felt her shoulders start to creep up.

It was the first time the hostess had inquired about Caleb, and it was surprising how much of a sting such a simple question caused. She'd had plenty of people ask about Caleb, plenty of people she'd had to explain the end of her marriage to.

But not at one of her *places.*

Frankly, it was surprising it had taken this long for it to become an issue. Probably, because she hadn't gone to many of her *places* in the last six months. She hadn't felt much like spending time with anyone aside from herself.

Aside from Luc.

Still, it felt odd to have to explain the situation with her ex-husband. Work had been easy—gossip flowed through the organization like water, and Luc had ensured that she hadn't needed to do an autopsy of the relationship with anyone there. Her other friends had been different. Worse because several had known about Caleb's cheating, which had instantly discounted them from her having any future relationships with them (because, seriously, what the absolute fuck? How could they keep something like that from her?) and the rest had fallen away into the background—either not as connected to her as they were to Caleb or moving on with their own lives when she hadn't had the ability to be a good friend.

She didn't blame them.

She just . . . this was one of their *places,* and it wasn't the same and—

Luc covered her hand with his, snapping her out of the spiraling. "He's not coming anymore."

The hostess's eyes drifted to her left hand (now sans ring) and then up to meet her gaze, understanding in the coffee-colored depths. But she didn't comment further, just nodded, patted their linked hands, and turned back to the counter, saying something to the chef behind it.

Sizzling covered the sound of his reply, and Lexi watched him move, so smooth and efficient. She knew it wouldn't be long before the food was in front of them.

"Want to talk about it?" Luc asked.

"God, no," she muttered. She'd just managed to shove the conversation back from the forefront of her mind. "I do have good news, though," she said, not forcing a smile. "The house paperwork went through."

A squeeze of his fingers. "So, that's behind you."

She nodded. "I guess, I need to go house shopping," she said, knowing it would definitely be a downsize. Hopefully, she'd be able to stay close to the office. Spoiled because her commute had been a max of twenty minutes, Lexi knew it would be difficult to adjust to something significantly longer.

More time for podcasts and audiobooks, she supposed, so it wouldn't be all bad.

Luc stroked his thumb over the back of her hand. "What just went through your mind?"

"I was thinking of podcasts."

His eyes narrowed. "What sort of podcasts?"

That narrowing was warranted, mostly because the last time she'd gotten to choose what played in the car on the way to their hike, he'd been forced to listen to a podcast about love. Which, under normal circumstances, wouldn't be so bad. Except this one hadn't been up his alley. She was a Lord of the Rings fan and had been utterly fascinated by the fan fiction turned real-life LARPing relationship. There had been some steamy online chats, lots of character interpretation and acting, and plenty of relationship drama.

She, for one (*literally* for one), had been riveted.

Luc, not much of a LOTR fan, hadn't.

"Not one requiring me to pull out my elf ears," she said, mouth tipping up at the edges. "Sad as it is to say."

He lightly flicked the top of one of her ears. "I don't know." Amusement danced in his emerald eyes. "I might be able to get into it if you were wearing one of those elf girl outfits."

Laughter boiled up within her, simmering up her throat, steaming out through her mouth . . . and nose, in a wholly undignified snort.

A tap to her nose. "You're cute."

"You just want to see me in see-through silks."

"Yes." A nod. "That I do."

Rolling her eyes, she nonetheless was smiling. "If you're good, I'll wear my robes for you."

"Why do I think that you don't mean the type of robes that you wear in the bathroom or over your pj's?"

It was her turn to tap his nose. "You'd be right."

The hostess came back, setting the steaming white bowls in front of them with a smile before heading to another table and wiping down a stack of plastic-covered menus.

"So," Luc said, picking up his chopsticks and digging in, "house hunting?"

"It'd be nice to get out of my apartment sooner rather than later."

"Not much of a garden in your current place."

"Exactly." She used the wooden spoon the hostess had set on the table and tasted the broth, nearly moaning when it hit her tongue. Perfect umami. "I can't wait to get my hands dirty."

A trace of heat drifting across his gaze had her smirking.

She lightly swatted his hand. "Ridiculous man." Then she picked up her chopsticks and dug in.

He slurped. *She* slurped.

Then he stopped slurping, met her gaze. "You could always save yourself the trouble of house hunting and just move in with me."

It took her a minute to process the words, she was so in love with her noodles, and then when she did, she nearly choked on her monster bite, coughing and sputtering over her bowl, her eyes watering, nearly spitting out the soup.

She met Luc's gaze, tears dripping down her cheeks.

Wordlessly, he pushed her glass of water toward her, reached across the table to dab her eyes with a napkin.

She set down her chopsticks, picked up the cup, and gulped the water down.

When she set it back on the table, empty, he covered her hand again, asked, "Do you want to pretend I didn't say that?"

Yes!

Yes, she fucking did.

And also . . . *no*. No, she didn't. She wanted—

What?

To move in with him? No, of course not. That was insanity. Except . . . *was* it? She'd already lived with him for a few months at the beginning of her separation. He'd been her friend for two years, her best friend for nearly that length of time. But he'd only been her lover for . . . two days?

She couldn't move into his house.

That was . . .

Impossible.

But *was* it?

"Eat now," he said, nudging her bowl toward her. "Panic later."

"I'm not panicking."

His brows lifted in question.

"I'm *not*."

A flash of dimple. "Sure, you aren't."

"Luc," she warned, even as his smile widened. Seriously, why in the fuck was the man so gorgeous? It wasn't fair. It was distracting and tempting and too freaking dangerous and . . .

He assumed she was going to say no.

She could see that in his eyes.

And some slice of devil was prompting her to call his bluff. Just pure mischief and wanting to see him scramble, not because she was in so deep as to *want* to move in with the man she'd been dating for only two days, not even a week after she'd finalized her divorce.

Lie, her heart yelled.

She wanted *that*. Maybe it was stupid under the circumstances.

But Luc was . . .

Luc.

Still, bluff and not, *want* and not, teasing weaved its way through her.

Which was why she picked up her chopsticks, said simply, "Okay."

His brows drew together, steam from his bowl flowing up in front of his face. "Okay, what? You're going to eat?"

A shake of her head.

"No."

More brow-drawing. More questions in his eyes.

"Okay, as in . . . I'll move in with you," she said as casually as she could muster, fighting a smile when shock shot through his gaze and his mouth dropped open.

His chopsticks hit the tabletop and rolled onto the ground.

"Really?"

She nodded.

He whooped, making her jump, their bowls rattling as he jumped out of his seat and rounded the table, tugging her into his arms. "Really?" he asked, pulling back to stare into her eyes. "*Really*, sweetheart?"

She bit her lip, nodded, hope and joy blooming inside her.

Another whoop, his arms tightening again.

Lexi threw her own arms around his shoulders, hugged *him* tight, shivered when he whispered, "All this time, all this fucking time, I was biding my time, trying to find the courage, to line up all the reasons to convince you to give me a chance." Her heart squeezed, eyes filling with tears. "I thought it would take many more months, *years*, to persuade you to give me a shot." His arms wound tighter. "I—" A sharp breath. "I just won't let you down. I promise you, I *won't*."

Caleb had once said the same thing to her.

Until this moment, she would have said she believed him.

Until this man, until her *Luc* made this pledge.

And she knew it would change everything.

CHAPTER THIRTY

Luc

A NAKED BODY in his arms was the best way to wake up.

The sun hadn't risen yet, but he'd tucked his cell under his pillow to mute the alarm for the early ass flight he had to take.

It was currently buzzing under his head.

Hating that he had to take his hands off Lexi, that he had to turn away from her in order to silence it, he nonetheless summoned the herculean strength to do so. Then decided that 5:20 in the morning was too early to think about words like *herculean*.

"Luc?" Lexi whispered.

He kissed her forehead. "Sleep, honey. I'm just getting up for my flight."

A nod, her pretty face burrowing into the pillow, her lips pursed into a pout.

A pout he kissed.

She smiled, rolled to face him, eyes closed, voice sleepy. "I'm going to miss you."

They'd barely had a week together, but now he was flying out with the team while they played on the road. He'd be going to the games, of course, but he also needed to meet with some agents to check out some players his scouts had highlighted. It would be some of the normal work that came with running a team, but with the added pressure of looking toward future seasons.

And the trade deadline.

Because they were now four and sixteen.

Horrendous.

The owners of the Breakers were breathing down his neck, and he knew that if things didn't turn around soon, he would need to look into making some coaching changes in addition to the roster changes.

The difficulty in that was that the Breakers were a family, and firing a coach or trading a player dismantled that close connection.

Yes, it happened all the time—not the firing so much, but the roster changes.

Yes, it sucked, because the team being a family wasn't just some bullshit he liked to spout off. He felt it, real and in his heart.

But the team was also a business.

So even though he got to know players' kids, their wives, and there were meal trains and team barbeques and holiday get-togethers, if the team wasn't winning, changes had to be made.

Warm hands on his face, tugging him down for another kiss. "It'll get better, baby," she murmured, her eyes still closed. "The team is young. They'll get their shit together."

Another reason why he'd been dragging his heels before making any changes.

They *were* young.

Most of the guys he'd won the Cup with were gone. Hell, most of the guys on the roster now were under thirty, and only two were married.

A different team.

And it was his job to figure out how to move the pieces around in order to get them to fit properly.

A puzzle.

But one that formed an actual picture of a winning team.

"Luc?"

Her voice was a little more alert now, and he didn't want her to wake up fully. He wanted her relaxed and settled. "Sleep, honey." He kissed her forehead.

She propped an elbow beneath her. "The team—"

He tugged the blankets up and over her, tucked them tightly around her, giving up on her going back to sleep when she opened her eyes and squirmed out from beneath the comforter, tucking it loosely around her breasts.

Shame that.

She could at least be topless if she was going to interrogate him at zero-dark-thirty.

"The team will be fine," he said.

Her brows lifted. "Will you?"

He laughed. "I'm not the one getting battered on the ice every night."

"Just up in the box every game," she said. "And *wishing* you were down there on the ice."

Truth, sometimes at least, but it sounded ridiculous to admit it, especially considering how old he was. Even without the wrecked knee, he was long past his playing days at this point. "I'm frustrated because the team is playing bad, honey, frustrated because I didn't put the tools together in the right way for them to be successful. But I'm not spending all my time being morose up in the box, dreaming about my playing days."

"Just *some* of your time."

He chuckled, despite himself. "Only when they're really playing like shit."

"You think you could do it better," she said. "If you hadn't gotten hurt, you think you could be down there."

A shrug. "I wouldn't be down there, regardless. Even *if* they were playing great." He sighed. "Look, this is just a storm to weather. God knows, I've been through plenty of them. This, too, will pass."

"And you think it will pass when you figure out the roster?"

"Yes," he said simply.

"You take too much on your shoulders," she murmured. "The team isn't just one person. It's not *only* your responsibility."

"Maybe not," he agreed.

"Why do I hear a but?"

"Because there is one." Smiling gently, he stroked a finger down her cheek. "*But* it does begin and end with me."

She sighed, rolled her eyes. "Broad shoulders you've got there."

"Subtle you are."

Laughter tinkled across the room, drifting to his ears, filling his soul with music. "Okay, Yoda," he muttered, tugging her toward him, slanting his lips across hers. He yanked the blankets back, loving the way she squealed as he lifted her up and tossed her over his shoulder like a fireman's carry. "Since you're up, let's go conserve some water."

More laughter, and although his work situation was shit, and he was going to have to make some really tough decisions, and probably make them soon, the sound of Lexi's happiness, the feel of her body was enough.

For the first time in a long time, his personal life was perfect.

———

HE'D HATED MORNING SKATES, even as a player.

He still hated them as a GM, especially after an early morning flight.

But it was his head coach's decision, and Tommy Franklin was an old school, by-the-books kind of coach, a head down, hard work, keep-pushing-forward coach.

And since that was normally Luc's *modus operandi*, they usually got along.

The shitshow on the ice, however, was telling him that something else was up, and he didn't think it was just feeling down because the losses were piling up. There was a feeling wafting up from the rink below, and it was in the way the players looked at each other, the way they looked at Tommy.

Something was wrong.

Something big.

And perhaps, he'd been too distracted by Lexi to realize exactly what was going on.

A bolt of guilt shot through him, but he pushed it away.

He was allowed to have a personal life, and he'd like to think that if this problem had been going on since the start of the season, he wouldn't just be clueing into it now. *Would like* to think.

"Fuck," he whispered, closing his laptop and standing up.

Well, even if he was an idiot and this had been going on for weeks, he wasn't going to let it go on any longer.

He made his way through the back offices, down the stairs, and past the guest locker room at the arena. It would have been better if they were at home, able to deal with the players on his own terms.

But they were on the road.

They were here, and things had to be done.

He waited by the edge of the rink, watching the practice wind down and nodding to the players as they moved by him when they got off the ice. Once the last player had gone by— Martin Robinson, their goalie—he waved off Tommy, the equipment guys, and trainers.

He then moved into the locker room behind Martin, shutting the door and throwing the lock.

He waited, arms crossed, as he leaned against the door.

It didn't take long. The guys weren't stupid. They'd had more than their fair share of coaching, of management. As soon as one player, Raphael Gomez, noticed it was him and not Tommy by the door, he nudged the guy next to him, who then nudged another, and pretty soon the room fell quiet, twenty-plus eyes coming to Luc and holding, understanding that the dynamic was about to change.

The silence was taut, rippling with tension.

But still, Luc didn't speak.

Tommy should probably be the one doing this, but as he'd told Lexi that morning, the responsibility for this team—for whether they succeeded or failed—began and ended with him.

Someone sighed, a sharp, short sound that pierced the silence.

Glares were exchanged, wet hockey gear remained on.

Luc continued to stand by the door.

For many, long minutes.

Until he was starting to think that this might not work. But then, they broke. Or he should say, one of them did. The source of the sigh, Marcel Aubert, began tearing tape from his socks, balling it up in quick, angry movements.

No one else moved.

And frankly, Luc was surprised.

Not by the rest of the team remaining still and silent, but by Marcel's actions. He was a quiet player. Not showy or egotistical. A hard worker who was a solid second liner.

Never had he given Luc one bit of attitude.

Until today.

He ripped off his jersey and tossed it into the center of the room, missing the bin that the equipment guys used to collect the dirties. Not that he got up and retrieved it, putting it where it belonged.

Instead, he continued, tearing off his shoulder and elbow pads then bent and went to work on his skates, yanking the laces, toeing them off. His hockey socks came after, uncovering his shin guards, which were next to hit the mat, his hockey pants a moment after that.

Then he sat back down on the bench, wearing a jock, his skintight undershirt, and the black socks he wore beneath his skates.

And glaring.

Couldn't forget the glaring.

That was angled in Luc's direction for a moment, then in the team's direction, then in the direction of one player in particular. In fact, *many* glares were pointed in that same direction.

Hmm.

Still, Luc waited.

Marcel sighed again, slumped back on the bench and crossed his arms.

Luc opened his mouth, thinking a demand to, "Talk," was overdue, but then he saw something cross Mark Shelby's face. He was the player on the receiving end of the glares, and the amusement in Mark's expression had Luc clamping his lips closed as he scoured his brain, trying to piece through every bit of information he knew about both players.

Mark was more talented. Their highest-scoring forward last season, in fact. A great skater with good hands, he was a definite force on the ice. Outside of hockey, he was single, no kids, family up in Canada.

Marcel was a rookie, a winger on the same side. Not as flashy, but a solid player. More likely to set up a goal than to actually score it. He had a girlfriend, and they were serious. In fact, last Luc had heard, they'd moved in together, and he was ring shopping.

So, more *hmm*.

"Anyone want to clue me in?" Luc finally asked.

Mark smirked, and it seemed like Marcel was going to launch himself across the room.

Suddenly, twenty-plus pairs of eyes were turned *away* from him.

Luc waited a few more moments, and when no one spoke, not even his captain, Oliver James, he slid his back down along the door, plunking his ass on the black skate mat and going back to waiting.

Eyes, once again on him, went wide.

He held each gaze in turn, waiting until last for Oliver.

Who stared right back at him, a muscle in his jaw twitching. He wouldn't be the one to speak, and everyone else was going to follow his lead.

Fucking hell.

Not like he didn't have work to do, a shit-ton of emails to catch up, meetings to get to, reports to review. Though, truthfully, nothing was more important than the team, than figuring this out.

So, back to sitting.

Back to waiting.

Though, this time, he added, "My ass is here until we figure out the bullshit that has you guys playing like fucking peewees. So until someone talks, until we sort this out, I'm not moving." A beat. "And neither are you."

Raised eyebrows all around.

Luc shrugged, settled in and opened his laptop. "I can do this all day."

And, finally, it was enough.

Mark broke. "That fucking pussy can't just get over it." He made a face. "Just crying about it all the time."

Luc closed his laptop, followed Mark's gaze—no surprise—to Marcel, who had gone from looking like he was going to throttle Mark to looking like he was going to stab him with his skate.

"You fucked my girlfriend!" Marcel snapped.

"Couldn't have been much of a boyfriend if she came looking for me," Mark said, snide in every letter.

"Fuck you!" Marcel was on his feet and across the room in a heartbeat, slamming his fist into Mark's face. It didn't miss Luc's notice that more than a few of the other players, including Oliver, could have stopped Marcel.

That none of them did, told him enough about where the rest of the team stood.

What else had Mark done? And how soon did he need to unload him?

The crunch of Mark's nose propelled Luc up, setting his laptop on the bench. But before he could reach the now-brawling, rolling-on-the-floor, fists-flying pair, Oliver and Ben, a second-line defenseman, were on them, each grabbing one of the men and hauling them away from each other.

Blood dripped down Mark's face. Marcel looked ready to explode all over again, despite knuckles that were split and abraded. Both of their chests heaved.

"What else?" Luc asked.

Silence, and fucking hell, were they going to go through this again?

Oliver glanced up, met Luc's gaze. "Plenty of *else.*"

That answered his question from before. He needed to unload Mark as quickly as possible.

"Let them go," he ordered.

After a pause, Oliver and Ben glanced at each other and Mark and Marcel were no longer restrained. "This bullshit ends here," he said, holding Marcel's eyes and then Mark's, in some sort of stupid ass alpha male nonsense. But he needed them, needed the team to function until he could off-load Mark. "James," he said to Oliver. "This is your team, and you need to find a way to fix this."

Let Mark think of this what he would.

If it got the team to a place where the hemorrhaging stopped while he navigated trade deals, then good enough.

He turned, snagged his laptop from the bench, moved to the door.

"Shower. Change if you want, but none of your asses are leaving this room until this is worked out."

With that, he strode into the hall and slammed the door shut.

CHAPTER THIRTY-ONE

Lexi

SHE WATCHED the Breakers win that night.

Adding a tally to one of the few they'd had that season.

Something had shifted, and it wasn't even that the announcers kept talking about how the lines had been "changed up." Instead, it was something deeper, something larger, as though the whole team was finally acting like an actual team.

They seemed like a completely different group of hockey players than she had watched previously.

Something had changed, and she'd bet more than her favorites from her collection of *The Lord of the Rings* memorabilia (which for the record and in proper order from least to most valuable—at least to her—were her replica ring, her signed script of *The Two Towers*, and a prop knife that one of the elves had actually used on set) that it was something deeper than a change in the team's lines.

Swapping players around didn't make that big of a shift.

Whatever it was, she was happy for Luc's sake that it was an improvement, at least.

She flicked off the TV, settled in under the blanket at her apartment. They hadn't had a chance to move any of her things over to his place, not with her just agreeing to live with him only the day before. And God, was it insanity to be moving in with someone after being together for a week? Who did that? Except . . . it didn't feel like a week, not they'd been working toward this for two and a half years. Which was why although it had been tempting to just stay in Luc's bed, she'd known she'd needed to take some time to wrap her head around everything.

Regret wasn't lingering about agreeing to move in with Luc.

That she was more certain of than anything else she'd ever chosen. Her future lay with Luc. She knew that in the marrow of her bones, in the beat of her heart, in the blood flowing through her veins.

Perhaps her life had always been leading to Luc.

Certainly, their friendship had been the best part of it these last two and a half years.

So why then was she feeling a little unsettled?

Because her life had taken another sharp turn? Or because something else, something that didn't involve her and Luc was on the horizon, another ax that was going to fall, to send her sprawling and reeling?

She didn't know yet.

What she *did* know was that come tomorrow, she was going to return to this space, pack up her apartment, and cram as much of the stuff—including her plants—into her car and take it over to Luc's place.

And then she would keep doing that until her apartment was empty.

Until Luc's house was full—and God knew that it *would* be full, considering she was going to cram in an apartment's worth of furniture into an already filled home.

So, maybe there *was* something waiting on the edges of her life, something that was going to throw her for another loop, but she couldn't focus on that now. Maybe she was being dramatic and had watched too many murder documentaries, or maybe that sense of bleakness on the edges of her mind *was* real.

But at moment, the only thing she could focus on was the thought of her plants cluttering up his living room.

And that made her smile.

After everything that had happened, she was just really happy to be smiling.

———

"SO, this is what it's like to be a hockey wife?" she asked into the phone, late the next evening.

Luc had called her after the game that evening, and it was the first time she'd heard his voice since he'd left.

They'd texted loads.

But he'd been busy—and she'd been moving. Still, his busy trumped hers, she realized as he told her all of what had transpired in that locker room. Sleeping with another player's girlfriend and more, more that even Luc didn't know, more that had festered and torn the team apart. But whatever, *however* the team had sorted it, they *had* sorted it.

They were a team again.

They'd won again.

The future looked a little bit brighter.

And the tension that had been in Luc's voice, more tension than she had even been completely aware of, was gone.

Guilt trickled through her, knowing she should have pushed more, should have fought more to shoulder some of his burden, knowing that she had been so wrapped up in herself, in her drama, her loss that her best friend's pain had been—partially, at least—hidden from her. *He* saw everything, and she'd missed precisely how much the losses were taking out of him. Oh, she'd understood that he was upset by the team's records, knew that he'd taken on too much of that responsibility.

But she hadn't understood until that moment how deep the wounds had been carved within him.

Deeper than she'd realized. Healing now.

And she wouldn't make that mistake again.

Luc focused on her more than himself, and she could do no less than the same for him.

That would keep the fear away. Stifle the fear lurking on the edges of her mind that she would do something to fuck this up, miss something and Luc would be hurt, that Luc would leave.

She would pay attention.

She would prove she could care for him just as strongly as he did her.

"Hockey wife?" he asked, drawing her out of her own brain, from her own thoughts of how she could show this man how much he meant to her.

"Yeah," she said. "Always stuck at home while you have all the fun."

"I don't always travel with the team," he said.

"Just most of the time," she countered, relaxing into the conversation, that fear drifting away.

This was just her and Luc.

And she'd meant what she'd told him before.

They would be perfect together.

Not because they would be without arguments or pitfalls, but because despite those speed bumps, they would still be good to each other.

Probably the romantic in her, to believe they would make their way to happiness, especially since they'd been together for . . . what was it? Five? Six days now? A week?

But she believed that.

Because they had two-and-a-half years of friendship under their belt.

Because Luc had shown her the type of man he was over and over again.

Because she liked the person she was with him.

So, that was why she didn't fear him, fear *them* together.

And that was why she was done dwelling on all the way things went wrong or could go wrong or how she might fuck up. She wanted Luc in her life. She was happier when he was in it. So, that was that.

His laughter trickled through the phone's speaker, and she wrapped it around herself as he said, "Yes, usually I do go with them."

"Because you love sightseeing?" she quipped.

"Something like that," he said, "if sightseeing involves boring ass meetings and wrangling annoying players."

Laughter trickled through her. "You love it."

"I do."

A blip of silence, not uncomfortable in the least. Just the moment of quiet as Lexi settled back—into Luc's bed. Because she hadn't been able to resist the temptation of it when she'd taken up an ungodly amount of space in his huge closet. "You have too many clothes, baby."

"Then throw them out," he said without hesitation. "We need to have room for your elf robes."

Laughter coiled inside her, exploded out through her mouth. "I knew you were into kink."

His voice went husky. "Oh, you have no idea."

"Hmm," she murmured, tapping her chin. "I don't know. I think I have a pretty good idea of the things you like. I did just spend the last couple of hours elbow deep in your closet."

He gulped. "What did you find?"

"Oh so, *so* much, Mr. Clotheshorse." God, the man had a wall of suits, more ties than she'd ever seen in her life.

"What did you find?" he repeated, sounding a little tortured.

"Regretting that key you gave me?" she teased.

"Never," he rasped, sending her pulse skittering. "I *am* regretting not being there right now because I'd be kissing you into telling me the truth."

"Kissing me where?"

More rasping laughter, sliding down her spine to curl between her thighs. "I'll show you when I get home."

Home.

She liked the sound of that.

Hadn't realized how adrift she'd been, how much Luc had been her anchor.

"Want to guess where I am?" she asked innocently, when that laughter faded and they'd spent a few minutes talking about his travel plans. He'd be home Saturday. Late.

And she'd be here.

Another wicked surprise.

"Where are you?" he asked huskily.

Figuring she'd show him, along with the "kink" she'd found in his closet, she hit the button to change the call to video.

It only completed half a ring before he'd picked up, giving her a gorgeous view of his naked chest. He was sprawled out on a hotel bed, the blankets and sheets tucked around his hips, the etched squares on his abdomen calling to her tongue, even though there were several thousand miles between them.

"Hi, baby," she whispered, plunking the hat onto her head.

He choked, then again when she deliberately angled the phone down, to show what she was wearing. "What are you—"

"Want to tell me why you have costumes in your closet?" She ran a hand down her stomach, nails grazing the white and red lace, then up, across the red cross over her left breast. "I did like this one, though." She met his eyes through the screen. "So, maybe you wanna play doctor, baby?"

His curse arrowed straight between her thighs. His emerald eyes were blazing through the phone screen. "I am so fucking tempted to get on a plane right now."

She grinned, rolled to her back, positioning the phone above her as she flicked open the button on the cropped white jacket of the nurse's costume she wore, exposing her breasts barely covered in sheer red lace. "And to think I was just going to send you a picture."

Another curse, and he sat up. "I'm getting on that fucking plane."

"Then you couldn't tell me what you want me to do to myself."

"I could *do* it myself."

She shivered, drew a finger over one breast and then the other, feeling her nipples harden, pebble against the lace. "I want you to watch."

His inhale rattled through the speakers. Moisture flooded between her thighs, and then even more when his voice, velvet and rasp, ordered her to, "Slip your hand beneath your bra."

"Luc," she murmured, her hand freezing on her chest, suddenly feeling a little shy.

"Get your hands on your breasts, baby."

She sucked in a breath, slowly slipped her fingers under the scalloped lace, trembling, desire gathering within her like a storm.

"Pretend it's me touching you," he murmured. "I'd drag my thumb over your breast, back and forth until I reached your nipple." She moved her fingers like he described, light, slow circles that drifted closer and closer until she reached the furled bud. "I'd make you wait for it, watch it get harder and tighter, begging for my mouth. I'd wait until you were trembling, until that gorgeous pink flush you get on your cheeks flared bright, drifted down your chest."

She was already feeling the heat on her face, between her breasts. Her muscles trembled. Her thighs pressed together.

And she hadn't even touched any of the good parts yet.

Her fingers inched closer.

"Wait for it, baby," he ordered.

She swallowed hard.

"Now," he said, his words sounding like they were gravel, "brush just one finger across your nipple."

She slid her finger down. Across, and her breath shuddered out, her spine arching as pleasure sparked through her—

The phone dropped onto her face.

"*Ow!*" she muttered, groaning and pressing a hand over her aching eye and nose.

Luc's worried voice took a moment to process.

Only her.

Only Lexi could have fucked up FaceTime Fun Time by dropping her cell on her face. She felt like she should be tasting blood, wondered if she should have a shiner, but . . . the major feeling that had gripped her was—

Laughter burst out of her.

Amusement.

Because, seriously, only her.

"Lexi!"

The panic in Luc's voice had her picking up the phone from where it had dropped onto the mattress. "Luc," she said. "I'm fine."

Piercing green eyes locked on hers through the screen, assessing. Then his expression softened. "Did you really just drop the phone on your face?"

Heat on her cheeks, this time not interlaced with desire. "Maybe."

"Are you bleeding?"

"Just in my soul."

He roared with laughter, not helping her alleviate her embarrassment in the least.

"You're an asshole."

"And you're the most beautiful woman I've ever seen."

Such intensity, blaring through the screen, filling her soul with fire, with . . . some deep feeling she didn't want to look at too closely yet, because that would mean what she was feeling was—

She dropped the phone again.

This time, thankfully, not on her face. It fell onto the mattress, the realization zipping through her, making her lungs tight, her heart pound until Luc asked, "Are you bleeding this time?"

She inhaled, a giggle bubbling within her, unlocking her enough that she was able to pick it up the phone again.

"Not bleeding," she whispered.

He smiled, and that slid her out of her brain, focus shifting back onto the gorgeous man, half-naked, all of his yumminess on display. "I have an idea," he murmured.

"What's that?" she asked, suddenly a little breathless.

"There's a phone stand on my nightstand." His lips quirked. "Use it."

Her mouth twitched. *His* mouth twitched. Laughter filled the air and speakers.

And then she set her cell on the stand.

"While you're sitting up, lose the jacket and bra."

She shivered at the order in his tone, but shrugged out of the cropped uniform top, flicked open the lace clip on the front of her bra, peeled it free and tossed both to the side.

His breath rattled through the speaker. "Fuck, you have nice tits."

Suddenly, her embarrassment was the last thing on her mind. The pain in her eye flitting away like a butterfly in the open air. "What next?" she breathed, hands drifting toward her panties. "These?"

"No."

Another order.

"Climb onto the bed."

She sprawled onto the mattress, angled the phone to make sure he could see everything.

"Touch your lips."

She rolled to the side, facing the phone and feeling all too wicked. "Which ones?"

A groan. "You have no idea how much I wish I was there right now."

"Will you touch yourself, too?"

A flurry of movement, his covers being thrown back, his phone being positioned. He was gloriously naked beneath those blankets, his cock hard, his hand descending to wrap around the straining length as he stroked once, twice.

Her lips parted on a shaky exhale.

"Run your finger over your bottom lip, your top," he said. "Pretend that my mouth is on yours."

She shuddered, almost able to feel the stubble on his jaw brushing against her skin, the weight of his body on top of hers, the warm press of his lips to hers.

"Now down, baby," he ordered. "Over your breasts again. Down," he added when she trailed her fingers along her chest, circling closer to her nipples—only this time without a side of cell phone in her face. "Slower," he murmured when she brushed one hard bud and moaned softly.

"I like—"

"When I run a finger over just the tip," he said. "I know, Lex. Do it now."

So she did.

And then when he told her to shift sides, to move to the other breast, she didn't complain, just followed his orders, her thighs pressing together, damp heat turning into more, until her underwear was soaked through. Both of their breathing had accelerated, and she could see that Luc's body was sheened in sweat, though his hand was no longer on his cock. Instead, it was braced next to him, the muscles of his forearm standing out in sharp relief.

The sight of that sinew, of the gleaming skin, had her desperate to reach between her thighs and alleviate the ache there.

But Luc hadn't told her to touch herself there yet.

Which was frustrating . . . and kind of sexy.

She liked being bossed around by him, hearing his gruff, sexy voice shake with need as he directed her to touch her breasts, her nipples, her throat and stomach and hips. His scorching gaze held hers the whole time, tracing over her body, a nearly tangible weight that razed through her every nerve.

And finally, when she felt as though she were ready to combust, he said, voice gruff, "Panties off."

She slid them down her legs, kicked them off somewhere.

"Get your fingers down there. Slow and steady. Tease yourself—"

"If I tease myself anymore," she said, tracing her fingers along her labia, shivering and jumping when she hit a particularly sensitive spot. "I'm going to explode."

Need in those eyes, a fierce smile on his lips. "Good. Because I am, too."

"You're not even touching yourself," she said, slowly shifting in and up, until she reached the spot—*the* Spot—not her clit, but just below it and to the right, a sensitive bundle that never failed to send her plummeting.

"I'm watching the most erotic show I've ever had the privilege to lay eyes on."

She stifled a moan as she pressed a little more firmly. "Put your hand on your cock."

"You giving the orders, now?"

Her head fell back, just for a moment, before she forced it up again, locking her gaze on the screen in time to see Luc wrap his fingers around his cock and start stroking. God, *that* was definitely the most erotic thing she'd ever seen. "I figured I like them so much"—a small moan slipped from her lips—"I might as well give some."

"Hmm." A beat. "Use a little more pressure."

She did, and oh, *that* was good "Can't help yourself, can you?"

A wolfish grin. "More, baby."

"Is that—"

His hand pumped faster. "*More.*"

She shut up, pressed harder, moved more quickly. Fuck, she was so wet and swollen, so sensitive, so . . . *close.* And based on the ragged breathing coming from Luc's end of the line, his glazed-over eyes, the way every muscle in his body was strung tight, he was close, too.

"Luc," she moaned, her voice choked. Flames were licking out from her center, turning the rest of her into kindling and then into small conflagrations . . . then into an inferno.

All the oxygen in her body consumed. Every cell and nerve wound tight.

And then . . . the blaze exploded, encompassing her.

She called his name again, heard his sharp shout of, "Lexi!" in return, barely managing to peel her lids back in time to see him come.

God that was a pretty sight.

His body, his face, his expression as he held her eyes.

Then the only sound was their breathing, rapid then slowing.

"You made a mess," she whispered.

He grinned, shook his head, used what looked to be a pair of boxer briefs to clean up. "You're a fucking vixen, you know that?"

"For the record, I wasn't the one who was slinging around orders."

He grinned.

She sighed, let her head fall back. "I like FaceTime Fun Time."

Luc was silent for a beat then busted up, still shaking his head, before he froze, stared into the camera, and said, "*Now,* you know what it's like to be a hockey wife."

She started laughing, feeling too lazy to do anything but lie there and appreciate him. Eventually, however, she got up to tug on some pajamas when Luc carried the phone into the bath-room to wash his hands.

Then they both crawled back into their beds and talked about everything and nothing . . . until at some point, she fell asleep.

CHAPTER THIRTY-TWO

Luc

HE'D COME in his hand the night before, Lexi's sexy, breathless moans in his ears.

It had been sexy as hell, but it wasn't nearly as good as coming *in* Lexi.

Two more days.

Three, technically, if he counted the fact that his flight wouldn't be landing until nearly ten on Saturday night. Which he *wasn't* counting, because if he considered that he still had seventy-two hours until he saw Lexi again, he might . . .

Do something stupid.

Like actually get on that plane.

And that was something he couldn't do, not when the team was finally getting their shit together. Not when he'd finally lined up the trade.

Giving up a fucking first-round pick, Mark Shelby, *and* a young prospect on their minor league team would be fucking painful. But necessary. They needed to purge the rotting, to get back on track, and based on the time he'd spent near the ice, in and outside the locker room, on the plane, adjusting the lines wouldn't be enough, even despite the wins they'd managed.

The guys needed to know they could trust Luc.

He'd assumed that, assumed they would come to him or Tommy with any of these issues—or at least that Oliver would —but clearly, he'd assumed wrong. Luc knew he'd been busy, wrapped up in scouting reports and business meetings, especially since the team had just finished negotiating a new arena with the city. That had taken up far too much time, and Luc understood now that he had been too busy with the business side of the organization, and not focused enough on the playing side.

The lack of presence meant that none of his team had felt comfortable coming to him.

He'd been too distant. Too disengaged.

Present in body, but perhaps in not in mind.

And that meant he'd let his family down, had allowed a snake in their midst, unraveling everything he and the guys had worked toward building. He was the delusional parent, thinking that his teenager wasn't having sex, even despite finding the used condoms in the trash.

In a word, Luc hadn't done his job.

So, he wouldn't be getting on a plane.

He was going to reset, to put in that hard work, and he was going to bring his family back together.

The first step would be being more engaged.

The second would be more open communication.

The third was . . . building those connections. Which was why he would be organizing some team-building activities when he got back to Baltimore. Trust falls or a room full of balloons with stuff written on them where they had to work together to find their match, or some other hippie shit . . . or maybe—he smiled now, his eyes taking in the text on his cell's screen—Lexi could give them a gardening class, and the player who managed to keep the plant alive by the end of the season would win a prize.

He tapped out the request.

Smiled when she immediately agreed.

Laughed out loud when he asked for her suggestion of a prize.

Then immediately thanked the hockey gods for bringing her into his life. Fuck, he loved her *so* much.

His phone buzzed.

Too much?

He typed out his reply.

Yes.

Another buzz. A crying face paired with a red heart that had him desperate to type out the words he held in his heart, even though he was desperate to tell her them in person. Then,

Good luck.

The urge to blurt out all those words in his heart grew louder. Because she'd remembered, even after their night had taken a delicious, wonderful turn that he certainly hadn't expected, one that had kept them both up into the wee hours of the night, she'd texted this morning, she'd remembered his meeting.

He sent back a thanks, along with a promise to check in with her later.

Then he got into the shower, put on one of the many suits and ties Lexi had teased him about, and headed to the arena, to the office he'd commandeered from Char. There were perks with remaining close with his former protégé, the current GM of the Gold.

He knew he'd have a quiet, hopefully soundproof, private space to conduct what was going to be a painful meeting.

————

TURNED out that soundproofing was key.

Because it turned one handsome, cocky, girlfriend-poaching Mark Shelby into a whining, screaming, hissy-fit-throwing crybaby.

At least no one could hear the bullshit he was spewing.

He was pissed that Luc had the "audacity" to trade him.

His words, not Luc's, and frankly, Luc was shocked the bastard had enough space in that brain of his to actually use big words, considering the size of the man's ego.

He'd conferenced in with Todd and Lexi, with Mark's agent, who was almost as much of a son of a bitch as Mark himself.

Not that anyone could get a word in edgewise, not with Mark's ranting.

But the deal was made, the ink was dry, and that was hockey. Players didn't always get a say in the teams they went to. And maybe because he was talented and put points on the scoreboard, Mark had figured he'd be with the Breakers to stay, and truthfully, until the toxicity had flared in the locker room and on the ice, Luc would have believed that, too. He would have been hard-pressed to give up his star player.

Things had changed.

Mark had changed them.

"Is this because I fucked that dumb bitch?" Mark snapped, shoving back his chair and pacing across the conference room. "She wanted it and . . ." He continued on with his ranting, but Luc tuned him out, not giving a shit at what he said.

Because it wasn't about Mark fucking around on Marcel.

It was about Mark being poison.

He was gone.

And the reality was that Mark didn't have anything in his

contract to prevent a trade, nor any clause within it that required Luc to run this decision by him. Luc had all the power in this decision, and Mark could yell all he wanted about it.

He would still be going to the Kings.

Heaven help the team there.

Hopefully, they'd better contain his bullshit.

But frankly, Luc didn't give a fuck. Mark would be out of his hair in the next hour—the ranting man had a flight to catch—and that wouldn't be coming soon enough for Luc.

He'd always thought that Mark was a bit of an asshole, but his skills on the ice had made him easier to put up with, easier to ignore and excuse his crappy behavior. Yeah, he was a bit of a loner, a bit distant with the rest of the team, but it hadn't appeared to impact much of anything until the beginning of this one.

Because for whatever reason, Mark had decided to torpedo Luc's family.

And no one fucked with his family.

So, Mark was out. Points or not. Abilities or not.

The points hadn't garnered the Cup, hadn't gotten the team a better record. The cost-benefit of keeping Mark around was just too great.

It was as simple as that.

Luc gathered his papers, ended the call with Todd and Lexi, Mark's agent signing off just as Mark whined, "I just bought a house and my stuff—"

Stifling a sigh, considering Mark's real estate woes were the least important things on his mind at this moment, Luc stood up, tugged open the door. "You'd better get to the airport. Traffic and—"

Mark's eyes widened.

"—all that," he finished.

"I—"

Char was waiting outside the door. Her sunny smile filled the space. "Just the man I was looking for," she said, eyes coming to Luc's. "I actually had a question about . . ." She trailed off, as though just noticing Mark for the first time.

What a good little liar she was.

"Oh, I'm sorry, I can come—"

"We're done," he said. "Come in," he added, sweeping a hand forward as though it were his conference room and not the one she'd loaned him for specifically this purpose.

Mark glared between them for a long moment, and then he sighed and stormed out, the door slamming behind him.

"You sure you want to lose him?" Char asked. "He *is* talented."

"Would *you* keep him?"

The expression on her face told him her answer.

"Ah, I have trained you well, young Padawan."

"And now your nerd is showing," she teased.

He grinned, hooked an arm around her shoulders. "Missed you, kiddo."

"Me, too," she said, smiling up at him before slipping out of his embrace. "Though I could do without the *kiddo* talk."

"Tough," he said, reaching out as though to give her a noogie.

She darted out of the way, made for the door. "Come on," she said, "Logan is going to meet us for breakfast. We'll play nice before he kicks your team's ass on the penalty kill."

He nudged Char out of the way, turned the handle, and opened the door for her. "Your guys planning to be in the penalty box a lot tonight?"

A grin. "*Your* guys planning to take a bunch of dives?"

He sniffed. "No, *my* guys aren't a bunch of little ballerinas falling all over the place."

"First," she muttered, jabbing him in the chest with her finger, "ballerinas are crazy tough. Second"—another jab—"a better comparison would be soccer players and their magic, healing water."

He laughed. "I think the soccer players would take issue with that."

"I think the ballerinas would, too," she said, her lips curving.

"So, maybe we just stick with hockey is better than every other sport?"

Her smile grew. "Exactly."

A tall, green-eyed man came around the corner, smiling like Char had hung the moon, and even if Luc hadn't immediately recognized him, hadn't once had Logan Walker on his own roster, Luc would have known the man because he tried to know every player in the league, and certainly the ones who'd been around for as many seasons as Char's other half.

"Molly's?" Logan asked, after greetings were exchanged and hands were shaken.

Char's brow creased. "You want to torture yourself on a day you can't eat it?"

A kiss to Char's cheek, a hand slipping around her waist, drawing her close. "It's your favorite," he said softly, as though that were explanation enough.

And for Luc, it *was* enough.

Because he felt that same breadth of emotion for Lexi.

Char glanced at him. "Talk some sense into him, Luc. We should go to the new vegan restaurant so he can eat something on his diet plan."

"Or he can eat what he wants," Luc said, lips twitching.

Char smacked him lightly. "Stop trying to undermine my players."

"We're going to Molly's," Logan ordered, tugging her closer. "You're getting that new apple-pear muffin you've been raving about, and I'm not going to eat, other than a cup of coffee because I had my meal plan breakfast, okay?"

A wrinkled nose—Char's not Luc's—but she didn't argue further, just allowed Logan to lead them to the arena exit.

And when the other man got pulled into a quick conversation with another player, Char glanced over her shoulder at Luc, love in her eyes, and whispered, "You sure you don't want to find this?"

He inhaled sharply, debated for a minute what to keep against his chest and what to tell her.

In the end, he said, "I have."

For a second, there was sad in her eyes. They were close enough that she knew only the barest details—he didn't date. Or *hadn't* dated.

"I have it *now*," he added.

Her eyes widened. Her hand found his, squeezed tight. "Tell me everything."

Logan's conversation wound down before he could even begin. "Later," he said.

A narrowed glance. "You promise?"

Logan came close enough to hear Char's question. "Secret GM stuff?"

Char met Luc's eyes, hers twinkling brightly enough that he laughed, and said, "Exactly."

"Damn," Logan teased. "I hate not knowing everything. Maybe I'll have to bribe you with muffins."

"I bet it would work," Luc quipped.

Char didn't even try to deny it, just glared at them both before striding off. The woman had had a love affair with carbs for as long as he'd know her.

Logan moved to walk after her, halting when Char whipped around, halting them both in their tracks with the fierce expression on her face. She pointed firmly in Luc's direction. "Next time you play us, you're bringing her."

He nodded.

Not because of the order or the fierce gaze, even though both were formidable.

But because he considered Char more than a good friend. Because she was family and wonderful, and he wanted Lexi to have that wonderful in her life, too.

With a sharp incline of her head, a clipped out, "Good," Char started walking.

Then whipped back around again. "And you're telling me *everything* on the car ride," she said. "*Not* over breakfast or sometime later when you turn the conversation back on me and my life, so you don't talk about yourself."

He hesitated.

"*Luc.*"

"Damn," he muttered. "I taught you to do the scary GM voice too well."

A flick of Char's hair, the red and gold and brown curls bouncing as she tossed them over her shoulder. "You taught me. I improved on the technique." A beat, those fierce eyes again. "You promise?"

Knowing he was trapped, Luc just nodded, said, "I promise."

Satisfaction in her deep brown eyes, but he only saw it for a moment because she tossed her head once more and pushed out of the arena.

Logan glanced back at him, eyes dancing, lips twitching.

Luc shrugged. "She doesn't lie," he said. "She did improve on it."

"Oh, I *know*," Logan said, laughter filling the air. "Believe me, I know."

They both started busting up, and then still laughing, they followed Char out into the parking lot.

Onward to muffins.

Plus, a side of Char-driven truth serum before they even got to the bakery.

CHAPTER THIRTY-THREE

Lexi

"NICE SHINER YOU'VE GOT THERE."

Lexi froze at her boss's words, taken off guard because she'd thought that the makeup she'd slapped on that morning had covered it well enough. Apparently, not enough, at least when it came to Todd's scrutiny. FaceTime Fun Time—or FaceTime mutual self-satisfaction—was a dangerous pastime.

She'd thought she'd broken her nose last night.

But then Luc's husky voice had coaxed her back under his spell, and she'd had a glorious fucking orgasm.

Courtesy of her own fingers, but only really because he'd talked her through it.

"That conversation with Shelby went well, huh?" she said, trying for distraction.

"About as well as expected." A beat, holding her stare. "So, what'd you do to your face?"

"Nothing," she said, too quickly, but when he kept looking at her like that, she found herself at risk of breaking under that intense blue gaze. "I just bumped into something." Except, dammit, not only was that a stupid excuse, but her cheeks flared—also something she knew that her makeup didn't cover, based on the way Todd's brows lifted.

"Now *that's* a story I want to hear," he said, eyes dancing.

"No," she muttered, "trust me when I say, no, you *really* don't."

More brow-lifting.

Then he shook his head, mouth tipped up at one corner. "You're probably right."

She cleared her throat, stacking the files she'd brought, just in case she'd needed them and hadn't been able to access some document on her laptop, for whatever reason. Unnecessary? Probably. But in her work life, she liked to err on the side of extra cautious and prepared. There was nothing worse than needing to pull out a piece of information and not having it, especially when she'd been in her early years as an attorney.

"Want to come over for dinner tonight?" Todd asked, leaning a hip against the table. "Holly was wanting to see you."

She shook her head, genuine disappointment threading through her because Holly was hilarious, sweet, and a fantastic cook. Lexi was going to miss a good meal *and* a fun night of teasing Todd. "I can't tonight," she said. "I'm packing up my apartment."

Todd had been reaching for the door handle, but her sentence had him freezing. "You bought a new house?"

"No," she said. "I'm actually moving in with—"

His phone rang. He reached into his pocket and silenced it.

"With whom, Lex?"

A tendril of discomfort weaved its way through her intestines, but she didn't try to hide the truth. It would be point-less with the way that gossip traveled through the front office.

"With Luc."

He relaxed, face softening.

"Not as friends," she whispered.

Todd's mouth dropped open. "What?"

"Luc and I aren't moving in together as friends." She lifted her chin, wondered if her friend would judge her, but once the shock faded, all that was left in his expression was . . . approval. A quick breath. "We're actually . . ." She trailed off, gripped tight some of that courage she'd been so hard-pressed to relocate, and her chin came up. "We're dating."

His face didn't change, just stayed locked onto hers. "Good."

Her jaw fell open. "Good?" She cleared her throat. "I mean, he's our boss and—"

"*I'm* your boss," he said, squeezing her hand. "And when you take over my job, sooner rather than later, you'll answer to the board and not to Luc. No issues on that front."

"But—" She suddenly felt a little insecure.

It had all been fine when everyone knew they were just friends, but would it be different if she and Luc were more than that? Would everyone treat her differently?

Because it wasn't a matter of *if* she and Luc were more, they already *were* more than friends.

Todd squeezed her hand. "But nothing, kiddo," he said. "Bottom line, you deserve to be happy. He deserves the same." Another squeeze. "That's it, and if anyone has a problem with that, you just send 'em to me."

Her heart thudded.

When had this man, one who'd been a peer and friend and now a boss and mentor, become more of a father figure than her own?

For a while now, she supposed.

"Todd," she began, eyes prickling.

His phone rang again. He silenced it again. Then surprised her by cupping her cheek, his words soft. "Happy. Remember that."

She opened her mouth, wanting to tell him how much that meant. "I'm—"

It rang for a third time, and he sighed, apology in his eyes as he yanked his cell from his pocket. "Just so you know, I'm really glad you're not moving back in with that twat-waffle, Caleb."

He pulled open the door at the same time he swiped, lifting the cell to his ear, his "Hello?" half cut off as the panel closed with a soft *snick.*

His other words, though, they stayed with her much longer.

Happy.

Yeah, she could do happy.

———

IT WAS SATURDAY MORNING.

Luc was coming home tonight.

And her apartment was nearly packed up.

Only her bed, couch, and dining room table remained. Items she was trying to decide if she wanted to keep or if she just wanted to give away.

She didn't particularly like them, having bought just enough cheap furniture to fill the apartment. She hadn't been able to stand bringing the stuff she'd shared with Caleb, so had only moved the few pieces she'd brought into their relationship, and hadn't been willing to buy something expensive, not when she'd barely known where she was going to end up.

Now she had a place, and that was enough.

She knew she'd need to decide on what to do with it in the next couple of weeks, but for now, she was focused on setting up her life with Luc.

After she'd unloaded this final carload. This final *full* carload, she thought, cramming the bag she was carrying into a tiny gap behind the front and back seat. Then she was sitting down, door half open, readying to turn on the car when she saw him.

Her heart stuttered; her lungs squeezed.

He sauntered over to the car, as though he had every right to be there, to waltz back into her life without warning.

"Alexis."

Her throat seized and she pushed out the single syllable. "Dad."

"Hi, honey."

Honey. *Honey?*

What in the absolute fuck was going on?

"Hi," she rasped, dropping the keys, and they fell into the gap between the console and the driver's seat. "Shit," she muttered, fumbling for the set as she felt her father come close, standing silently next to the car.

She could brush a finger along the keyring but couldn't actually reach the fucking set. Now she'd have to get out of the car and interact with her father.

Who'd called her honey.

An endearment she hadn't heard for more than seven years.

She didn't want to hear that. She *didn't.*

"I was hoping we could talk."

Fucking hell. Now? Why, after all this time? Because she'd made him feel guilty on the phone and now, he suddenly had a conscience?

Well, fuck that.

He didn't owe her an explanation for why he'd disappeared. She was a grown woman and could take care of herself. And she certainly didn't own him anything, not after everything that had happened that he hadn't been here for.

Monthly calls that lasted all of five minutes.

That wasn't a father's love.

She needed to get out of here.

But her fucking keys were . . . just . . . out . . . of . . . reach. She'd need to either learn how to hotwire her car or maybe go Inspector Gadget and extend her fingers so she could grab them . . .

A sigh.

Or maybe . . . she just needed to step out of the car, put her feet onto the asphalt of the parking lot and see what her father wanted.

Adulting.

She hated it.

Stifling a sigh, she slid out of the driver's seat and turned to face her dad. "What did you want to talk about?"

"I—" His gaze darted over her shoulder then back to hers, staring deep into her eyes with a set that was almost identical to her own. "Did you want to go somewhere to talk?"

"You mean somewhere *other* than the empty parking lot with rain threatening?" she asked sarcastically.

The first hint of humor in his brown eyes. "Yes, honey. I had hoped we'd talk somewhere without risk of getting poured on."

She resisted the urge to cross her arms. Just barely. "About what?"

His gaze darted to the side again.

And she decided that she didn't want to have this conversation.

"Now's not a good time."

His face fell, and a bolt of guilt slid through her, but she buckled it down. What did she have to feel guilty for? He was the one who'd pushed her away for so long. And maybe it was a dick move, but she wanted to get to Luc's. She wanted that comfort and security. She wanted to continue moving into Luc's place, wanted to keep on making it *her* place, too.

She was busy.

She was . . . also avoiding whatever shadows were in her dad's eyes.

If he was looking for forgiveness, Lex didn't think she had the strength to absolve him of anything, not at this moment, not after all this time, not after Caleb and everything she'd gone through the last six months. She was just finally getting her feet under her again. She'd just found a slice of happy.

And what fucking right did her absentee father have to waltz back in?

Adult. Adult.

She was an adult.

Inhaling, she tried to force herself to calm. He'd been grieving, and she didn't need—

A flicker of rage. Because, know what? Fuck that. Yes, she was an adult, had been an adult when he'd disappeared into his grief. But also, she'd still been his daughter, and *she'd* been grieving, too. She'd needed him, and he hadn't been there.

No one had.

She'd pulled herself out and had dived headfirst into Caleb.

If her dad had been around, maybe she would have seen through the act, realized Caleb's love hadn't been—

And *that* wasn't fair either.

She needed to own her own shit. Not blame her failed relationship on her father. Just like it wasn't *her* fault that Caleb was a serial cheater.

"You're moving?" her father asked, pulling her out of her own brain.

She cleared her throat, turned back to her car, bending around the driver's seat and reaching beneath it to snatch up the keys. Once they were in hand, she straightened. "Yeah," she said. "I'm moving."

Silence.

"Can I ask where?"

"With my boyfriend," she said.

Eyes widening, his lips parting, but no sound came out for a long time. Then he said, "Is Caleb—"

"I believe I mentioned I was getting a divorce during one of our calls," she said, ice creeping through her veins. "Though, that you don't remember certainly isn't a surprise."

A raindrop plunked onto her shoulder.

"Alexis."

"Lexi," she corrected.

"Can I ask who?"

No. He couldn't. "I should go," she whispered.

"Can I help you with carrying in the boxes?" he asked so

softly she could barely hear him. "I could follow you to your new place."

Her lungs froze. "Thanks, but no." She jingled the keys in her hand. "I need to—" She broke off at the flash of pain darting across his face, more guilt weaving through her. And even still, she couldn't summon the words.

"Go," he whispered, nodding and stepping back. "Bye, honey."

That guilt struck again, stronger this time, and Lexi opened her mouth to say he could help her . . . right when the skies opened up.

Her dad nudged her into her car. "Go, honey."

She sat down, legs buckling, the door closing before she had a chance to say anything else.

And by the time she pushed her hair out of her face, got the keys in the ignition to run the wipers, her dad was gone.

Good.

That was what she wanted.

But . . . she found herself searching the parking lot when she pulled out.

Just to make sure she didn't run him over.

CHAPTER THIRTY-FOUR

Luc

"Was that better than FaceTime Fun Time?" he asked, his heart still thundering in his chest, the sweat still coating both their bodies.

"Hmm," she murmured, rolling in his arms, her hand pressing to the spot over his heart, probably feeling it thundering under her palm. "I'm not going to commit to that."

He mock-gasped, flipping them so he was on top, his cock stirring even though he was a forty-year-old man who definitely shouldn't be ready to go this quickly again.

Especially when that last orgasm had threatened to blow his spine out.

Her eyes were wide but filled with happiness, and for a moment, he couldn't catch his breath. It wasn't from any exertion on his part but instead from the impact of the breadth of his emotions. *How* did he feel this much for her? Literally *how*? He'd been in love with her for two years but unable to act on it, and now to be here, with her, with her in his life like *this* . . . it was just so much better than he'd ever imagined.

"What is it?" she asked, her hand cupping his cheek.

"Nothing," he said, pushing down the sappy, too big for this early in their relationship emotions, and tickling up his hand up her side. "Except for the fact that you're comparing my in-person sex skills to my phone sex skills."

She giggled and tried to squirm away, but he just let his hips fall heavier on hers.

A gasp, a trace of heat in her eyes. "Already?"

He nipped her bottom lip, smiled when she nipped back.

It was late on Saturday night, actually almost very early on Sunday morning now. He'd come straight from the airport, hoping to see Lexi in that nurse's outfit, but even more over-joyed when she'd been sitting up waiting for him, wearing one of his hoodies, the gray cotton dwarfing her frame, her hair piled on top of her head, the delicate lines of her face high-lighted from the screen of her laptop as she'd sat at the kitchen island.

She'd closed the laptop the moment he'd come through the door.

Then had stood, and he'd seen that she wasn't wearing any pants, the sweatshirt hitting her at mid-thigh.

And no surprise, they'd ended up here about three-point-six seconds later.

"Tell me about what you did today," he said, running his hand up and down her side.

"Worked."

"On a Saturday?" he asked.

"Well, someone was all bossy about getting me moved into his house this week."

He rolled his eyes because their first-ever argument as a dating couple had been about her waiting until he'd gotten back so he could help her do exactly that.

"So," she said, "because of this extremely stubborn person"—he tweaked her nipple and she coughed, squirmed—"stubborn *female*, I spent all week lugging around boxes."

"Well, at least you got your workouts in." He bit back a

smile and trailed his hand down her side. "You know what they say about women who just sit around and—"

She caught his hand. "And *you* know what they say about men who dare to finish that statement."

He barked out a laugh, pressed a kiss to her mouth. "Save any of those boxes for me?"

Humor glimmered in her eyes. "You saw the living room, didn't you?"

No, he hadn't. He'd been too focused on that bare expanse of thigh in his kitchen, on their days apart.

She patted his shoulder, a knowing smile on that kissable mouth. "Don't worry. I'll put you to work in the morning."

"Deal."

"Although . . ." She trailed off, lips curving.

"Although?" he asked.

"Maybe, I could put you to work now?"

He grinned. "Again?"

She nodded, eyes flicking down. "Since you're . . . up."

Laughter in his chest, his throat, his bones and blood, and then his mouth. And from Lexi, when she kissed him, floating from her body to his.

He pulled back. "Just so we're clear . . . exactly how many boxes are there?"

More laughter.

More happiness.

More love.

Then he tugged her closer, pressed his lips to hers, and showed her just how *up* he was.

———

"AND THEN," Lexi ordered, "that one goes there."

He paused, holding the planter aloft, waiting for her to change her mind. *Again.*

"No, wait," she said. "Put it over by the window."

Still, he paused, just in case there was a third change in direction. Which earned him a light swat . . . and then a peck on the cheek. "By the window," she repeated.

He lugged it to said window, the bright purple flowers catching the sunshine.

But when he turned back, ready to grab one of the final two planters that she'd left just inside his front door (heavy as fuck, and it made him a little crazy that she'd thought it was a good idea for her to move them by herself from her place—but they would talk about her stubborn refusal to use him as a pack mule later), he saw she'd gone still, panic written into the lines of her face.

"What?" he asked, immediately crossing to her.

"Is it too much? Am *I*—too much—" She swallowed. "With the plants and the house and the taking over?"

"No," he said immediately, but he could see she didn't believe him, so instead of returning to the other planters, he took her in his arms. "Have I given you any indication that it's too much?"

"No, but . . ."

"But what?" he asked. "When have I ever not told you what I was thinking?"

She frowned, tried to push out of his arms. "Um, seriously? How about the fact that you apparently were *into me* for the last few years?"

"*Into you* is the mildest description of what I feel for you," he said.

Her lips parted on a shaky exhale, she stopped fighting to escape from his embrace. "I feel a lot for you, too," she whispered. "But I—" She broke off, shook her head. Then took another breath and said, "I didn't know my husband was cheating. I didn't know you felt more for me than friendship. I didn't know *I* felt more."

"Caleb is an asshole," he snapped, and her eyes flared. "And neither of us were in a position—"

"But *why*?" she exclaimed, interrupting him. "I knew I was close to you, knew you were my best friend, knew that I loved spending time with you." Her voice dropped, shame in every word of her next question. "So, why did I never consider cheating with you? Why did I think I was so happy with Caleb? Even despite our problems, I thought we'd be together forever."

Some of these questions, he'd heard before. Some were new, were probably because she was with him now, and he knew it had to be bringing up insecurities, especially since they'd jumped into this pretty quickly. Some were old because although Caleb was out of the picture, those kinds of wounds didn't just disappear. "You didn't cheat because you're a good person," he said fiercely. "Same as I shut down all those feelings for you from the moment I found out you were married."

"Not *all* the feelings," she murmured.

"What do you mean?" he asked, genuinely confused.

"I mean, if you'd truly shut everything down, you probably wouldn't have been my friend, right?" She bit her lip, waited.

He cupped her cheek. "Yes," he admitted, knowing it was the truth. "It probably would have been easier if I could have just cut off all ties with you, rather than continuing to torture myself." He tucked a strand of hair behind her ear. "But I knew from the moment I heard you laugh, I wanted to be the one to make you do it again and again." He tugged lightly on her earlobe. "And the reality is I couldn't have pictured a future without you in it. In *any* form."

She was quiet for a long time, golden-brown eyes on his, searching his for . . . something. "I felt that, too," she whispered. "Not about the laughing, but . . ." She softened, ran her fingers over his jaw. "From the moment I met you, you fit into my life without effort. Like there was a line drawn from you to me, and maybe I was good at ignoring the attraction beneath until I was free to do so, but I knew from the first time we met that we were going to be in each other's lives. Which"—she inhaled, released

it slowly—"I get, sounds like complete and utter foolishness . .
."

He stroked a finger down the soft silk of her cheek. "From
one fool to the other then."

Her face gentled. "Exactly that."

I love you.

The words were there.

But not yet . . . not yet.

He moved back to the pots. "Where does this one go?" he
asked.

Happy on her face. Joy in his heart. She was here in his life,
his house, and that was enough.

"By the fireplace—" He lifted, started to move that way.
"Oh, wait, maybe by the couch—" He paused. "No, no, the
stairs." He waited until she nodded. "Yes, definitely the stairs."

He hauled it that way, started to set it down.

"Or maybe—"

He almost sighed, but the humor in her voice had him
glancing up. "Now you're just torturing me."

"No," she said, eyes sparkling. "That'll come later when I
bust out the nurse's outfit. Which," she added, surveying the
room, "I just realized you never explained to me why you have
all that lingerie in your closet. Is there something you need to
tell me? Something you need to *confess?*"

Unbidden, heat rose to his cheeks.

She gasped, lurched toward him. "Oh my God, there *is*," she
exclaimed, clasping his hands. "Tell me. Why do you have
them?"

"Well, I . . . um—"

"Or . . . is it your kink?" She wrinkled her nose. "I mean, I
guess I could get into it, if you like to dress up—"

"They're not mine."

"An old girlfriend's?" A flicker of jealousy had him tempted
to say, yes, just to see what she would do.

In the end, he decided, "No," was safer.

"Hmm. Your sister's?"

He shuddered. "God, no."

"So, what?" she asked.

"It doesn't matter," he said, and yeah, maybe he was being evasive, but it wasn't a very exciting story, and—

Her brows rose, teasing in her expression. "Right. So they're not an old girlfriend's, not your sister's, and they wouldn't fit you very well, would they?" she said, tapping her mouth with a finger. "Not with those broad shoulders of yours. Maybe we need to go shopping for your size—"

"Lexi," he warned when her eyes continued to dance. "I didn't buy them. They were a gift."

"Oh?" she asked archly.

He snagged her around the waist, hoisted her up, twisting so she was between him and the wall. "Yes, *oh*," he muttered. "The guys got it for me as a gag gift last year."

Those brows arched even higher.

"Why would the team get you a gag gift of lingerie?"

Okay, he was explaining this poorly.

"It was the White Elephant party at Christmas time. You know, the one where everyone had to buy gag gifts. That was"—a wince—"the one I was stuck with."

Her eyes went wide. "And you . . . decided to keep it in your *closet?*"

Yeah. No. He'd *thought* he'd thrown it away, but he'd also been pretty drunk. He remembered stumbling into the house . . . and that was pretty much it. "No," he said. "But . . . I can't say I'm sad I got to see you in it."

"Well, I have to admit, I *am* a little disappointed," she said. "I saw the gift bag and new lingerie with the tags still on . . . and I thought it was for me."

"Should I rewind and lie, tell you I went shopping and they're for you?"

A little of the humor left her eyes. "No," she whispered. "Don't lie to me, okay?"

He sucked in a breath through his nose, calling himself an idiot six ways to Sunday. "I won't," he promised. "Not ever."

Teeth nibbling at the corner of her bottom lip.

"I swear, honey. Okay?"

Those teeth released, but she nodded. "Okay."

"Now," he said, leaning a little heavier against her, loving that the closer contact between their bodies chased the shadows from her gaze. "I think that pot looks perfect by the front door, don't you?"

"I—" she began.

He shifted his hands to cup her ass then lifted her off the wall, started striding for the stairs, bounding up them.

"I—"

He dumped her on the bed, dropped down on top of her.

Her hands came to his shoulders. "I think it looks perfect there, too," she said, a little breathless. She tilted her head to the side, allowing him better access to her throat.

And he forgot all about lingerie *and* plants.

CHAPTER THIRTY-FIVE

Lexi

"How did you hurt your knee?" she asked, Thursday during lunchtime. "You've never told me exactly what happened."

They were sitting in Luc's office, downing salads.

He froze with his fork halfway to his mouth. "Why?"

Her brows came up at his tone. She'd never heard him use it with her before. "Because we're dating, and I want to know everything about you?"

"I took a bad hit in a game."

She waited for him to say the rest of it. Because surely there was more. She knew he'd been a promising young player, and she'd overheard enough conversations and interviews to understand that his knowledge of the sport wasn't from merely studying the game. He'd been *on* the ice.

"Then what happened?"

"Surgery."

She waited until he'd taken a bite before asking again, "*Then* what happened?"

"Rehab. A few games. More surgery," he clipped out. "More rehab. And eventually . . . released from my contract."

"Luc," she murmured, reaching over and taking his hand. "That must have been really hard."

"It was what it was." A shrug. Another bite. "But it was a long time ago."

She scooped up salad on her fork. "You know, I really hate that saying."

He shrugged again, ate some more of his greens. "I don't know what else to call it," he said. "I was injured. I tried to come back, but my knee was never the same again. Thankfully, I was lucky enough to have been given the opportunity to take a position with the team."

"And how did it feel?" she asked. "I mean, your dream was taken away from you, that had to be really hard."

"It sucked. But I can't change it, and"—he reached over and squeezed her hand—"I'm happy with where I am now."

He wanted to gloss over the past.

She got that. Oh, *how* she understood that.

She'd spent the past six months in misery, in second-guessing every action. But . . . she also knew enough now that she couldn't just ignore everything and expect to move forward completely unscathed.

It would creep back in.

But maybe he was well over it. It was almost twenty years ago, wasn't it? He'd had plenty of time to deal with the trauma of it. He wasn't like her, a raw wound just scabbed over.

Except . . . there was that sharp edge to his voice, the hint of darkness in his expression.

"You made the most of that opportunity," she said.

He finally looked up from his food and smiled, and there he was again. The light was back. "Yup. Made it all the way up to GM. Not too shabby, huh?" He took a bite, eyes still on her, and when he finished chewing and swallowing, he asked, "Did you find a place to take your big furniture yet? Or do you want me to rent a truck and bring it over to the house?"

She'd hardly spared a moment to think about the furniture,

about her apartment, and certainly not since Luc got home. Not when he was there, and there were so many fun things to do with him.

Hot tub. Check.

Planting new flowers in his back yard. Check.

Going to the cute farmer's market downtown. Check.

Cooking in his kitchen and eating meals while holding hands, showering together to conserve water (even though they ended up not saving much because showering together inevitably led to lots of sexy time). And all that conserving was usually followed up by cuddling on the couch or in bed, watching a movie.

Check times three.

Everything with Luc was easy and comfortable and so totally effortless.

Unlike . . . her relationship with her father.

That was a dumpster fire of epic proportions, her fury and frustration and hurt all tangled up. She still couldn't believe the gall he'd had in just showing up at her apartment. Totally fucked up and unfair, and she knew Luc would be on her side about it. Which was probably why she found herself blurting, "My dad came to see me."

Surprise had his fork freezing again. "When?"

"Last week."

He set down the fork. "And you're just telling me now?"

She matched him, placing her own fork on the lid of her Tupperware. "I . . . it's . . ." What? "Strange," she said. "You know, he called me that day a while back. We talked, sort of. It was mostly the normal stuff. An update on where he was, and then I mentioned my mom."

And her had dad sounded guilty.

"What?" Luc asked.

"He said some stuff, like about how he'd been a shit father since my mom died"—a shake of her head—"not those words exactly, but it seemed like he finally recognized that—" She broke off and stared at the floor.

"That he'd been a shit father?" Luc asked dryly.

She nodded. "Yeah, *that*." She picked up her fork again. "So, he was outside my apartment, and I was surprised. I mean, I didn't even think he had the address." Her shoulders rose and fell on a sigh. "Maybe I emailed it to him? I don't know. I guess I probably did, but it's not like he ever replies back to me and then—"

"He was there."

Her lips pressed flat. "Exactly."

"Did you guys talk?"

"No." Her voice sounded cold, even to her own ears. "And I don't think I want to. I mean, it's been seven years of once or twice monthly calls, and I stopped looking for anything from him a long time ago."

But *had* she really stopped looking?

Or was there some small ache in her heart that had always remained, desperate for him to come soothe the hurt?

She didn't want to think about that right now.

She *wanted* . . . to be done with this.

She and Luc had been having a perfectly nice time talking to each other and ignoring the past, until she'd brought it up. They should *keep* doing that—the whole having a nice time chatting, not the languishing in the past. Luc didn't want to talk about his injury, and Lexi found that, despite her blurt, she didn't want to discuss her dad or the complicated things he made her feel. She'd had enough betrayal to last her a lifetime.

For now, she wanted to focus on salads and the handsome man who might or might not be sporting a hickey below the collar of his button-down.

Yes, a hickey.

Because they were apparently trying to act like teenagers again.

And she was loving absolutely every minute of it.

"Let's talk about something else," she said, and he nodded, his eyes soft, telling her that he was going to let her off the hook of continuing to talk about the past. "I think the front yard needs another tree. I was thinking of a maple, but I don't know if it can withstand the cold. I'll have to research—"

"Doesn't syrup come from maple trees?"

She blinked at the left turn in conversation. "Um, yes?" she said, more question that statement.

"So . . . doesn't most maple syrup come from Canada?"

Her brows drew into a frown. "Among other places, yes?" Another statement that sounded like a question.

"Okay . . . isn't it cold in Canada?"

Ah. Now she saw where he was going, the pain in her ass.

And speaking of . . . she wondered if he was into anal. She'd tried it a few times and had liked it. Maybe they could . . .

"What just went through your brain?" he asked.

She smirked. "Nothing," she said. "So, you're saying that because it's cold in Canada, we can plant a maple tree here in Maryland."

He dumped his salad in the trash, pushed up to his feet, and rounded the desk, heat in his eyes. "Never let it be said I can't use logic." He sat on the edge of the desk, those strong thighs on either side of hers. "Now," he murmured, his voice like silk, stroking across her nape, sliding down her spine, curling between her thighs, "what were you just thinking?"

How much she'd like that monster cock of his in other places. Her mouth. Her ass. No big deal.

Her cheeks were hot. She knew it.

She wasn't normally a sex machine. She liked to have sex, don't get her wrong. She'd slept with more than a handful of people and wasn't shy when it came to asking for what she wanted between the sheets. She even liked her body. Yes, it had lumps and marks that weren't perfect. Yes, she maybe wished her stomach was flatter, her thighs less jiggly. But she liked tacos, okay?

And nothing was going to stop her from eating udon.

"Nothing," she said again.

He trailed the backs of his knuckles over her cheek, down her throat. "What?" he pressed.

She shook her head.

"*Lexi.*"

"*Luc.*"

He bent until she could feel his breath on her lips. "Should I kiss you until you tell me?"

"You think that'll work?" Big words, big talk.

Except that her voice was husky, and the desire in it was palpable.

Because she *knew* it would work.

A soft groan. "I know it will." His mouth brushed hers as he spoke. "Now, tell me, honey. What made all that heat trail across your face?"

She shuddered when his knuckles drifted lower, trailing down the V of her shirt. Her nipples beaded against her bra. Heat and need and desire made her thighs tremble, her skin feel too tight for her body.

But she wasn't going to give in and just tell him.

Even if she felt like her spine was going to melt out of her body and into a puddle right in the middle of his office floor.

A raspy growl. "Lexi baby."

Her heart thudded against her ribs. "I'll tell you later." A beat. "*If* you're good."

"Hmm." His knuckles shifted to one side, brushed lightly across her nipple, and she had to bite back a gasp. Then he did it again. "How can I be good?"

Closer now, her body drifting closer, until his hand was trapped between them.

His cock was hard, and she was desperate to rub against it. *No.* She was desperate for it to be inside her, especially when his emerald eyes were so bright, so molten, so filled with the desire she knew was mirrored in her own gaze. She swallowed several times, trying to get her throat to unstick.

"If you tell me," he murmured, his mouth coming to her ear. "I promise that I'll be good. I'll be very, *very* good."

She shuddered.

Fuck this power trip she was on. She was going to tell him.

"I was thinking about your cock—"

He started to smile, pleasure drifting into his face.

There was a knock at the door.

She jumped back.

He cursed.

And speaking of cocks, her eyes caught on the erection that was tenting his slacks.

"Ignore it," he muttered, reaching for her.

"The cock or the knock?" she asked.

"Either. *Both*."

She giggled, but then whoever was on the other side of the door rapped a fist against the wood again, and Luc sighed, stepped back.

"Sorry," he murmured.

"No apologies," she said and waved a hand at his chair. "Sit. Hide *that*." Then she moved to the door.

"And you say *I* give orders."

Her lips curved, laughter in her chest as she turned the handle and tugged open the door.

Oliver James, captain of the Breakers, stood on the other side of that wooden panel.

CHAPTER THIRTY-SIX

Luc

HE WATCHED LEXI LEAVE, hating that he had to do real fucking work . . . instead of real *fucking* work.

But . . . Oliver was in his office, seriousness in his expression. Luc understood better now that his captain was a quiet man who liked to keep things on the ice and in the locker room. So, despite the interruption, the delay in his delving into Lexi's brain, his discovery of whatever had sent that red flaring across her cheeks, the trace of wicked in her eyes, Luc was glad Oliver had come to talk to him.

They'd spoken after Shelby's trade had gone through, and Luc had made it clear the captain needed to talk to someone— whether it be him, a coach, or the newly hired team psychologist, Hazel Reid—when shit got serious enough that Oliver couldn't handle it on his own. Luc knew that wasn't easy for him.

There was a reason Oliver had been chosen captain, despite being a man of very few words. He was dedicated, one of the hardest-working players, a natural-born leader without ego.

And that was a rare thing in this league.

But he wasn't exactly *open*. He liked to clutch his cards to his chest, and while there was a rapport with his teammates, there had always been a very clear line between Luc, Tommy and the rest of the coaching staff, and Oliver.

One side was the players.

The other was management.

Luc had thought that made everyone more comfortable on the work front, especially when there didn't seem to be any of that distance when it came to the team events.

Hell, he didn't have family, so he considered everyone in the organization to be part of his.

But in keeping that distance in the organization, he'd allowed Shelby's bullshit to fester, to have a place, and make it so that no matter how much rebuilding he did, no matter how many talented players he'd brought to the roster, the Breakers would never rise from the surf again.

So, Oliver being here was important, something that would inch the team out of those pounding waves, and something Luc wouldn't jeopardize.

Period.

Later, he'd ferret out the secrets in Lexi's mind.

"I'm sorry to interrupt," Oliver said, and Luc tore his gaze from the door that had just clicked closed.

"Don't apologize," Luc told him, focusing on his captain. "Everything okay?"

"It's about Shelby."

Of course, it was.

"What can I do?"

Oliver's gaze skated to the side, quiet descending for long moments.

Having the sense that his captain was gathering his thoughts, Luc didn't push. Just waited until his eyes met Luc's. But he wasn't nearly prepared for the shock that Oliver's words delivered.

"I think you should pick someone else to be captain."

Oliver had been in the position for barely more than a year —just last season and the half of this one. He was a solid player. He was good at leading the team. That he was wanting to step down when the team was just rebounding after weathering some serious shit—they'd gone five and one over their last games—was concerning, to say the least.

"What did he do to you?"

Silence.

Heavy, dread-filled quiet.

"It doesn't matter," Oliver finally said. "He's gone now, and the team is all the better for it."

"I agree the team is better." Not that whatever had happened didn't matter. "So, tell me why it would be better without you wearing that C."

Shame in his pale blue eyes. "I couldn't shut that shit with Shelby down, couldn't bring us together. The team needs someone who's able to do that."

"Yes, they do."

Oliver nodded. "So, you'll pick a different captain?"

"No."

Also, no hesitation in Luc's mind or in his answer. Because Oliver coming here, Oliver being concerned more about the team than his own ego was the most important thing. He wasn't perfect.

But the Breakers didn't need a perfect captain at the helm.

They needed someone who would continue moving forward despite the bumps in the road, the mistakes that were made.

They needed his stability, his constant calm, his perseverance.

Luc knew that if he told Oliver that, he wouldn't absorb the compliment, wouldn't understand that what made him a good man inside was what the team needed. Luc didn't even think Oliver would consider himself a good man, not when it came to hockey, at least.

Not with the struggles the team had been through these last few seasons.

Ever since Shelby had joined the roster.

"I made the choice to bring Shelby to the team," Luc said quietly. "I signed him because I was looking at stats and skating ability and the fucker's golden hands. But I ignored the fact that he had a reputation for starting shit. I wanted to get us back to the Cup as quickly as possible." He tapped his fingers on the edge of the desk. "I wanted that big win again. But I forgot that there's no easy fix. That's on me. Not on anyone else, ultimately, except for me."

"I should have handled it," Oliver muttered. "And barring that, I should have gone to Tommy or you. Certainly before the GM of the whole fucking organization had to come into our locker room, dress us down, and then keep us inside like a bunch of children."

There was that.

"Why didn't you?" Luc asked. "When it wasn't going well, why didn't you go to Coach, to me?"

"I was trying to fix it. I thought I could help Marcel get over his girlfriend," Oliver said. "I thought I could deal with . . ."

Luc's eyes narrowed. "Deal with what?" he asked, when Oliver trailed off.

A long pause. "All of it."

"Did you feel like you didn't have a safe space to come here, to talk to Tommy?"

"No," he said. "I just thought the team should be taking care of itself." He shook his head. "I understand now that was a mistake."

More of that separation.

More of Luc understanding that it was what made this situation escalate. If it wasn't there, then perhaps Oliver would have felt more comfortable coming to him before things had gotten so bad.

He needed to fix this, bridge the gulf.

He needed Oliver to continue to reach out, especially with the big, deep shit that required more help than he might be able to handle. The guys needed someone who could handle the team *and* liaison with management.

And as far as Luc was concerned, he didn't think Oliver had been given a fair chance to do that.

He was still getting his feet underneath him.

And the team had already been in a bad place when he'd jumped in.

He couldn't work miracles, and Luc didn't expect him to.

"I think you should pick Smitty," Oliver said.

Conner Smith—solid defenseman, six years in the league. He was already an assistant captain, so it wouldn't be that much of a stretch to ask him to step up.

Except . . . he didn't have that spark Luc had seen—*still* saw —in Oliver.

The kid had something special—broad shoulders to carry the responsibility, ability to own mistakes, and . . . a glimmer of greatness.

Oliver was a player who could lead them to the end.

They just needed to get the right players around them . . . and perhaps, to punch out the dents in his confidence.

Steepling his hands in front of him, Luc sat back in his chair, and debated how to accomplish that.

Oliver was quiet, not moving, his gaze steady.

"We're going to set up a weekly meeting. You'll bring any concerns to me—playing time, injuries that might have been missed or are unaddressed, personality issues. If someone's dog died, I want to know."

Oliver's brows dragged together. "You want me to tattle on the team?"

"No," he said. "I want to see the speed bumps before my car is barreling over them, throwing the suspension off. I want to know the things that are weighing on the guys. I want to understand the *concerns*." He sat up. "And I need the team to understand they can come in here, talk to me or Tommy or any of the other coaches or Hazel without consequence. And I need you to provide stability," he added, when the protest was still in Oliver's expression. "We've got a mess to clean up in front of us, and I've never known you to be the type of person to shy away from hard work."

Silence.

"So . . . are you with me?"

More silence.

Then Oliver nodded. "I'm with you."

It was a start.

But Luc knew it was a good one.

CHAPTER THIRTY-SEVEN

Lexi

THERE WERE twenty-three sets of eyes on her, each belonging to a sexy, successful professional athlete, and Lexi was elbow deep in potting soil.

Though, she supposed, there were more than twenty-three men staring at her.

The four coaches—Tommy Franklin, the Breaker's head coach, along with Steven Balko, Aiden Philips, and Tomás Petin, all assistant coaches.

Then there was Luc.

Her Luc, who had stared at her with pride as she'd put the guys to work, and who, perhaps a bit too gleefully, had been more than happy for her to direct his players to dig a ton of holes to help rehab this community garden. Trees—and not puny ones, either—had now been planted all along the far end of the field. They would provide a windbreak from the intense gusts that sometimes drifted up from the river and whipped through this neighborhood.

She was on the committee for this community garden, and while most of the year's crops had been harvested and eaten by the locals (providing quality fresh produce to people who might not otherwise have access to it), there was still an entire section of winter squash and carving pumpkins that would be used in the next few months.

She couldn't wait to see what carvings the kids would come up with.

Now, however, the competition began.

"You all have pots and supplies in front of you," she said. "You'll each pick a flower, name it, and then plant it in the pot. The player who manages to not kill it, and/or whose flower is the healthiest by the end of the season will win a prize."

"What if we all kill it?" one of the players, Theo Young, asked.

Theo was a man with a wicked smile, a beard that many a woman had swooned over, and a pair of piercing gray eyes. He was young, like his namesake, and the requisite "funny" man.

Lexi didn't normally have patience for class clowns, but she liked Theo.

He was a good kid.

"Then the one who kills it the least will win."

He grinned.

"And"—she met each of the guys' eyes in turn—"I've already spoken to each of your girlfriends, your partners, your wives . . . your *mothers*. They all know they are not to touch these plants."

Brows lifted.

She heard a muttered curse.

"No cheating. No teaming up. No sabotaging teammates' plants," she said sternly. "I'll be requiring daily pictures."

"What about when we're on the road?" Luca Castillo, one of the defensemen, asked.

"That's the only time you can leave it in the care of those partners, girlfriends, or parents." She smiled. "*If* you trust them to not kill your chance at winning the prize." Then she shrugged. "Either that, or you can bring them with you."

"This is like some fucked up version of that baby project from high school," Flynn Robertson, the first line center, grumbled.

"Ridiculous," someone on the end muttered.

And Lexi started to feel a bit disheartened.

Maybe this was a stupid idea. Maybe she should have just stuck with digging the holes and planting the trees. They'd all been smiling and joking then, instead of the frowns and shifting and sighs.

"This—"

Shit.

Her heart pounded. Her palms grew sweaty. Luc took a step forward, mouth opening, eyes flashing.

"Mine's name is KiKi," Oliver said loudly, grabbing a flower from one of the containers in front of him. "And she's going to kick all of your flowers' asses."

Silence.

Then Conner Smith spoke. "No way," he said, reaching for a flower. "This bitch is the winner—" He froze when Luc cleared his throat, glanced up at her. "Sorry," he said, and she found herself shrugging and shooting him a smile. Such a loose cannon, that one. "This beautiful flower, Betty, is gonna win, mother—*Mofos.*" A dancing brown gaze met hers, and he winked.

Theo grabbed a pot and a flower, got busy with the soil. "I give you Plantessa," he declared.

And suddenly, there was a mad rush for plants, a bit of jostling as the guys hustled to grab the flowers they thought would grow the best, their competitiveness finally coming to the forefront.

More soil was dispersed, flowers were transplanted, questions were asked of her.

Some questions she answered for the group at large (what the supplies in front of them were used for), some she left up to them (how often to water, how much sunshine, how much plant food), even though they were good questions.

This *was* a bit like that baby project, bringing home the crying, pooping/peeing doll for a night, except that it was a plant, and required significantly less care.

She'd also picked a hardy flower.

It would take a lot to kill it, so she had faith that more than a handful of them would survive the season.

But the task was onto them now.

And she hoped their competitive natures would bring about some good-natured ribbing and maybe a little bit more closeness at having to undergo this "torture" together.

Fingers trailed down the back of her arm, and then Luc was in front of her, his thumb brushing across her cheek. "You had a little dirt," he said, when she raised her brows in question. "Sorry, the guys were . . ." He trailed off, shot a glare at the team, though they were all now dutifully planting their flowers. "Assholes."

"They're not so bad," she said, leaning against his side.

He kissed her, not lightly, but also not shoving his tongue down her throat. Team event tongue, if that was a thing, just a little flick against her bottom lip, inducing the perfect amount of heat, enough so that she relaxed, the rest of the tension from their flower plan not going over quite as well as planned disappearing.

"Thank you," he murmured, cupping her cheek for a moment before turning back to survey the tables that now appeared to have seen a tornado rip right through them.

Soil bags were torn open, dirt scattered into piles on the ground, on the wooden surface, brushed across the guys' clothes and faces. Empty flowerpots littered the space, along with the plastic plant tags she'd noticed only a few of the guys paid attention to in their hurry to get their flowers planted. The name tags she'd brought were being decorated with paint pens (which she'd also brought), and she saw that

Plantessa (oh, Theo, he sure did make her laugh) had gotten hers, along with a Danielle, a Frances, a Barbie, a Tricia, and even a Frank.

At least there was one male flower.

Amusement curling through her, she saw a few of the players track Luc's hand around her waist, her body cuddled up to his, knew some had seen the kiss, and though a few sets of eyes widened, most of the guys just seemed to shrug off the change in relationship, though a few smiled widely. Conner winked at her.

Her cheeks heated, but she merely winked back, knew that some teasing was going to come, especially with what Luc was trying to do, trying to strengthen the team's bonds.

Teasing and razzing were part of hockey.

She'd been around these guys enough to know that in her heart.

Lucky for her, she knew how to hold her head high . . . *and* how to tease back.

"Kiss her again," Theo called. "Maybe then she'll answer some of our questions."

Luc growled.

Lexi laughed and turned in his arms, kissed Luc soundly on the lips. "Still not going to answer your questions," she said, once she'd pulled away.

"Oooh," Luca called to Theo over the laughter.

"I'm going to go check on the pumpkins," she murmured to Luc. "I'll leave you to your hooligans," she added, a little louder and with a look slanted in Theo's direction.

He merely grinned and waved, his fingers covered in dirt. "We're all just glad that you decided to finally give him a chance."

Oliver chucked an empty pot at Theo. It bounced off his chest, leaving another smattering of dirt there.

"Dude," Luca muttered.

Conner shook his head. "Dumb ass kids."

Luc glanced down at her, apology in his eyes, fingers drifting up her arm.

"Don't you dare," she said, smoothing a hand down his chest. "This is good," she told him. "The guys are coming together."

He made a face, grumbled, "Still want to dump that bag of soil on Theo's head."

"Save it for the pumpkins," she teased, slipping out of his arms and heading around the corner, past the small shed where they stored their supplies, and to the large green vines that tended to take over. A few of the gourds had slipped off the mint-colored plastic cradles that helped to prevent the pumpkins from getting lopsided and rotten when grown solely on the ground.

She straightened them, checked on a few others, counting to make sure there were plenty along with a few extras for the kids —in case the squirrels got busy—and had just bent to adjust the drip line to ensure they got enough water when she felt a prickling along her spine.

Her eyes flicked behind her, but the guys were occupied in the planting.

She should have looked in front of her.

Because when she pushed up to her feet, brushing her dirt-covered hands on her jeans, she saw him.

And her heart seized.

Fuck, she'd been so happy, and now *he* was there.

Her dad. Again.

Why was he here?

He should be off in his RV, soothing his soul with solitude, ignoring her existence and everything their life had been before.

The urge to turn and flee was strong, but she lifted her chin, pressed her feet into the earth, and held her position as he closed the distance between them.

"Hi, baby," he murmured.

The endearment tore through her, anger in its wake. Such

red-hot fury that she was almost surprised by its intensity, how hot it burned. "Don't," she snapped, that rage making the word almost guttural, choking off more words that threatened to emerge.

Probably a good thing.

Because she'd gone from feeling slightly guilty to wanting to lash out, to be cruel, to unburden all her fury and hurt and grief of losing her mom and make him *hurt*.

"You were good with the team."

Her shoulders tightened, tension coiling in them, leaking down into her spine. How long had he been here, if he'd seen them interacting? Was he spying on her? *What* else had he seen? And seriously, why hadn't he just *gone* already?

So many questions, but she didn't want to open herself up to conversation, to allow him in.

Who knew when he'd take off again?

Especially because this was probably some guilt-ridden penance for her mentioning her mother weeks before.

"Thanks," she said, shoving down the anger because she didn't want to lose her cool within earshot of the team then retreating a step when he came closer. "I should get back."

"Lexi, baby, I need to apologize." An intensity to the statement sliced clean through her. And a battering ram to her stomach, her lungs freezing.

"Don't," she whispered, curling forward, her arms crossing over her middle.

Pain flared across her father's face. He reached for her.

This time, her feet couldn't stay in place. She stumbled back a step.

And then . . . there was a warm hand on her back, Luc's voice in her ear, his body covering hers. "You okay?"

She shook her head.

He glared up at her father. "You need to go."

"I'm not leaving until I speak to my daughter."

"You had that chance," she whispered. "You had it so many times over the last years, a-and you didn't bother."

Luc tucked her closer when her voice broke. "This isn't the right time," he told her father. "You can't just waltz back into her life and disrupt it when she's working."

"I know I treated you abhorrently," her dad said, his eyes, more brown than gold in this light, were locked onto hers. He ignored Luc, still speaking in that same intensely quiet voice that had torn her insides to ribbons. "I was so worried about what I'd lost that I didn't do a good job of looking after you."

She'd been thirty.

Old enough to look after herself.

But . . . still needing her dad.

Maybe that made her pathetic. Maybe that anger and resentment that still flowed through her, twisting this way and that, vast rapids of fury with hidden dangers beneath, made her just as weak. None of which changed the fact that she'd practically been an orphan the last years.

Tiptoeing through their brief, halting phone conversations, not daring to bring up anything about her mom.

Because then she wouldn't get a phone call.

And then even the scraps would be gone.

No phone calls. No emails.

Six months the first time. Longer the second, until she'd thought that, perhaps, she wouldn't hear from him again.

Not answering her calls. Not returning her messages. *Nothing.*

She'd had her work and friends, and then she'd had Caleb, and he'd become the center of her universe until—

He'd gone, too.

More pain ricocheting inside her like a barbed pinball.

Because now, Luc had taken that top spot, and what she felt for him was so much bigger than what she'd felt for Caleb, and now she was wondering what in the fuck she was doing. Her dad had wounded her, sliced her to pieces deep down, burying her beneath the rubble of her grief, her loneliness. Caleb had rebuilt her, brick by brick, but without mortar, stones so precariously stacked. And then when he'd felt like it, he'd shoved at that tower of rock and sent it collapsing to the ground.

But Luc?

Luc went so much deeper.

He was built of blood and bone, of heart and soul, and she knew that if he ever decided to hurt her like Caleb had, like her father had . . .

There might not be anything left to piece together.

The thoughts in her head felt so dramatic, so over the top and ridiculous.

And yet, she didn't doubt them.

Broken. She'd been broken twice before, and she didn't think she could stand it a third time.

Luc held her against him, his body strong and capable.

He wasn't broken.

He was whole and hearty and amazing and . . . how long would it be until he sent her careening to the floor, to shatter into a million pieces.

The first had taken thirty years. The second only seven. The third would . . .

Fingers under her chin, tilting her head up, green eyes fierce. "No," he growled, and she saw the breadth of emotions in those emerald depths, the way they seemed to scream *I am not like them.*

For a moment, she didn't believe him.

For a moment, she wanted to hang onto the fear and protect herself from any future hurt.

But . . . Luc.

That heart and soul. His patience and perseverance. The sense of coming home every time she was with him. He *wasn't* like the others. He was what she'd had growing up. He was her mother. He was the safety and security, the peace inside . . . the love filling her to the brim.

That was Luc.

He relaxed at whatever he saw on her face, his arms wrapping around her even more tightly, and she pressed so close, his warm body familiar and comforting, his hand stroking a gentle caress up and down her back.

And . . . his ear was right there, so close and tempting.

The words were bubbling up on his tongue.

She gave into the moment.

Maybe this was backward. Maybe she should pick a sweet, romantic moment to tell him all she held in her heart, not blurt out something right after he came to the rescue again, when he was still struggling to hold the broken pieces of her together.

But maybe it was the perfect moment.

Because he'd been the glue, the mortar so many times. Because . . . she was done being broken. Because there wasn't any point in waiting for a perfect time. Life was built in the imperfect moments, cobbled together with pain and love, sacrifice and joy. It was fitting together pieces of a jigsaw puzzle that never seemed to sit correctly. And it was . . . soft hands on her back, tugging her toward a warm chest. It was lugging her plants around, opening his home and heart without question. It was light in his eyes, gentle kisses on her forehead.

It was . . . Luc.

It was *her* with Luc.

So, that was why she rose up on tiptoe and brought her mouth close to his ear, whispered, "I love you."

He turned into a statue.

His arms clamping around her tightly, his shoulders going taut, his lungs seeming to stop working.

Then he shuddered out a breath. "What did you say?"

"I said—"

He weaved his fingers into her hair, tugged her back enough so he could see her face. "What did you say?"

"I love you," she murmured.

Emerald eyes flaring, his fingers trembling as they slid from her hair and traced across her cheek. "I—*how?*"

Her heart squeezed. "Because how could I not?" she whispered. "How could I not love someone as wonderful as you? How could I not be so fucking happy to wake up beside you, to feel your touch, to see your smile?" She covered his hand with her own. "You're my home, my heart. I think I knew it from the first time in that bar two years ago. I certainly had never wanted a friendship with another guy, let alone to allow our lives to become so intertwined." Her lips turned up as she tapped her chest, right above her heart. "You stitched yourself right into here, and even though I should be terrified of being hurt again, all I know is that I trust you to keep me safe."

His eyes glimmered with tears. "Lexi," he rasped.

"So, I know you might not feel the same—"

"I do."

Said so quickly that she blinked.

Her skin was silk on his hand. "Even when I had no hope in my heart that I'd be here with you, like this, I still loved you."

Happiness bloomed within her. "Really?"

He nodded, fingers flexing on her cheek.

And then his mouth lowered to hers, and they were kissing. At what was definitely the wrong time for declarations and bone-melting caresses. At what was also certainly the perfect time, because life was messy and things could change on a dime, and if Lexi didn't grab onto her chances, then she might miss out on her slice of happy.

So, she ignored the fact that one of the players could come around the corner of the shed, that her dad was still just a few feet away and hadn't yet gone, though he'd stopped talking, and she fell into the kiss.

She loved Luc.

Luc loved her.

That was enough.

Eventually, though, they had to fall *out* of the kiss, and when she pulled her mouth from his, chest heaving, the sensations she'd been lost in dissipated, she blearily remembered where she was. Remembered the joy in her heart from loving this man, remembered the hurt and the devastation whose talons had gripped so tightly, the same claws that Luc had so deftly removed, and looked up, preparing herself to deal with her father in front of her, once and for all. She'd set the terms. She would rebuild their relationship, and its wall, its mortar and supports would be crafted by her. She would be the one deciding to let him in, or maybe she would move on with her life this time, without wondering for once why it had been so easy for him to leave her.

"I love you," Luc whispered, holding onto that moment for just a few seconds longer. "Until the day my heart stops beating."

Her eyes burned, but it was with happiness, and she found herself kissing him again, just a brief slide of her lips against his. And when she finally managed to tear her gaze off Luc, off his glistening green eyes, his kiss-swollen lips, and returned it back in front of her . . .

Her father was gone.

Right.

That wasn't a surprise.

CHAPTER THIRTY-EIGHT

Luc

THERE WERE plants on the plane, glittering name tags hot glued to the ceramic pots, a line of them carefully buckled in with seat belts.

Luc bit back a smile then a laugh when he saw that the coaching staff had brought theirs along as well.

"You don't even know what the prize is," he said, pausing in the aisle.

"It's about pride, now," Tommy said. "None of us bastards are willing to back down."

Luc smothered a smile, quickly snapped a few pictures, and fired them off to Lexi then settled into his seat and pulled out his laptop. Always emails. Always so many emails.

And they never seemed to stop.

But at least one of them sitting in his inbox made him happy.

And hard.

Thankfully, it had been sent to his personal email, and not . his work one. *Thankfully*, she'd included a NSFW warning so he was able to open it carefully, no nosy eyes allowed to creep in.

Unfortunately, he couldn't do anything about the racy picture she'd sent him, in that gag lingerie. This one wasn't a nurse's outfit but the maid's uniform, complete with a feather duster and a little white cap.

And black lace.

See-through black lace.

Thank God, they were flying back after the game tomorrow.

Because he needed to have a conversation with this woman about the timing of her sexy lingerie exploits.

With him.

She needed to be playing dress-up with *him*.

He told her that. Both in the email and in the text he sent afterward. After which, he made a mental note to order some lingerie—lingerie he'd only give her when he was actually with her.

Then the plane doors closed.

He shut down his phone and laptop, knew that the emails would continue to pile up and that they wouldn't be nearly as fun as what he'd seen in Lexi's.

But, for once, he couldn't bring himself to care.

He shut his eyes, dreamed about Lexi bending over, *way* over, to dust the baseboards.

———

THE ICE WAS SHIT, but the team was playing well despite the bounces that had been keeping the game close enough that neither the Breakers nor the Rangers could eke out a definite lead.

It was just back and forth all night.

And though he could feel the guys getting frustrated, could feel their discouragement when they'd pulled ahead and then had been scored on just thirty seconds later, tying the game again, they were holding it together.

The wheels stayed on.

Their determination renewed, and they went out there and skated hard for the next shift.

Marcel had been moved to the top line, and he, Oliver, and Flynn had good chemistry, but their line was the only one that hadn't scored that night.

They were due, and Luc could feel in his hockey bone—

Also . . . that was *not* a term he should be using on the regular.

Anyway, there were twelve minutes left in the third. Oliver, Flynn, and Marcel's line had been on the schneid all night, and they were going to get one before the end of this game.

Luc knew that.

Not just in his hockey bone.

Biting back a grin, he studied the arrangement of players on the ice and then settled back onto his seat and braced himself for whatever result this game would bring.

He was betting on his guys.

They'd won eight in a row.

They were on a hot streak, and a win tonight would mean they were at five hundred (the team would have equal wins and losses) for the first time that season.

Not exactly the auspicious start he'd been hoping for going into this year.

But it was something positive, and the team was coming together, and there was still half a season yet. The Breakers could make a run for it.

They just needed to keep battling, continue moving forward—

In a flash, Marcel was carrying the puck up the ice, Oliver streaking next to him. They crossed the blue line, Marcel faked a shot, passed the puck to Oliver, who danced around a defenseman and passed it back to Marcel. A quick flick of his stick and the biscuit went to Flynn, who'd trailed behind and high in the slot. A gentle tap of his stick sent that puck to the backdoor, to Oliver, and . . .

Goal.

The crowd groaned.

Luc grinned.

Yeah, they just needed to keep battling.

————

HE DIDN'T UNDERSTAND EXACTLY how he knew something was wrong, but the moment he entered the house, there was a stillness in the quiet.

Yes, it was late.

Yes, he was tired after the travel and game and work.

But, no. This wasn't anything to do with that.

Luc's stomach knotted as he moved through the house then checked the back yard, half looking for Lexi and half double-checking that all the doors and gates were closed and locked. They were, and he armed the alarm before he moved up the stairs.

The light in their bedroom was off, along with the bathroom light, though the space was steamy, as though she'd taken a bath not too long before.

He was just starting to worry that he might have missed her in the yard—perhaps she'd been dozing and he'd accidentally locked her out—and had turned to move back downstairs, to look again, when he spotted the line of light under the closed closet door.

It was a little late for reorganizing, though he knew she still had a few boxes left to clear out, so maybe she couldn't sleep and thought to get ahead.

"Lexi?" he called.

No answer.

His heart gave a little pulse, and worry crept in. Maybe she'd dropped a box on herself or fallen while trying to put something up on one of the high shelves.

Frowning, he quickly crossed to the closet, opening the door carefully, in case she was behind it.

But he needn't have worried about that.

She was sitting cross-legged on the floor, wrapped in her fluffy bathrobe, her hair piled on top of her head, and an open box on the floor in front of her.

"Hey, baby," he murmured, relaxing . . . until he realized exactly *which* box lay open in front of her.

Her tear-streaked face lifted, devastated eyes drifting up to meet his.

Oh. Shit.

CHAPTER THIRTY-NINE

Lexi

SHE HADN'T MEANT to knock down the box.

She'd been trying to shove a bin of her summer clothes onto the top shelf of Luc's—well, *their* closet—and the box had fallen.

Snooping—aside from her stumbling onto the gift bag overflowing with lingerie on the shelf where she'd been stashing her jeans and having some fun—wasn't her usual *forté*. She'd done her level best to leave Luc's things where they were, well aware that she was the one coming into his space.

But he'd taken one look at her clothes crammed into the few empty spaces, and had ordered another dresser, then had purged a bunch of his stuff, making more room for her clothing.

She hadn't asked him to.

He'd done it anyway.

Because he'd seen that she was overflowing, that she needed something—even as simple as closet space—and he'd given it to her.

It was no surprise why she loved the man.

And had made a vow to make sure she gave him just as much attention and insight and caring back.

Then . . . the box.

And she had begun to wonder about everything.

At first, the contents had made her smile. Old pictures of him as a little kid, wearing superhero costumes, in hockey gear that made him look like a giant marshmallow. Him with his parents—both gone now, they'd passed when he was in his early thirties. Photos of him with his friends, with a prom date.

And other photos.

Of a beautiful blond woman, wearing a sparkling ring. A wedding dress. A bikini while on a white sand beach. Luc, younger and tan, posing with her, carefree and loose, happiness in every line on his face.

He hadn't told her.

Ever.

And . . . he had secrets.

Like Caleb.

Heart pounding, she carefully laid the pictures out in front of her, studying his face in them, trying to find a sign of that same person in the man she loved.

But she couldn't find it.

Luc wasn't unhappy now, far from it, actually. But he also wasn't blithe and untroubled, blitzing through life with hardly a care like in the photographs. He had responsibility, a weight and heaviness that had come from his injury, his change in career, and . . . quite certainly, from whatever had happened with this woman and her shining blond hair.

She placed the photographs carefully in a half-moon, studying them closely, knowing that she was intruding on something he probably hadn't wanted to share, and yet not able to stop herself from digging deeper into that box, pulling out picture after picture, until her fingers eventually grazed the bottom of the container, and there was nothing left.

Except, a ring.

There, glittering in the bottom corner.

She picked it up, examining the perfect princess cut

diamond, the shrine to a life she knew nothing about, and felt her stomach roil and twist.

She was going to puke.

She was going to—

The closet door pushed open.

Luc took one look at her face and dropped to his knees in front of her. "It's not what it looks like," he said, the words tumbling from his lips. Which was pretty much the one thing he could say to make her feel worse than she already did.

Because it always was what it looked like.

Always.

Eyes burning, she dropped her gaze to the pictures and brushed a finger over his smiling face.

So young and so handsome.

"Baby," he said, settling on his knees in front of her, scattering the photographs. "This is old stuff I never look at. Shit that was shoved into a box and forgotten. My ex-wife has been out of my life for fifteen years. None of this means *anything*." He began snagging the pictures of him and the woman, crumpling them together before she could tell him it wasn't the fact that he had been married, but rather that she hadn't known something that big about him. She didn't give a fuck about the marriage, but he'd promised to never lie and then hadn't told her that, and she was fucking terrified because if she didn't know something as big as that, then what else might she not know?

"*You're* the most important thing," he said, shoving the photos into an empty trash bag he or she had left in the corner of the space. "You're the one whose photos I want on my wall. You're the one whose finger I want my ring on"—his eyes dropped to the circle of metal and diamond that rested in her palm—"You're the one I want in my life."

She inhaled, released it slowly.

"Luc," she whispered, feeling the edge of that stone dig into her skin. "Why didn't you tell me?"

"Because it didn't matter." He peeled open her fingers,

snagged the ring, and shoved it into the bag along with the pictures. She started to protest—he couldn't just throw *that* away—but he kept talking. "Caterina and I have been done for years. Nothing of her still exists in my life. I promise you."

That made her heart squeeze.

She opened her mouth.

But he continued talking.

"I'm not the kind of man to cheat. I promise you that. I would never *ever* do that."

She knew that.

His fidelity wasn't what was making pain blaze across her nerve endings.

It was the secrets. It was the pain hidden beneath a wall of "Everything's fine." It was that he knew all of her hidden hurts —Caleb, her mom, her dad—and she didn't know *this*.

Because he'd never mentioned an ex-wife. A divorce.

Because she'd had to tear any information about his injury out of him.

She understood not wanting to rehash everything, not wanting to go back to the miserable, unhappy days.

But . . . he'd seen so many of hers.

And, while he didn't owe her an explanation of every moment of his past, of the things that still stung his soul, it continued to play into his life today. She could see the hurt in his eyes, the panic that made his hands shake, the fear that made his voice tremble when he said, "Please, don't leave me."

Eyes burning, she swallowed. Hard. Her own voice shaking when she whispered, "Luc."

A mistake that.

She should have made the promise first, because while she knew that she loved him, that she wasn't going to walk out just because he had secrets—no, she was going to be a battering ram and get through his walls even though the bricks reinforced with extra mortar—*Luc* didn't know that.

He cursed, pushed to his feet.

And then he was gone.

The shock of his sudden departure froze her in place, mouth open, words stoppered up in her throat, her hand extended.

Then the rattling of a garage door rolling up shuddered through the house.

And Lexi unfroze, feet moving beneath her, pushing her up to standing, knees shaking as she stumbled out of the closet.

Through the bedroom.

Down the stairs.

To the kitchen. The garage.

Empty.

The door just settling down against the concrete, the fumes from his car's engine still in the air, heat lingering from the gasoline that had burned.

Luc was gone.

CHAPTER FORTY

Luc

HE DROVE FOR A LONG TIME, the dark of night morphing into the barely gleaming morning sky, until tendrils of pale orange and blue drifted up and grasped onto the bleak black, tugging it away into nothingness.

Sort of what was coursing through his insides.

Blissful nothingness.

And then the occasional punctuation mark of pain.

Pathetic. He'd begged Lexi to not leave him, and . . . she hadn't made that promise. Bitterness, long forgotten, after he'd spent years pretending it had disappeared like the darkness of night, reared its ugly head, gripping him in its talons and shaking fiercely, until he'd had to pull over on the side of the road just to breathe.

She'd left.

Not Lexi. But Caterina.

He'd loved her so much, had *needed* her with an intensity that blazed through him like the sun on a blistering summer afternoon.

And it paled in comparison to what he felt for Lexi.

And Lexi hadn't promised.

He loved her until it felt like his insides were going to be shredded . . . and she wouldn't promise to stay.

Pain lanced through him, knowing that it wasn't a fair thing to ask of her, understanding that with the way her asshole of an ex, the piece of shit who called himself her father had treated her, it was probably a promise she wouldn't ever be able to make.

Yet, he'd asked it anyway.

And when she hadn't been able to make it, he'd been right back in the past. Lying in the hospital bed, the surgery that was supposed to have pieced him back together just complete, the IV still in his arm, the pain medicine making his brain hazy.

Caterina tugging the rings from her finger.

The *clink* as they'd been set on the faux wood table in the corner of the room.

The pull of his skin on the staples as he'd tried to shove his elbows beneath himself, tried to sit up. The agony when he'd shifted toward her, blasting away any relief from the morphine.

And the look on her face when she'd left.

As though he were the most pitiful creature she'd ever laid eyes on.

That had been in Lexi's eyes, though she wasn't cruel, wouldn't give a promise she might potentially break. Instead, he'd seen the pity . . . and the hurt.

That was nearly as bad as the self-loathing, the feelings of being unworthy.

He'd hurt her.

The one promise *he'd* made. To not lie.

And though it hadn't been a direct one, he was guilty of lying by omission, of deliberately avoiding talking about the past and his injury and Caterina . . .

Because it hurt.

But nothing hurt more than seeing the pain in Lexi's eyes, the pain he'd caused.

So he drove, aimlessly, the grip of dawn firmly yanking the night into day, and he didn't feel any better. Not as he drove out of town, slowed a bit by the early morning rush hour traffic, nor as he pulled into the gravel parking lot, nor as he walked along the quiet trail, the trees' branches intertwined like lovers' hands overhead, nor as the hush of mother nature closed in around him.

He needed to find some way to get Lexi to forgive him, to understand, to . . . terror gripped him, pushing right through the heavy, creeping amber that had dripped over him, encasing his heart, his mind, his limbs in a slow, stifling death.

He'd begged her not to leave.

And he'd gone instead.

Like *they* had.

So what if she couldn't promise to stay with him? Who gave a fuck, if she had pity in her gaze, if part of her thought he was pathetic? Yes, it stung. But it wasn't anything he didn't feel himself, and if he could compartmentalize it away, then he could do the same with her looking at him that way.

It wouldn't be easy.

It would burn like the bile scalding the back of his throat in this moment, understanding for the first time in hours that he might have blown his chance with the woman who lived in his heart.

And that hurt with an intensity that made her pity feel like a light spring breeze.

He would take any part of her she was willing to give.

He would crawl. He would beg. He . . . would give up everything for her.

Because some part of him, a quiet whisper buried under the shards of the past, understood that she would never ask him to do that. She, who had been hurt and left broken, who'd stitched herself into something beautiful and wonderful, would never ask that of him.

The realization had his feet stalling, the scrape of his now-ruined dress shoes on the dirt loud in the nearly silent forest.

The wind shifted, bringing a scent he recognized. Or maybe, he caught the glimpse out of the corner of his eye, his gaze moving from his wrecked shoes and up beyond the trail.

Or perhaps, he'd felt it in his heart. Felt *her* there.

From the moment he'd seen her those two years before. And again, now. And all the time in between.

Because Lexi stood in their clearing.

Run.

He needed to *run*.

CHAPTER FORTY-ONE

Lexi

HE'D GONE SO STILL.

And then he'd moved like the wind, running again.

Only this time, he was running *toward* her, tearing across the meadow—their meadow—and closing the distance between them almost faster than she could process, skidding to a stop in front of her, bits of grass and moisture flying up around them.

It had taken mere heartbeats, and yet, his chest rose and fell like he'd run a marathon.

"Lexi," he murmured, reaching a hand up, tentative, almost as though she were merely an apparition, but then his fingers touched her cheek, and she watched the panic slide out of his expression.

"I'm here," she said, covering his hand with her own. "And I'm not going anywhere."

His lips parted, a breath sliding out.

"How?" he whispered, and she didn't think he was referring to how she'd found him—thank you, Find My iPhone, and the fact that they'd long ago linked their cells on the tracking app.

"I love you," she answered. "More than anything."

That seemed to unstick him. "I should have told you," he said, his fingers flexing on her cheek, his body coming closer. "I don't know why I didn't. I"—his eyes darted away—"I guess it was done with, and so I just wanted to not think about it and—"

"It hurt," she whispered.

Another breath, this one grazing her cheekbone.

He nodded. "Yeah," he said. "It hurt, and I buried it deep. Because . . . I'd trusted Caterina, and she shoved me down when I was at my lowest."

"I'm sorry," she said softly.

"You have absolutely nothing to apologize for." He stepped back and thrust a hand through his hair. "I'm the one who didn't tell you. I'm the one who ran away."

"Bullshit."

His eyes narrowed.

"Okay," she said. "I'll give you that you ran." It wasn't like she could say he hadn't, not when she'd literally had to chase him down on the app, but, "I didn't give you a reason to stay." She placed her hand on his chest. "You fought for me for two and a half years. Fought to make a space for yourself in my life, fought to be my friend, my *best* friend. You've been there for me, over and over again, and never once did you ask anything of me."

That was what pained her now.

He'd supported her, had literally held her more times than she could count while she fell apart.

And, never, *never* had he expected anything in return.

She'd thought it was because he was a generous man—and he certainly was *that*—but now, she understood that it was more than that.

He didn't *expect* anything in return. Not just because he was giving, but because some part of him thought he wasn't worthy of it.

Her breath slid through her, a slow inhale-exhale.

She'd had her moments of that same despair, of not feeling worthy, and he'd held her tight until she'd found her own value, until she'd stitched herself back together.

Now, she needed to help him do the same, to heal a wound so old he'd almost forgotten about the injury it had done to his heart.

Until she'd shoved it in his face.

So, two things for her to be guilty about.

Two things she couldn't do a damn thing about now, not really. She couldn't take it back. She could only do her best to make it right.

"I'm sorry," she said then added, placing a finger to his mouth when she saw the protest form on his lips at her apology, "Let me say this?"

He nodded.

She took a breath then said, "You give the appearance of an open book, of someone to take totally at face value. And you *are* that man, in so many ways," she hurried to say, when a trickle of hurt crept into his emerald eyes. "You are what you seem. Wonderful and kind, on the surface and beneath." She shifted closer. "You *are* my friend—the best one I've ever had."

"But," he said before she could.

"But, you're also responsible." She grinned when he blinked, confusion drifting into his face. "And truly, it's not a bad thing. I just think that sometimes you take on so much responsibility for everything, even things that aren't your fault, or not entirely your fault, anyway, and I think that sense of responsibility . . . does damage."

He inhaled sharply.

"And I know—I *know*—that a marriage takes two people to hold it together, two to tear it apart."

Fury in his eyes. "Caleb—"

"Is an asshole," she interrupted. "But he wasn't the only one in the marriage, and if I'd been more honest with myself, I would have understood what wasn't working before things went as far as they did. I was gripping, holding tight to a happy memory, onto the safety and comfort the marriage brought." She slipped her arms around his shoulders, leaned against him. "And I wasn't looking beneath. But it was there," she whispered. "The fractures were present. I just couldn't see them."

"Like the ones inside me," he said, holding her tight. "It was so long ago that I thought I was long past the pain. I didn't realize how much it *still* hurt, how much I'd avoided anything that might be a deep connection with a woman. Until you. Until you became the most important thing in my life."

"And until you thought that I was going to leave you." Like Caterina had.

Throat working, he nodded. "She . . . it . . . the breakup was brutal."

She wanted to ask what had happened, but she was content to wait, content to just know what he'd given her already, to understand what was in his heart, and to be patient for him to be ready to share.

But he gave her the rest without hesitation now.

"I was devastated, my career imploding, my body broken, and she left me right after I came out of the second surgery, after the first one failed. My knee hadn't healed right, so the surgeons went in again," he added when her brows went up. "I remember waking up, staples in my knee, and watching her take off the rings, setting them on the table."

She gripped his hand but didn't speak.

And he kept going.

"She said she hadn't signed up to take care of a husband. She'd married me because I could take care of her."

Fucking. Bitch.

Luc was one of the most caring people she had ever met, and she didn't think that was a quality he'd developed later in life. His kindness and generosity were intrinsic to his being, and she'd been on the receiving end of that often enough to understand it was just part of who Luc was.

He didn't think about it.

He just *was*.

And for that bitch to not be willing to reciprocate that same care had Lexi's blood boiling.

He went on, "She'd cleaned out our bank account by the time I made it home from the hospital and served me with divorce papers even before the stitches were removed."

"So, you lost your career and your marriage, all in one fell swoop."

He nodded.

Lexi burrowed deeper into the circle of his arms. "But you're not going to lose me, baby," she promised, leaning back enough to see his face. "I see you for who you are inside, and I love that man."

His nostrils flared.

His hands tightened.

And the final bit of weariness disappeared from his eyes.

"I love you," she said again. "And I promise you that nothing you can show me will make me run."

His lips curved.

He drew her nearer, a glimmer of humor in his eyes. "Nothing?"

She found herself grinning. "Except . . ." A tap of her finger to her mouth as his brows lifted. "If you touch my chocolate."

Laughter in the air.

A wonderful man bringing his mouth close to hers.

"I promise that if I touch your chocolate, I'll be the one who's doing the running." His smile grew. "To the store." A beat. "To buy you more chocolate."

Her hands cupped his cheeks, her mouth close enough to his that she could feel his breath on her lips. "I love you."

"You're my heart," he said simply, and the words sealed themselves inside hers.

"Luc," she whispered.

Straightening slightly, he brushed back her hair. "What?"

"Now's the time to kiss me." She drew him down again. "Chop. Chop."

A chuckle. "God, I love you."

"And yet, I'm still waiting for a kiss."

Luc went still, and then he roared with laughter.

And *then* he kissed her.

CHAPTER FORTY-TWO

Luc

HE AND LEXI were in the back yard planting when it happened.

And by planting, he meant that he was watching Lexi bend over in tight, ripped jeans, and pretending to dig the occasional hole, when her father appeared.

He held a large bag printed with red bows and paused just inside the gate, halting when he spotted the two of them.

"I'm sorry," he said, looking older than Luc had seen him appear a few weeks before. His shoulders were bent and curved, his face haggard, his hair limp and askew. "I just didn't want to leave this on the front porch."

Lexi had frozen, soil falling through her fingers, the carrot seeds she'd been planting, scattering onto the ground. "What are you doing here?"

A cold question.

One that filled Luc with dread.

Because this thing with her father was eating her up inside, just as much as Caterina and his divorce, the betrayal, the loss of playing hockey had affected him.

And he didn't want it to continue, didn't want her to hurt like he had.

God knew, she'd suffered long enough already, *hurt* enough.

"I wanted to see you," her father said.

"Well," she said. "I don't want to see you. Not yet," she whispered, low enough that Luc knew the other man wouldn't hear. She turned back to the soil, started picking up the seeds, voice rising, "You should go."

"I'm sorry," her father said. "For everything. I know there's nothing I can do to rebuild what we had. I know it won't be the same, but I've wasted so much time already, and I-I was hoping we might find a way for us to move forward."

Lexi opened her mouth, and Luc could see the sharp retort on her tongue, and he knew, even despite the pain her father had caused her, that some part of Lexi would feel guilty for the angry words later.

She was love and kindness.

Not fury and cruelty.

But that viciousness was bubbling right near the surface, readying to explode outward from her lips and tongue . . . it *would* be cruel.

And she would regret it.

This was the third time her father had shown up without warning, somehow knowing where Luc lived, knowing that Lexi would be here. Watching her, perhaps, or maybe he'd paid more attention to his daughter's life than Lexi had thought.

Because he *was* here.

And he'd come back a third time, even though his reception during the previous visit Luc had witnessed had been anything but warm, and despite, presumably, the initial meeting going the same way.

So, maybe Lexi and her dad would never have a father-daughter relationship, not like they'd once had.

But maybe she could find some peace.

Which was why he interrupted before she could snap out her retort, saying, "Have a seat on the deck?"

Lexi's mouth dropped open, fury in her golden-brown eyes when his own eyes made contact with those scorching depths.

Her father, however, seemed to understand what Luc was trying to do. He moved quickly to the small table on the back deck, its umbrella and cushions already removed and stored away because winter had arrived, and took a seat.

Peace.

Luc wanted it for Lexi.

Frankly, he didn't give a shit about her father. Part of him would always hate the bastard for what he'd done to the woman he loved.

But Lexi deserved that peace. Resolution. Those final broken pieces swept away, reformed into something changed, but something whole.

Luc didn't tell Lexi to sit—not that she would have listened anyway.

Instead, he moved to the table, sat next to Lexi's father.

And he started a conversation, sticking out his hand and saying, "I'm Luc, Lexi's boyfriend."

Cool fingers grasping his. "Sam." He set the present on the table, his gaze shifting toward Lexi, who'd dropped back into the dirt and was digging furiously. Probably a pit to bury him in.

This was a minefield he hadn't been prepared to navigate, but Luc would do it for Lexi, for the woman he loved. So, despite the awkwardness in the air, the way that Sam could barely concentrate on the conversation, Luc began asking questions about his travels, his RV, his favorite place he'd visited, sports. Hell, he even asked what Sam thought of the weather.

The. Weather.

It wasn't scintillating.

It was quite painful, actually, to continue yanking one-word answers out of Sam, but Lexi hadn't run screaming out of the yard, and even as she continued digging furiously in the dirt, she was moving a little closer. Planting things in the beds near the deck, her head tilted a way that told him she was listening.

Sam seemed to know it, too.

His answers got longer.

Lexi moved closer still. Not looking at her father but standing behind a chair, her dirt-covered fingers gripping its wooden back.

Luc glanced up at her, caught her gaze, expected to see anger at him.

But instead, there were tears in her eyes.

He reached for her.

She allowed him to pull her onto his lap, still not speaking but listening carefully, and that was enough.

Sam stopped the story he'd been telling about a bear that had run in front of his RV in the middle of nowhere in Montana and stared at Lexi, quiet falling around them. He pushed the present closer, near enough that Lexi would have had to be blind to not see it.

Still, she ignored it, ignored her father.

But she was there. In Luc's lap, three feet from her dad, listening and quiet, the tension gone from her frame.

"I'm going to go now," Sam said. His eyes went to Lexi's. "I know you have no reason to believe me, but I'm not going anywhere. I'm not going to disappear again. I'm not going to be that person." His breath shuddered out. "I will find a way to make these years up to you."

Lexi went still, a muscle in her jaw twitching, but to Luc's surprise, she nodded.

No words.

But a nod.

Some progress.

"If . . ." Sam took another deep breath. "I'd like for you to open this." A beat. "When you're ready."

Hope in golden-brown eyes so like Lexi's, his gaze tracing

every line of her face before drifting to Luc. He inclined his head, gratitude shining brightly. Luc nodded back.

And then Sam was gone.

Lexi sat in his lap for a long time, quiet and still.

But eventually, she got up, set about finishing the planting, filling in the large hole she'd dug. He helped her, not relaxing until she brushed her fingers to his, until she allowed her shoulder to bump against his.

They worked until dark descended, until the temperature dropped.

But when they went into the house, she picked up the present from the table.

Then later, after she opened it, after she read through the stack of letters inside, ones that appeared to have been written over the course of seven years but never sent, after she flipped through the album her father had put inside the bag, she cried, big heaping gasps, cathartic cleansing sobs as she gripped his shirt.

Eventually, though, the tears stopped . . . and the next day, she wrote a letter of her own.

Peace—working toward it.

Life moving forward.

And perhaps, broken pieces mending once more.

CHAPTER FORTY-THREE

Lexi

SHE AND LUC had spent a glorious month without drama—no personal dramas, no running, no new divorces cropping up (and her being able to joke about that made her proud of how far she and Luc had both come), and no surprise visits by her father.

Because . . . she'd had a *non*-surprise visit.

Or perhaps, better explained, she and her father had exchanged a few letters, and then, almost to her own surprise, she'd invited him to lunch.

They hadn't talked about anything important.

But they *had* talked.

And Lexi had come to some painful realizations of her own, thinking back on the conversations, on the effort she put into the relationship, and wondering if perhaps, she had been avoiding her father as much as he had avoided her.

Oh, there was no doubt he'd done some brutal things, disappearing and not taking her calls when she'd mentioned her mother for months at a time, being the worst of them.

But . . . maybe it hadn't been quite that simple.

Because maybe she'd needed to forget, too. Forget that she had a big, gaping hole in her life and to focus on something different, something that wasn't painful. Maybe he'd given her the perfect excuse to forget about the emptiness her mom had left behind and to discover something completely new. Something that was light and different and cotton candy and *Caleb*. Something that would dissolve easily, even if she hadn't been able to see it at first.

So, she was working through that.

Aside from the personal revelations and the work she still needed to do on that front, Luc hadn't had any issues with the team—no trade deals that needed to be negotiated well into the night. Although, only about half of the team's flowers were alive, and they'd had a plant funeral the other day—the guys making tiny tombstones emblazoned with the names of their flowers and having a procession to the compost bin, complete with a depressing-sounding dirge.

The other plants were looking good, however, and Oliver, Theo, and Luca all looked like they might win the competition.

Speaking of which, she snuggled up to her sexy boyfriend, letting the covers slide down her bare back and propping her chin on her crossed arms that lay over his chest. "What does the winner get?"

He frowned, his body still lax from the way they'd celebrated his return from the short road trip—she missed the man far too much.

Okay, she missed the man perfectly.

Because they were perfect together.

Not perfect in the sense that there weren't any hurdles to make it over, or that they didn't bicker about what to eat for dinner, or that she didn't invariably fall asleep on the couch every single time they tried to watch a movie together.

Rather, they were perfect in the way they came together, how they cared for each other, how their broken pieces fit together, filling in the gaps and crevices, formed something that was whole.

So . . . perfect.

In the cup of coffee Luc left on the nightstand for her when he was home.

In her search for a substitute for his favorite beard oil, when his preferred brand had been discontinued. It had taken her eight (*eight!*) tries to get the ideal match.

In Luc carrying her up to bed every time she tried to stay up to watch a movie snuggled together on the couch, and every time only lasting at most, twenty minutes.

In the special recipe she'd created for him, combining his two favorite things, peanut butter and pumpkin, into peanut butter chip pumpkin bread.

It was perfect because they gave a shit, because they each wanted to make the other's life better, and because there was love in every moment . . . even the ones where they were irritated with each other.

Now, Luc peeled back his eyelids, sleep already written into the lines of his face. "Huh?"

She'd have about two minutes of lucidity before he passed out.

She'd better make the most of them.

"For the plant competition," she said, resting her ear against his chest, listening to the solid, steady heartbeat underneath. "Since you didn't go with *my* choice of prize—"

"I'm not buying them lingerie," he muttered. "There's been far too much of that going around."

"You liked it," she said.

"Yes." He had.

"So, what's the prize?"

Luc chuckled.

"What?" she asked.

"It's nothing." A shrug, somewhat awkward considering he

was lying down. "A stupid little prize I saw in the airport and picked up."

"Show me."

He sighed. "I'm comfortable."

She stuck out her bottom lip. "Please?" she asked. "Just tell me where it is, and I'll go get it myself."

"I'll get it." He nipped the tip of her nose. "I'm putting this on your tab, though."

Lexi rolled her hips against him, sighed and pressed the back of her hand to her forehead, all fawning maiden. "However will I work it off, good sir?"

A wolfish grin, a laughing kiss. "I've got some ideas." He nudged her off his chest, moved into the closet.

"Oh, God," she said as he emerged with a red bag that matched the one she'd found moving in not long ago. "Tell me you weren't joking before."

He frowned.

"Because looks like the lingerie bag I found before," she said, "and I was just kidding about that being a good prize."

His laughter filled her with warmth. "It's not lingerie, love."

He set the bag in her lap. "See for yourself."

She tugged out the tissue paper that had been jammed into the top and then shuddered. "Good God, what the hell is that thing?" she asked, pulling out the creepy stuffed animal. "Does it have real *teeth?*"

Luc chucked. "Teeth, yes." He flicked a finger against the plastic chompers. "But not real."

"It's creepy," she said, tracing her hand over soft, fuzzy blue fur and deliberately avoiding the gaping mouth, the pot-smoker eyes, the teeth that looked too real that were sticking straight out. "And it's wearing underwear."

Indeed, it was. A tiny pair of white skivvies, probably the only cute thing on the creature.

"It's a Fuggler." Luc made it dance in the mangled cardboard box it came in, and she shuddered again. "His name is Mac, and he's adorable."

That was not the word she'd choose, but Luc seemed unreasonably happy about the terrifying creature, so she just carefully tucked it back into the bag, making sure to cover its face with the tissue paper.

A fact which he noted, if the smirk on *his* face was any indication.

He just took it from her lap and carried it into the closet, tucking it into whatever dark corner it belonged, but when he came back out, his hands weren't empty, as she'd expected.

Instead, he held a box.

A slender, navy, velvet-covered box.

"Merry Christmas," he murmured, setting it on her lap.

"Christmas isn't for two days."

He shrugged. "Merry Early Christmas then." A nudge, sliding it closer to her fingers. "Open it."

She reached for the box, opened it, the little hinges making a soft *creaking* sound.

But she barely heard it over the sound of her gasp.

Inside wasn't filled with diamonds or other precious gems. Instead, there was a simple charm bracelet, and on many of the links were bright, colorful charms—a bright purple flower, a gardening shovel, a hockey stick, a briefcase, a wave, a tub of popcorn. But many of the others were empty, and she felt her eyes sting when she met his gaze, knowing that he'd left space for the memories they would make together, the private jokes that were theirs alone, all of those perfect moments that were theirs alone.

"You like it?" he asked.

She nodded.

He put it on her wrist, and she admired the charms, running her fingers over the colorful pieces of silver, the weight of the metal comforting on her skin. "Good," he said, "because when I look at you, I know that my heart beats only for you."

Her breath caught. She couldn't speak, not with her throat so full of happiness, tangling up with tears.

"When I close my eyes, I dream of you," he murmured, his thumb brushing along the inside of her wrist. "When I wake up, I am so thankful you're next to me. When I hear you laugh, I can feel your joy inside my heart."

This man.

He melted her from the inside out.

Luc brushed away a tear she hadn't known had fallen.

"I love it," she murmured, managing to push some words out. "I love *you.*"

His smile lit up all those formerly dark and empty places inside her, blasting them full of fire and light and joy, and she knew that she'd never go back there. Not ever again.

Once she'd been broken.

And now she was whole.

EPILOGUE

Luc

I<small>T WAS</small> the night before the final game.

The final round of the playoffs.

Three wins to three wins against the Kings.

The winner of the next game would take the Cup.

If *anyone* had thought the Breakers would be in the finals with the way their season had begun, Luc would have said they were missing more than a few screws. But despite their horrendous start, they *were* there.

The final match would be here in Baltimore, and he should probably be inside, sitting at his laptop, searching for last-minute information about the Kings, something the team might be able to use for the game.

But . . . they'd prepared.

They'd practiced and played their asses off.

Whether they won or lost tomorrow, the team had given every bit of themselves to the pursuit of that dream.

A soft hand trailing across his shoulders. "Are you going to get any sleep tonight?"

His heart was full, and he slid a hand around Lexi's waist,

tugging her down into his lap, her stomach slightly rounded, her eyes tired but happy.

Five months along.

Their whoops.

But the best *whoops* of Luc's life.

"I was catching up on my reading," he said, holding up the book he had, in fact, been reading, although not absorbing much, considering his mind had been on the game tomorrow.

She'd added plants to his trio of trees.

He'd added a comfy outdoor couch with extra pillows and a bin of blankets within arm's reach.

She'd continued leaving her books out here.

He'd found her a waterproof box to leave them in. Not that she remembered. If a book was left behind, it wasn't on purpose. It was closed between two cushions, a receipt in between its pages to mark her spot, or propped open on the arm of the couch, or on the table, a leaf becoming a makeshift bookmark.

God, he loved this woman.

"I wondered where that had gone," she said, snagging it from him and pressing a kiss to his cheek. "Thief," she teased.

"Pregnancy brain," he teased back. "Or whatever the occupational equivalent of pregnancy brain is."

"Space cadet?" she asked, nestling closer.

"Never." He pressed a kiss to the top of her head, shifted her so he could wrap his arms around her and stand.

"I'm too heavy," she protested.

"Never," he repeated, walking through the meandering path and up the stairs onto the deck, moving into the house.

Lexi snuggled closer, yawned. "I have a good feeling about the game tomorrow."

He moved upstairs, into the bedroom, set her on the bed, tugging off her shoes, but just as he was about to take them into the closet, he saw something sparkling out of the corner of his eye.

His jaw fell open.

Lexi's eyes twinkled with humor . . . but that wasn't what had caught his eye.

"You've been snooping again," he murmured, prowling back toward the bed, taking her hand, running a finger over the ring she wore on her left hand.

"Somebody left this right out in the open," she said.

His brows rose. He distinctly remembered hiding it in a certain box.

One that was sitting closed at the end of the bed.

"Really?"

She sat up, mischief reigning supreme. A foot with pink-painted toenails nudged the box toward him. "I was adding something to it."

Brows drawing together, he nonetheless snagged the box when she pushed it closer.

Pulled off the lid.

And . . . felt his eyes burn.

Pictures of them. Not just from the months they'd been together but from their entire friendship. Silly hammy selfies. Posed pictures on their hikes. Breakers events in formal wear. Sharing a bowl of udon.

Their life.

Happy memories, two whole people filling up a box that had once been overflowing with pain.

"There's something else in there," she whispered, wiping the tear he hadn't known had escaped.

His fingers brushed a velvet bag.

"Wh—?"

She closed his hand around it. "Open it," she whispered.

He tugged the drawstring, dumped the contents into his palm, and felt his heart squeeze tight. A charm shaped like the Cup . . . and a ring.

Not sparkly.

Instead, a simple, plain band. One that he knew instinctively would fit his finger perfectly.

And it did.

But when he went to attach the charm to her bracelet, she stopped him.

"Tomorrow," she whispered.

He tucked it back into the bag, slipped it into the box, and set it on the nightstand. Then he slid into bed next to the woman who held his heart.

"For the record," she murmured sleepily. "I said yes."

Luc fell asleep with a grin on his lips.

EPILOGUE

Oliver

They were tied.

They were exhausted.

It was double-overtime, his legs were dead, plays were getting sloppy, and the game-winning goal would probably be some garbage shot that ricocheted off a trio of players before creeping home.

But for whose side, he didn't know.

Oliver hoped it would be for them, of course, but truly, it could go either way.

Marcel banked the puck off the boards, and Oliver could see it wasn't going to clear the blue line, so he hauled ass to pick it up, to clear it out.

He did, managed to get it over that line, to give his team a little breathing room, to get it deep enough to get fresh players on the ice.

But he paid the price, taking a hard slash on the wrists, pain lancing up his arms.

He nearly dropped his stick, his hands going numb for a brief moment, but he powered through it, held tight, and continued driving forward.

Even though he took another hit, this one to the back.

Not that the refs were going to call anything.

Double-overtime in the final game of the playoffs? Yeah, no. Nothing outside of the most egregious of hits was going to be called.

But, fuck, he'd appreciate it if Mark Goddamned Shelby would stop trying to pound his spine into his body. Oliver knew that he'd be black and blue tomorrow. Totally worth it, though, if he was able to hoist the Cup.

Still, he worked along the boards, gaining a few inches.

But when he glanced over his shoulder, saw Mark was winding up again, Oliver let his instincts take over.

He kicked the puck forward, dodged to the right.

Shelby missed the crosscheck and stumbled.

Oliver saw the empty lane ahead. A sudden surge of adrenaline had him bursting forward on tired legs to retrieve the puck, to pick it up on his stick and streak toward the Kings' net.

He had space. He had opportunity.

He was going to end this.

Fifty feet from the net. Thirty. Ten.

Just him and the goalie . . . and a glimpse of an opening on the short side.

He held his breath. Fuck, maybe he even closed his eyes when he shot that puck. Maybe that was why he didn't see it.

But whether it was a mere blink or an unconscious close of his eyelids, they snapped open at the sound.

Thunk.

Not the *ping* of a crossbar or post being hit, the puck deflecting out without crossing the goal line, but the solid *thunk* of the biscuit colliding with the wrapped metal support . . . at the back of the net.

The buzzer went.

The crowd erupted.

And in all that joy and cacophony and chaos, he didn't see Shelby coming.

Just felt the heavy impact.

Saw the ice coming up fast.

Then pain, so much pain . . . and the world went black.

BOLDLY

Don't miss Oliver's story in Boldly, coming August 31, 2021.
Preorder your copy at www.books2read.com/BoldlyEF

———

Hate missing Elise's new releases? Love contests, exclusive excerpts and giveaways?

Then signup for Elise's newsletter here!

http://eepurl.com/bdnmEj

———

ALSO BY ELISE FABER

Billionaire's Club (all stand alone)

Bad Night Stand

Bad Breakup

Bad Husband

Bad Hookup

Bad Divorce

Bad Fiancé

Bad Boyfriend

Bad Blind Date

Bad Wedding

Bad Engagement

Bad Bridesmaid

Bad Swipe (June 28th, 2021)

Gold Hockey (all stand alone)

Blocked

Backhand

Boarding

Benched

Breakaway

Breakout

Checked

Coasting

Centered

Charging

Caged

Crashed (July 27th, 2021)

Cycled (October 5th, 2021)

Breakers Hockey **(all stand alone)**

Broken

Boldly (August 31st, 2021)

KTS Series

Fire and Ice (Hurt Anthology, stand alone)

Riding The Edge

Crossing The Line

Leveling The Field (June 14th, 2021)

Love, Action, Camera (all stand alone)

Dotted Line

Action Shot

Close-Up

End Scene

Meet Cute

Love After Midnight **(all stand alone)**

Rum And Notes

Virgin Daiquiri

On The Rocks

Sex On The Seats (April 26th, 2021)

Life Sucks Series **(all stand alone)**

Train Wreck

Hot Mess

Dumpster Fire

Clusterf*@k (August 16th, 2021)

Roosevelt Ranch Series **(all stand alone, series complete)**

Disaster at Roosevelt Ranch

Heartbreak at Roosevelt Ranch

Collision at Roosevelt Ranch

Regret at Roosevelt Ranch

Desire at Roosevelt Ranch

Phoenix Series **(read in order)**

Phoenix Rising

Dark Phoenix

Phoenix Freed

Phoenix: LexTal Chronicles **(rereleasing soon, stand alone, Phoenix world)**

From Ashes

In Flames

To Smoke (October 18th, 2021)

Stand Alones

Someday, Maybe (YA)

ABOUT THE AUTHOR

USA Today bestselling author, Elise Faber, loves chocolate, Star Wars, Harry Potter, and hockey (the order depending on the day and how well her team -- the Sharks! -- are playing). She and her husband also play as much hockey as they can squeeze into their schedules, so much so that their typical date night is spent on the ice. Elise changes her hair color more often than some people change their socks, loves sparkly things, and is the mom to two exuberant boys. She lives in Northern California. Connect with her in her Facebook group, the Fabinators or find more information about her books at www.elisefaber.com.

facebook.com/elisefaberauthor

amazon.com/author/elisefaber

bookbub.com/profile/elise-faber

instagram.com/elisefaber

goodreads.com/elisefaber

pinterest.com/elisefaberwrite

Made in the USA
Las Vegas, NV
24 February 2023

68041351R00173